THE TRAVELS OF IBN THOMAS

James Hutson-Wiley

Published by New Generation Publishing in 2020

ISBN

	Paperback	978-1-80031-544-0
	Hardback	978-1-80031-543-3
	Ebook	978-1-80031-542-6

www.newgeneration-publishing.com

 New Generation Publishing

ACKNOWLEDGEMENTS

The Travels of Thomas ibn Thomas, the second book in the Sugar Merchant series, would not have been written without the encouragement of my readers and the unwavering support of my wife for which I will always be grateful.

Dr. James (Ted) Blanton once again provided substantial assistance in ensuring that the narrative is as historically accurate as possible. Dr. Blanton also supervised the construction of travel maps drawn by Alex Fries of the University of Alabama Cartographic Research Lab. Any historical or geographic errors, purposeful or not, are entirely my responsibility. The editors at Writers Services Ltd. also provided significant contribution to the narrative.

The Authors Confession

Sometime in the eleventh century, an Arab philosopher claimed that the relating of an untrue tale is the greatest waste of one's time. But what is truth? Many believe the only valid source is revelation from God. Others rely on a narrator's integrity. Often we trust only those facts which are both observable and verifiable. I would like you to believe, as many late medieval authors claimed, that the Travels of ibn Thomas were discovered in a dusty corner of the Escorial in Spain. The chronicle of Usamah Ibn-Munqidah, the 12th century travel writer was, indeed, found there. But my assertion would be a lie. About that transformational era, firsthand accounts, whether Arab, Jewish or Christian, are rare. Notable examples are 'A Monk's Confession', a memoir written by Prior Guibert of Nugent in about 1130 and 'The Travels of Ibn Jubayr, written around 1185. In the following pages, I have avoided falsehood to the extent feasible within the confines of a fictional work. Many characters described were actual participants in the tumultuous events of the early twelfth century. When in doubt, I have followed the example of the first historian, Herodotus: if truth is unclear or unknown, fabricate it.

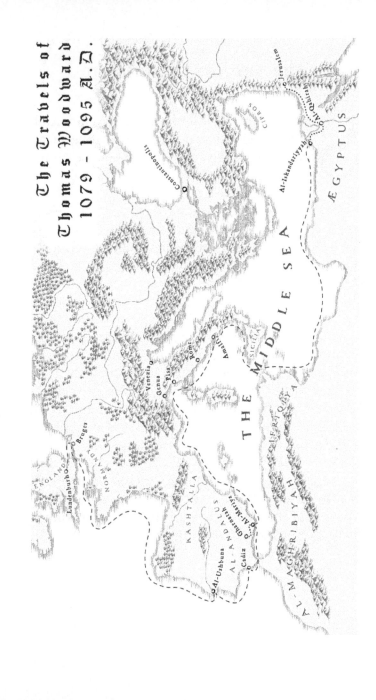

The Travels of
Thomas Woodward
1079 – 1095 A.D.

Constantinopolis

CIROS

Jerusalem

Al-Qhirah

Al-Ishandariyyah

ÆGYPTUS

THE MIDDLE SEA

SICILIA

Amalfi

Roma

Pisa

Genua

Venezia

IFRIQIYAH

AL-MAGHRIBIYAH

ENGLAND

Lundenburh

Bruges

NORMANDY

KASHTALLA

Ghirnatah

Al-Mariya

AL-ANDALUS

Al-Ushbuna

Cadiz

4

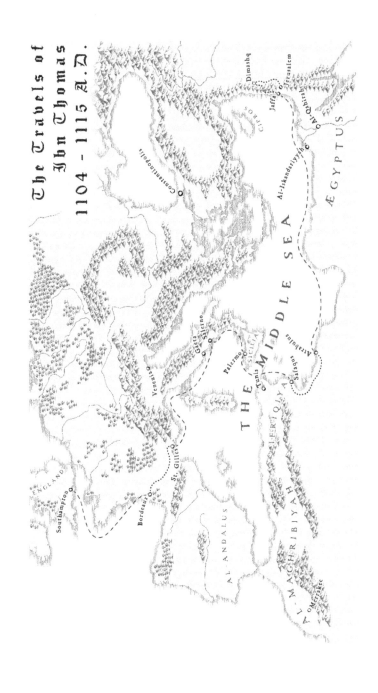

The Travels of Ibn Thomas 1104 – 1115 A.D.

ENGLAND
Southampton
Bordeaux
St. Gilles
Venezia
Constantinopolis
Genoa
Salerno
Palermo
SICILIA
Tunis
IFRIQIYA
AL-MAGHRIBIYAH
AL-ANDALUS
Ommartikee
Safaqus
Atrabulus
THE MIDDLE SEA
AEGYPTUS
Al-Iskandariyyah
Al-Qāhirah
Jaffa
Jerusalem
Dimashq
SYRIA
CILICIA

AD 1115
AH 508
AM 4875

My grandfather and uncle call this city al-Quds, or sometimes, Bayt al-Maqdis, the House of Holiness. My adoptive uncle claims there are seventy-two names for it. Yerushalayim, the City of Peace, is the most common. Christians call it Jerusalem. To all of us – Jew, Christian and Muslim – it is the Holy City. On my first visit, it was neither holy nor peaceful. It reeked of excrement and rotting food. Most of the ragged knights and their shabby retainers who remained in the city were suffering the effects of last night's indulgence in cheap wine. If they were not sleeping, they were fighting among themselves or aimlessly roaming the city, kicking beggars from their path. King Baldwin had dispatched his able warriors to aid Prince Ruggiero and the Atabeg of Dimashq in their battle with the Turks. Those left behind were recovering from wounds or lacked the sobriety and health required of an effective force. It was hard to imagine the Apostles and Our Lord Jesus trudging through these narrow, trash-strewn streets. Surely the Romans kept this place in better condition during their rule.

I had entered through St. David's Gate which, although guarded by a great citadel, involved no difficulty in passing through. The soldiers lounging there were indifferent to us pilgrims. Although they sullenly demanded a few coins for entry, they left us in peace. There were many entering the city that day. Those I accompanied were much like me: dark skin and brown eyes, with unkempt black hair and untrimmed beards. Most of my fellow travelers were Eastern Christians from Arminiya and greater Suriya. The Muslims call them the Rum. Most were intent upon reaching the Chapel of the Condemnation. There they would begin the Way of the Cross and seek salvation. That was not my goal. I had come to learn the fate of my father, who had traveled here so long ago.

Perhaps I should commence my tale from the beginning.

I

EYNSHAM

AD 1104
AH 497
AM 4864

I was about twelve years old when the white-robed monk extracted me from my home in Eynsham. I had not been happy there. To be fair, most of the Brothers treated me kindly. Postulates were beaten for failing to study their lessons or for committing other infractions of Benedict's Rule, but not me. I was different. The other boys did not fail to note this discrimination. Not only was my appearance strange, with my darker skin and black hair, I was ignorant of scripture and did not know the words of the chants we sang at mass. Worse, I spoke Latin with an unusual accent. The others spoke either Norman or Saxon. In my early years, I was not proficient in either language. Thus, my fellow students rarely spoke to me. I thought the nature of my origins was held in confidence. Of course, in that closed monastic community, there were no secrets. When they had the opportunity, students called me the Halfling Moor. Even my formal name, Thoma ibn Thomas, was a source of ridicule. I began to insist that my name was just 'Thomas'. For the balance of my life, Christians called me by that name. For others, I was known by my true appellation. I introduced myself using the name that I believed acceptable in the circumstances. Once, an older boy called me an infidel bastard. For this insult, I attacked him with my small fists. As you might expect, he responded with greater force. It took weeks for my bruises to heal.

My tutor, Brother Robert, insisted I ignore these affronts and accept with grace that I was, indeed, different. That was not easy. Contrary to the teachings of Saint Benedict, I was proud of my heritage; of spending my early years in the land of the Moors. I had vague memories of my English father, whom I had not seen since his departure for Jerusalem. I wanted to believe he carried out great deeds. My mother, who died in my infancy, was a Moor, as was my grandfather, Terryn, and my uncle, Assad. Their partner in commerce, Jusuf, was a Jew. Before coming to the abbey, I spoke Arabic fluently. I had learned the rudiments of reading and writing in that language and had memorized several surah of the Holy Book of Islam. Everyone at Eynsham was clear in their faith. Although I attended mass each day, I remained confused.

I came to Eynsham from Aegyptus at the age of eight. My exit from Iskandariyyah had been both sudden and disturbing. On the morning of my departure, my grandfather introduced me to a kind, but gruff, man named Rowan. He was the captain of my uncle's fleet and would take me to the homeland of my father. Rowan spoke for a few moments with my grandfather, who had tears in his eyes. As my guardian he had a duty to perform before we boarded his ship. He asked Terryn if he wished to accompany us. My grandfather shook his head sadly and said, "No, do what you must." With that short statement, he kissed me, turned his back and walked silently away. Rowan took me by my hand and together we walked to a Funduq belonging to merchants of Genoa. There I met a Christian priest who asked me a few questions: did I believe in God, did I believe in Jesus Christ his only son, did I believe in the Holy Spirit? I dutifully responded yes to all those questions although I knew nothing of any Holy Spirit nor did I know anything about Jesus except He was an important prophet. When this short ceremony was over, the priest suddenly, and without warning, dunked my head in a bowel of water nearby. I thought he was going to drown me, and I cried aloud. My cry, for some reason, pleased the priest. He made a sign over me and Rowan took me immediately to a large vessel in the port. We were, he said, bound for a place called England.

On the long voyage from Aegyptus, I came to know my guardian well. He taught me understanding of the stars and the currents of the Middle Sea. It was through Rowan that I learned something of the Saxon and Norman language, though not enough to speak fluently with others at Eynsham. This first journey was filled with fear, overwhelming excitement and deep sadness. I was leaving everything I knew behind.

All this set me far apart from the postulates at Eynsham. My father had disappeared. I had no mother, no brothers or sisters. When I was older, I received letters from Jusuf, who insisted I call him uncle, and from my true uncle, Assad, and my grandfather, who grieved they were unable to travel to visit me. I still felt alone. I desperately wished to be like the others. I arduously studied scripture and joined in the singing of mass with enthusiasm, but I could not hide my doubts and questions. There was no escape from my difference. Half Moor, half Christian; half English, half Arab; I had no place to call home except the abbey. When the white-robed monk took me away, it was a great relief. Perhaps I could find a new life in another place where there were others like me.

My introduction to Brother Jehan, who collected me from the Abbey, was troubling. He was a thin man, not much taller than me and in his middle years. His skin was sun weathered and his shaven countenance severe. I thought he looked weak, but I was wrong. He rarely spoke and when he did, his voice was gruff and sullen. He had a noticeable limp when he walked. During our first meeting he stared sullenly at me for no obvious reason. I did not like him. He was, he declared, a 'frater conversus' at the Hospice of St. John in Jerusalem. Like most of us, I was familiar with the Hospice and its role in protecting pilgrims in the Holy Land. I knew that lay brothers, not bound by strict Benedictine rules, ran this institution. I wondered what business he had with me. Our abbot, Columbanus, was present as well. Their relationship was anything but cordial. They often glared at each other. Brother Jehan expressed his disapproval aloud when our abbot showed me the letter and manuscript which changed my life.

"Abbot, there is no reason for the young man here to read that now. It will take him all night. It is a waste of precious time. We must leave today. I protest!"

Abbot Columbanus looked at him with displeasure and ignored his complaint. "Take this," he said, and handed me a document written on thin, yellowed sheets of fiber. The document was unusual, as most manuscripts in the Abbey were written on vellum. "I want you to read it. Go to your room and read. Come back when you have finished. If that takes until tomorrow, so be it," he ordered.

In my room, I pored over the document for the balance of the day and well into the night. Some of the manuscript was written in cypher. This presented a difficulty until I re-read my father's introductory letter. In it, he wrote that the first words of Saint Paul in his epistle to the Ephesians, and the Saxon language, were the key to understanding. That forced me to visit the scriptorium, where I spent hours translating the Arabic number cypher into words. I wept when I had finished reading the manuscript. I did not know what to think. It contained revelations I could never have imagined. It was shocking to learn my father had been a spy for the Church. At a young age, he had been selected for this role and received training at Eynsham, from a priest named Ogier, and a monk called Leofric. Ogier was a leading member of a group, reporting to the Pope, calling themselves 'frumentarii', whose task was to protect the interests of the Church. Like Jehan, Leofric was a frater conversus. Once, he had been a skilled mercenary warrior. He was assigned to instruct my father in the art of using a staff for defense. This weapon could be used to disable an opponent but, ordered Leofric, not to kill. He commanded my father to swear before God not to violate the sixth Commandment. On completion of my father's training, Ogier dispatched him to al-Andalus and eventually Aegyptus. There he was to gather ancient texts held by the Moors, seek friendship with the Fatimid rulers and establish himself in the world of commerce. Along the way, he had befriended a skilled Muslim merchant, my grandfather, who called himself Terryn, his son, Assad and the Jew, Jusuf. Against all odds, he succeeded in fulfilling his tasks. Together with Assad and Jusuf, he had created a massive enterprise, a Collegantia they called it. Their commerce was based upon the production and distribution of al-sukkar. In my father's time, al-sukkar was well known in the Muslim world but not within Christendom. Everyone knows what it is. We call it 'sweet salt'. Against the wishes of both the Church and Qudis, or religious judges of the Islamic faith, my father married a Muslim, Terryn's daughter, and Assad's sister. To secure permission from the ruler of Aegyptus for this marriage between Christian and Muslim, my father promised to raise his son, if he had one, in the faith of Islam. Although my mother died shortly after my birth from an illness which afflicted most of the population, my father made good on his promise. This was why I knew so little of the Christian scriptures and so much about the surah of the Quran.

According to my father, the original intent of the armed pilgrimage was to support the Greek Emperor in driving the invading Turks from his lands. Everyone hoped that such support would bring the two branches of Christianity, Roman and Greek, together under common leadership. Years before, the Turks had captured Jerusalem from the Fatimid. The Turks had forbidden Christian pilgrims from visiting the city. Both the Roman and Greek churches had agreed to encourage the Fatimid rulers in Aegyptus to regain control of the city, providing Christian pilgrims were once again permitted to freely visit the Holy sites. To honor his commitments to both the ruler of the Fatimid, al-Afdal, and Father Ogier, my father was asked to aid in securing a Fatimid victory over the Turks and set free the Holy City. To this end, he was to undertake the perilous journey to Jerusalem with a small band of warriors armed only with staffs. Once there, they were to discover a way to open Jerusalem's gates for the Fatimid army.

Before he departed on this mission, my father feared for my safety. At the time, many believed that armed pilgrims would attack and destroy al-Qahirah. Thus, he sent me to Eynsham on a Collegantia vessel, captained by Rowan, the master of their fleet. My father had given specific instructions to the Abbey regarding my education and care. In the event of his death, he bequeathed his interests in the Collegantia to me and required the Abbey to hold those interests in trust until my majority. Then he violated his marriage vows by asking for me to be baptized and taught the Christian faith. If I ever returned to Aegyptus, he warned, I might be accused of apostasy which, he warned, was a grave crime.

Now, I knew my origins; why I had been raised in the faith of Islam and why I had been sent to the Abbey. Now I understood how it came to be that my uncle was a Moor and my adoptive uncle a Jew. That was a relief and a misfortune. I was, indeed, different. At least I knew the reason. By the morning of the next day, I had completed my reading and, with effort, composed myself. Our abbot called me to the chapter house. He spoke softly.

"My son, you now understand. Eynsham has fulfilled its obligations to your father. We have taught you the Quadrivium and the tenets of faith. We do not have the ability to advance your learning further. We, both Eynsham and the Church, owe a debt to your Father and must do more."

Jehan scowled at this last declaration and spat on the floor. He mumbled something under his breath. Our abbot glanced at him scornfully but ignored his crude interruption.

"You have been bequeathed great wealth, which we manage in trust on your behalf. We have maintained correspondence with your uncle and his partner, the Jew, to tell them of your progress. They too have protected your interests. We have done our best. It is time for you to leave this place. Your education must continue if we are to honor your father's wishes. Brother Jehan will accompany you to the Salernitan School, where you will study with others like yourself. It is a long and difficult journey. However, I believe you will not be disappointed. Will you assent?"

Although I wanted to affirm my agreement immediately, I had questions.

"Reverend Abbot, Brother Jehan, what do you know of my father? What was his fate? Could he still be alive? Why have you kept this from me? He left me behind when he journeyed to Jerusalem. What happened to him?"

The abbot slowly shook his head and remained silent for what seemed an eternity.

"Thomas, we have no answers to your questions. Years ago, we made inquiry. We received only silence. We know he left for the Holy City and that al-Afdal, the Fatimid ruler of Aegyptus, captured it from the Turks. Was your father in the city when we took if from the Fatimid? We are uncertain. He never returned to al-Qahirah. Neither your grandfather nor your uncle learned of his fate. Brother Jehan was present at the city's capture and says he knows nothing." Jehan nodded his head in agreement but was otherwise silent.

"You have heard what happened in Jerusalem after our conquest. I am sorry. We believe he died fulfilling his duties. He is most certainly with God."

I knew what had happened in the year of our Lord 1099. Everyone did. The conquering armed pilgrims had massacred thousands of the Holy City's residents after the fall of Jerusalem. No one was spared. Women and children, Jews and Rum Christians were massacred without mercy. The sole exception was a small group of Fatimid warriors who surrendered after bravely withstanding the siege. These few were permitted to return to Aegyptus. My father was not one of them. I did not say this, but I determined I would devote my life to discovering his fate. In the meantime, the Salernitan School, whatever that was, would take me away from Eynsham and closer to finding an answer.

"When do we leave, Brother Jehan? I am ready."

II

A.D. 1104–1109
A.H. 497–502
A.M. 4864–4869

THE JOURNEY TO SALERNO

The following morning, we made ready to depart. I had said farewell to the Brothers I knew so well. I assumed we would walk to our destination. The satchel containing what few belongings I owned had, however, disappeared. I thought it was awaiting me outside the walls of the Abbey. To my surprise, the satchel was indeed outside strapped to one of two gigantic horses. Brother Jehan impatiently gestured for to me to mount the smaller of these beasts. I hesitated.

"You have not ridden horses before?" he asked.

When I shook my head in the negative, he declared, "Well, you will learn. It is a long journey we take."

And with that declaration, he reluctantly helped me to mount and handed me the reigns. I was sorely afraid of falling or, worse, losing control of the animal. Thanks be to God, it was well trained. I had simply to maintain my position on its back and the creature docilely followed Brother Jehan's horse as we left the

Abbey behind. As we rode, I noticed Jehan wore a long straight sword beneath his cloak. A sword-bearing monk was a sight I had never seen. My curiosity got the better of me.

"Brother Jehan," I shouted. "You are wearing a sword. Why?"

He turned in his saddle and said, "It is wise to be prepared." With that simple explanation, he turned away from me, riding on without saying anything further.

By the time we reached Southampton, I had grown accustomed to my steed. The rear end of my body had not. The welts on my bottom gave me much discomfort. To make matters worse, it rained for most of our three-day journey. My woolen robe became soggy. I was cold and miserable. The weather did not disturb Brother Jehan, who rode in silence and without complaint. He was indifferent to my condition. Otherwise, the three-day journey south had been uneventful. We stayed each evening at Benedictine Abbeys, where we were always welcomed and well-fed. At each stopping place, I dried my robe by the fire until we left in the morning and, once again, found myself reduced to misery. Brother Jehan spoke little and then only if necessary, so I had time to ponder. One specific question among many concerned me. I mustered the courage to ask.

"Brother Jehan, why has the abbot allowed us to use mounts as fine as these? Surely Eynsham cannot afford the coin for their hire."

"Eynsham cannot afford horses like this," he answered. "These are yours. You have paid for them. You are bearing the cost of this journey. What good is wealth if it is not spent on good works? I, myself, follow the Rule of St. Augustine. I have no need for coin." That was all he had to say on this subject. I wondered just how much wealth I possessed.

Southampton was much like other seaport towns in England, except most of the inhabitants were Normans. The buildings were all wooden, even the castle. Given the seemingly constant rain, however, there was no danger of fire. Within the town each trade was concentrated in its own muddy street. It was a major transit port between the King's city of Winchester and Normandy. That, said Brother Jehan, is why we had come to this place. It was also becoming the home of many who followed the Augustinian rule.

There is no merit in describing our journey to Salerno in any detail. We loaded our horses in a large, flat-bottomed cog and crossed the English Sea to the port of Bordeaux. My father had written of the illness that befell him on his first journey by sea. I did not escape that fate. The vessel's rocking motion produced the expected consequence and I spent most of the day at the rail voiding my stomach of all its contents. Brother Jehan cared little for my discomfort. I even once caught him smiling at my distress. From there, for the sake of safety, we joined a merchant party traveling to the Kingdom of Arles. When possible, we followed ancient Roman roads which had fallen into decay and were often merely muddy tracks. Long ago, scavengers had removed most of the stones used in their construction. Over the long and uncomfortably wet days of travel, I amused myself by listening to the merchant's tales and improving my familiarity with the language of the Normans. Brother Jehan did not speak but did nothing to disguise his displeasure with the task he had been assigned. There was a single event on that tedious journey I should relate.

An incident on the road; we are joined by a new attendant

Our merchant companions halted in the city of Toulouse to conduct their affairs. Brother Jehan insisted we continue alone. There was, he said, no time to waste. We had ridden for about four hours when a fallen tree limb blocked our path. Jehan silently motioned for me to halt and slowly drew his weapon. Without warning, four rough looking fellows, all carrying rusty swords, rushed at us from the brush on our left. Our foes had made an error. They had attacked as a group from one side and had not realized Brother Jehan was armed. It was over in moments. Jehan casually struck the arm of the first of the brigands with his blade. The recipient of the blow gave forth a terrible scream as he discovered his sword arm was lying on the road. Copious amounts of blood spurted from the stump of what remained. The other three brigands stopped dead in their tracks as they witnessed the plight of their comrade and realized we were not simple travelers they could rob with impunity. All but one ran. The remaining thief stood motionless, in shock. He was just a blond-haired boy, no older than me but much taller. He fell to his knees, begging for mercy, shaking so badly with terror that I thought he would fully collapse. I too was quaking with fear. I had never witnessed violence like this or seen blood spilled from such a wound. It had happened so fast.

Brother Jehan said nothing. He dismounted and tore a strip of cloth from his own cloak. He quickly bound the wound he had caused to staunch the flow of blood. From his pack, he extracted a thick poultice which he applied to the weeping bandit's stump.

"You may not die," he pronounced. "Be gone, find a barber quickly. Reflect on your sins. As God has commanded, you must not steal. There is still time to repent and make amends." He turned to the boy, who had soiled himself from fear.

"Why are you with these people?" he asked in Norman. "You see what happens to those who accost peaceful travelers. Have you no home?

The boy understood the question and responded at length in a language the likes of which I had never heard. Brother Jehan scowled and replied, in the same strange language, asking more terse questions to which he received even longer replies. As I listened, I found that I partially understood what was being said. Many of the words were unfamiliar to me. When it became clear I did not fully understand this discussion, Brother Jehan turned to me and explained.

"This boy speaks Limousin. It is the language of these parts. His mother apprenticed him to these ruffians a year ago. They are followers of a Cathar Parfait, who believes Satan rules our Church. They only steal from those who do not believe their heresy. 'Parfait' is what they call their own religious leaders. His name, he says, is Roland. His mother told him his name is the only gift she could give. Since Roland was a hero who defeated the Moors, perhaps, she said, so would he become a hero someday. I am sorry to say his father was a priest of our faith who abandoned his mother after his birth. I can understand why she so easily subscribed to heresy."

"Who are the Cathar, Brother Jehan?" I asked.

Jehan scowled. "This so-called faith teaches that there are two Gods. The one who rules this world is evil; the other, who rules all things spiritual, is good. Their ignorance is like that of the Moors and the Jews. These beliefs are anathema. May God destroy them and preserve us from wickedness."

Brother Jehan's face became flushed with anger and I began to fear more violence. After a few moments, he calmed himself by mumbling a payer.

"Roland claims his mother was too poor to feed him any longer. She believed an apprenticeship with these heretics would be to his benefit. His mother, he says, believed they merely charged tolls to travelers to support their religion. He has spent two years with this band. They have attacked and robbed travelers many times. His task was to help in laying the ambush and carrying away the stolen goods to be distributed to the poor and members of the Cathar community. He has not, he swears, ever hurt anyone but he claims he knows how to use this piece of trash he calls his sword. He says he has knowledge of the roads hereabout and begs that we take him with us as a servant. He has nowhere else to go."

"Let him ride with me," I said. "Perhaps he will be of use."

"I doubt that, but very well, you can take him if you wish. Perhaps there is some hope for him. We will take him to St. Gilles. I have friends there. I will deposit him at the priory. The Brothers may find a use for him and, God willing, rid his mind of evil beliefs."

With this declaration, Brother Jehan, wiped the blood from his sword, ordered the boy to mount behind me and we traveled onward.

Roland proved his worth by directing us along old Roman roads which followed the coast of the Middle

Sea. Besides his vile odor, he had another bad habit. He talked incessantly. He was indifferent to the fact that many of his words were incomprehensible to me. Over the next few days, this became irksome. I wondered how he had time to breathe with his nonstop jabbering. To pass the time, I tried to teach him the Latin names for what we saw near the road. Roland would repeat each word perfectly and then would launch into a long discourse in his own tongue. Often, he would laugh loudly at his own wit. I longed for quiet and secretly wished I could stuff a rag in his mouth. Brother Jehan ignored us both and rode on as if he were alone.

Given its location, the city of St. Gilles provided a large hospice to care for pilgrims making their way to Santiago de Compostela. It was also a port of embarkation for the sea voyage to the Holy Land. It was from here we would sail to Salerno. Brother Jehan did not wish to follow the northern land route through the mountains. There was, he claimed, no time for such a journey. When I asked why we were in such a hurry, he gruffly responded.

"It takes too long. I must deposit you in Salerno before classes begin. I have much more important duties to attend to than escorting Moorish children to a school full of infidels."

That was an insult and I felt my face turn red in anger. It took all my willpower not to respond. There was, I thought, something very wrong with this man.

We deposited Roland with the brothers at the priory, who happily received him into their care. Many of them spoke Limousin and, upon our departure, were listening to what I presume was Roland's wordy description of our journey and his many trials and tribulations. I left him behind with profound relief.

Brother Jehan sold our horses to a merchant in the city and deposited the proceeds of the sale in his own purse. In his manuscript, my father had explained the basic rules of negotiation and trade he had learned from my grandfather, Terryn. Jehan, clearly ignorant of these fundamentals, accepted the first offer made. He did not bargain. I asked about this, and Jehan sourly replied.

"I am no merchant. I have faith that God's will was done."

I was certain God was indifferent to this transaction but held my tongue. We then searched for a vessel bound for Salerno. Jehan once again failed to bargain and paid the asking price for passage. I could only shake my head in wonder at his casual use of my funds.

I am admitted to the Schola Medica Salernitana

The captain of our vessel had no knowledge of navigation, so we followed the coastline to the city of Salerno. It was a long and uneventful voyage. Thanks be to God, the seas were calm and the sky cloudless.

This time I avoided becoming sick. On one of those dull days, I mustered the courage to ask Brother Jehan a question.

"Why do you bear such hatred for the Moors and Jews?"

Jehan turned to me, his face growing red with fury. He almost shouted his response.

"Boy, if you had battled the Moors for three years as I have; if you had witnessed their perfidy and cruelty; if you had seen your friends butchered by infidel demons in the fields of Dorylaeum; if you had heard the shrieking ululations of their women as they castrated the wounded, you might understand. And you ask about Jews? If you knew the consequence of moneylender avarice; their Christ-killer ruthlessness when it comes to collecting their coin, then you might share my views. They were most pleased to lend me the funds to join the pilgrimage to the Holy Land. They bowed with their oily smiles and complimented my courage as they provided funds for my journey. When I could not repay them at the agreed time, they took my lands. They destroyed my honor. Those usurers dismissed my explanations. I had risked my life for the Lord and, unlike others, I had not engaged in plunder to repay them on the day they wanted. I pleaded for more time to regain my wealth. My entreaties were ignored. They cared not that I would be unable to take a wife if I were left with nothing. They would not listen to reason. I had no alternative. The only choice was to seek absolution from my debt. Thanks be to God, I have found refuge in the Church as a lay brother among others sharing my convictions. We must purge this world of the enemies of our Lord Jesus. Deus lo Vult; God wills it."

Brother Jehan took a deep breath, spat into the sea and continued.

"The worst of this lot are those who claim they have converted to the true faith. They lie. Their sole reason for accepting our church is to gain wealth for themselves or avoid tax. Many are traitors! These are the worst," he mumbled, looking directly at me.

I did not know how to respond to this diatribe. He clearly thought of me as one of the 'worst sort'. I was filled with anger at his words but, once again, said nothing. I avoided him for the rest of the day. How, I wondered, could a man of God speak in this way? What rot afflicted his soul to produce such enmity for those who were not followers of Christ? What did he mean about traitors?

I begin my education

We arrived at the port of Salerno, and it was with relief that I stepped on dry land. The city was a bustling home to thousands of residents. Arabs in their brightly colored turbans, black bearded Greeks, Normans and Jews all roamed the streets, engaged peacefully in their commerce. It was not always easy to see the differences. Often, for example, Merchants of the Jewish faith from al-Andalus wore turbans no different from those of their Muslim brethren. Normans wore tight wrappings around their lower legs; but often the Greeks did the same, as they wished to follow the latest fashion.

The city did not rival Amalfi as a trading center. Its primary attraction was the Salernitan School of medicine. Students came from all over the world to study at this institution. And a great institution it was. With towering battlements and fragrant gardens, the school's imposing edifice overlooked the sea and the busy port. We climbed the hill to the entrance gate and Brother Jehan demanded an audience with the famous physician, Johannes Planterius, who was to become my tutor. After the customary introductions, Johannes explained I must demonstrate understanding of logic and the Quadrivium. If I did so, I would spend five years at this school studying the structures of the body and the means to preserve health and cure disease. For the first two of these years, I would be confined to the boundaries of the school. This restriction, he said, was for my own good.

"Patients with considerable wealth travel here to find cures for their illness. Although we often accomplish just that, many have conditions that are not curable. These poor souls often became prey to charlatans. Rogues are happy to offer potions and salves at great cost which have either have no effect or are mortally dangerous. Many seek to corrupt our students with their evil. We do not want you to have any contact with people of this sort."

As we talked further, Johannes was delighted to learn of my knowledge of Arabic. There were, he explained, many texts written in that language. The school had an extensive library of Arabic, Greek and Hebrew writings on the art and practice of medicine. Some, I thought, might even have been those rescued by my father from the House of Wisdom in al-Qahirah. Of these, the work of Ali ibn'Abbas, the Persian Ibn Sina, Ahmed al-Jazzar, Galen and the Jew, Isaac Judaeus, were of note. The Church had specifically approved the use of Galen's texts as, they claimed, he would certainly have been a Christian if he had been born after the resurrection. The Muslim and Jewish writers were not officially approved but were not forbidden to us. I must, Johannes insisted, exert considerable effort to succeed in Salernitana. That effort would be to my benefit. If I did well and served an appropriate apprenticeship, I would never suffer from lack of gainful employment. Of course, he cautioned, the cost of my study and residence would be considerable. Brother Jehan assured him I had the means to pay. The church, he declared tersely, would make all necessary arrangements on my behalf. Clearly, I had no choice in this matter. My excitement overcame any concerns.

We toured the grounds to find a place for me to sleep. Brother Jehan shook his head in disgust and muttered to himself. I ignored him. For me, it was clear our abbot had chosen well. Many of the people we encountered on our path were just like me. The students and teachers were Arabs, Jews, Greeks, Normans and others from all over the world. They spoke Norman, Greek, Arabic or oddly accented Latin. For the first time, my own appearance and speech were not unusual. Even more wondrous was the fact that many were women. I was too young at the time to appreciate this benefit but found the female presence to be strange and somehow comforting. In my limited experience, I thought women merely cared for domestic matters like cooking, cleaning or child rearing. Some in the lower orders wove cloth in their homes. They certainly did not engage in other pursuits. This was not the case here. Much later, I studied under the most famous of the women teachers, Trota de Ruggiero. She was famous for her text on the process of childbirth and the ailments of women.

Brother Jehan left me that day. He was content that he had discharged his duty and rid himself of his association with me. He did not say 'God be with you'. He merely walked away saying that he might return in time. I was too interested in my new place of residence to have any regret or fear when he departed. I understood why our abbot had chosen this place for me. I was no longer alone.

I will not waste words describing the five years I spent in Salernitana. Suffice it to say I was one of the youngest students. I passed my examinations in the Greek language and the basics of the Quadrivium and thus avoided the necessity of devoting an additional three years of study before learning the physician's art. Although we sang mass every Sunday, priests and monks rarely bothered us. The school covered its costs through the fees paid by the students and by wealthy patients who came for cures. The church contributed nothing. Salernitana was, therefore, not beholden to Rome. As a result, everyone was free to practice their faiths in ways that suited them. At the time, my own beliefs were ill-formed, and, in this way, I was still different. Whether other students were Jews or Muslims or Christians, each was clear in their own convictions of truth. There was no ambivalence. I met no one who shared my own history of being raised in two faiths. When we were eventually permitted to leave the grounds of the school, members of each faith tended to congregate together. What was common to all was our deep belief in the power of our common God to heal or, in the case of those patients who committed sin, to punish. All of us studied the astrological charts. We understood that the position of the stars, as determined by God, had much to do with the treatment and outcome of illness. To be honest, there was little time to devote to meditations or prayer even if I had been inclined to do so. Raised in the faith of Islam, taught as a Christian and having a Jew as an adoptive uncle made it easy for me to befriend students and teachers regardless of their convictions. The women were a different matter.

The first two years of the medical school were difficult. From dawn to dusk I studied the structures of the body and then, by candlelight, read translations of the basic Greek and Hebrew texts which formed the foundation of our learning. The most important documents, however, were written in Arabic. I worked hard and my ability to read this language improved. This was to my advantage as the Latin translations of these texts were full of errors and, often, omissions. During my first year, I made friends with Johannes' son, Matthaeus, a brilliant student. Unlike his father, he had a caustic sense of humor, which he often employed. Having spent his entire life at Salernitana, he was comfortable talking to the women students and often engaged in easy banter with them. I, of course, had no experience with these creatures and was ill at ease in their presence.

Each year, Brother Jehan visited me at the school. Other than paying my fees, he spoke little to me. He made no effort to conceal his distaste for the place. He stayed long enough to discover if I was diligent in my studies, but that was the extent of his interest. He always gave me the impression that the school was nothing but an evil smell in his nostrils and he could not wait to leave.

"Are you going to mass each day?" he gruffly inquired.

I confessed I went each Sunday but did not attend other services. Brother Jehan found this response troubling.

"You of all people should take your faith more seriously. You should be concerned for your soul. This place breeds temptation and evil thoughts. Unbelievers are everywhere. You must show more devotion. Keep your distance from the Moors and Jews so God will forgive your transgressions."

I had no idea of what transgressions I had committed. Was being raised as a Muslim in my childhood a transgression? Matthaeus told me he had overheard Jehan asking his father if I was cultivating friendships with nonbelievers. Johannes responded angrily that I had made friends with many of the other students, regardless of their faith, and that it was not the duty of the school to govern such matters.

I receive an important visitor

In the late spring of my second year, I received another visitor who shed light on my situation. I was deep in my studies when Johannes sent a servant to my room, who told me to dress in my best robe and present myself in the master's chamber without delay. When I did so, I was surprised to find that Johannes was entertaining a man I did not know. He was in his middle years and carried himself with great dignity. His robe, embroidered with gold and silver, was a thing of beauty and must have cost a fortune. I remember his eyes. Complementing his sharp features, they were a striking hazel color. They reflected his wisdom and seemed to pierce my soul. I did not know what to say. Why did this obviously important man wish to see me?

"Thomas," said Johannes. "This is Cardinal Deacon de Gaeta, the chancellor of the Roman Church. He pays us a great honor by visiting our humble school. He has asked me many questions about you which I have answered truthfully. I do not know why, but he wishes to speak with you in private. I will leave you now." With this simple statement, Johannes left me alone with the cardinal.

The cardinal inspected me closely and said nothing for what seemed an eternity. I was uncomfortable under his gaze. Finally, he spoke.

"My dear friend Father Ogier, may he rest in peace, believed you would resemble your father."

In my nervousness, I could not contain myself and said, "Your Eminence, I have knowledge of Father Ogier. How did you know him? Did you know my father?"

"Yes, my son; I should explain. Abbot Columbanus wrote to me from Eynsham. He tells me you read your father's manuscript, so you must know something about Ogier's role. Is that correct?"

"Yes, Eminence, I read that Ogier was an important member of a group within the Church keeping the Pope appraised of important events in the world and carrying out other tasks. I know only what my father related."

The cardinal motioned for me to remain silent. He had more to say. "Thomas, I knew Ogier well. We both worked closely with Desiderius, the abbot of Monte Casino, who later became Pope Victor III. We all believed it was in the interest of the Church to maintain relations and even friendship with the Fatimid rulers. At the time, they controlled most of Ifriqiya and parts of the Holy Land. All changed when Pope Urban came to power and began the armed pilgrimage. He sought reconciliation with the church in the east and agreed to assist Alexios, the ruler of the Greek Empire, in regaining his lands from the Turks. There were many who believed it was our duty to go further; that God wished us to liberate Jerusalem and rid the Holy Land of the Moors."

Again, I interrupted the cardinal. "I am aware of this, Eminence," I said, "but what does it have to do with me?"

"I want you to understand your situation," he answered. "In the course of his duties for Father Ogier, your father not only performed great service but amassed a fortune. He endowed Eynsham with a large bequest and transferred his commercial interests to the Church to be held in trust on your behalf. I think you know this. The cost of your education was to be paid from the trust. If he died, he required all remaining amounts, together with his ownership interests, to be given to you on your majority. For many years, his partners in commerce sent funds to Eynsham. At last counting, this was almost fifty thousand dinars. That does not include the continuing interests in his enterprise. I don't have to tell you this is an exceptionally large sum."

It was true that I had never wondered how my expenses at Eynsham and the Salernitan School were paid. This was indeed a large amount. I lacked for nothing and was ashamed I had never questioned this fact. I waited for the cardinal to continue.

"I have told you your wealth was administered by Eynsham Abbey. That was true until two years ago. It was then that Robert Bloet, the Bishop of Lincoln, ordered all coin in your trust be transferred to Rome. Bloet is a married man who has no respect for monks. He enjoys a high position in the court of King William. Abbot Columbanus had no choice but to comply with this command. This is the crux of the problem. As chancellor of the Church, it is my duty to be aware of any large holdings. In this case, I am not. You must know why this is important?" he asked.

I did not. "Eminence, I have little knowledge of anything outside my studies. The demands of this school are such that there is little time to learn of events outside."

"Then I will explain briefly. You see, we are in dispute with the Holy Roman Emperor, Henry V. Like his father, the Emperor does not believe the Pope has ultimate authority. He claims it is the right of temporal rulers to invest Bishops and other officers of the Church in their own lands. That cannot be. The Pope is God's chief representative in the world. This truth must be upheld at all cost. What will become of the world if God does not command all? The dispute is serious, and we fear war will result. The Church needs all the coin it can muster if we are to avoid such a conflict. I had hoped to ask your permission to borrow from your trust, but I cannot locate the funds. Do you understand?"

"I understand the need, Eminence, but I know nothing of this matter," I replied. "What can I do?"

"Two things," said the cardinal. "The first is to sign this document, which authorizes me to temporarily make use of your trust in any way necessary to serve the interests of the Church." He handed me a parchment to read and execute. "I also ask that you advise me if you learn anything that will help discover where these funds have gone."

I quickly read the document and signed it, but I had no idea how I could help otherwise. Brother Jehan had access to the funds. That is how he had paid for my journey to school and the fees for my education. Jehan would know the answer to his question. I said as much to de Gaeta.

The cardinal nodded his head in understanding. "So Jehan has knowledge of this," he murmured. "This presents a difficulty. I must seek guidance from the Pope. There is nothing you can do."

I asked de Gaeta why this was a problem, but he refused to answer. He buried his head in his hands, deep in thought. Finally, he addressed me.

"Thomas, continue your studies here and leave this matter to me. However, you must be careful. Trust no one. Your life may be in danger. I will reach out to you when I know more." With that disturbing remark, he dismissed me from the chamber.

Why should my life be in danger, I wondered? I was studying to be a physician. Affairs of this sort had nothing to do with me. I thought about our discussion for several days and could not reach any conclusions. I put the matter aside. I had no time to ponder a question to which there was no answer.

The dissection of a body

Every five years, the Church allowed the school to cut apart and inspect a human body. Matthaeus and I were fortunate to witness this event. The body itself was that of an old, presumably unbaptized vagrant, removed from an unconsecrated grave outside the city walls. It was in the final stages of rot. We gagged at its sickly-sweet smell. Despite our distress, to see the complexity of how the body is composed and closely examine its various parts was to become convinced of the greatness of God and His creation. I shared this revelation with Matthaeus. He observed that what we were chopping to pieces could not possibly be a marvelous creation. In its putrid smelling, semi-liquid state, this example, he claimed, must have been a rejected error. His amusement was soon stifled. As the least experienced students, we were instructed to put the pieces together in their original form. For this task, it was necessary to learn to sew so we could reattach the parts with thread made of gazz. The revolting odor of the cadaver coupled with its slimy state made us both sick. We were unable to eat for days after.

When we had passed examinations for our basic understanding of the body, we commenced what Salernitana considered its most important instruction: the causes and cures for afflictions of all kinds. A fundamental principle was the need to provide fresh air and a clean environment to patients with disease. Likewise, for wounds, rose water mixed with wine or saltwater and vinegar should always be applied to prevent rot. For excessive body heat, the bark of white willow trees, ground to a powder, was proven effective. More important, however, was our need to understand the various substances which either alleviated distress or cured disease. This required study of the Antidotarium Nicolai, which contained recipes for one hundred fifty different medicines. We memorized all of them. This was a daunting task. We learned not only the construct of the formulations but their effect on illness and their proper application. This text was based on the work of a teacher once resident at the school called Constantine the Ifryquian. I count my blessings that I studied the works of this incredible man.

A common belief amongst Arab physicians was that most illness results from the ingestion of substances which either were not perfectly cooked in the stomach or easily discharged as waste. If the heat of the stomach was incorrect, they argued, these improperly processed substances would result in an imbalance between the humors and thus cause disease. A proper cure, they insisted, was to withdraw food from the patient until the evil substance was gone. This would permit the stomach to regain its proper heat and the humors restored to balance. Constantine found this reasoning to be wrongly considered. There were, he wrote, several ways to restore balance that did not involve the withdrawal of sustenance but, rather, the introduction of certain potions. Medicines when properly applied and when combined with purging, prayer and bleeding, could, he claimed, aid the body in naturally treating affliction and thus achieve proper balance.

Constantine had once been a follower of the Islamic faith. He had studied and practiced medicine in Ifriqiya and elsewhere in the Muslim world for years. During that time, he had developed his own list of medicines derived from plants, minerals and animals based on evidence of their effectiveness. This list eventually became the Antidotarium we studied. It was complementary to Ibn Sina's masterful Canon of Medicine. Constantine also found instances when growths and boils needed drainage or even removal. Such treatment was painful. For that, he also developed solutions. His favorite cures for pain, for example, involved the juice of the poppy flower, which in Arabic is called 'Af-Yum'.

Matthaeus and I secretly sampled many of the cures suggested by Constantine. Since we had no underlying illness, it was not possible to corroborate their effectiveness. Worse, the cures often had unpleasant effects. We assumed in those instances we had either failed to measure the ingredients properly or prepared the formulations wrongly. I remember one instance which almost destroyed us.

It had been a long day of study and the sun was setting over the harbor. Matthaeus, panting with excitement, entered my room with a cup of thick brown liquid.

"Thoma," he said. "I have discovered an improvement to the potion for pain. We need to sample it now! We will become famous if I am correct."

Matthaeus may have been an excellent student, but I had no faith in his alchemy.

"What have you made?" I asked cautiously.

"I believe it to be a miracle. Do not ask; just sample it with me. First, we have to inflict some pain." And with that declaration he stuck me in the arm with his eating knife and performed the same act upon himself. He acted so fast that I had no time to protest and immediately felt the pain. Fresh blood stained my blouse.

"Drink half of this. I will drink the remainder and let us discover the results."

Foolishly, I did so. The liquid had a bitter and thoroughly unpleasant taste. Within moments, the pain in my arm became a dull ache. I was struggling to stay awake.

"What is this, Matthaeus? I slurred.

Matthaeus, now feeling the effects of his potion, looked at me, his eyes glazing over. He groggily responded.

"I told you, it is a miracle; Af-Yum, ground root of valerian, crushed passionflower and Massiltanum. Galen writes that Massilitaum is very raw wine and it can be used as a poison. That is not true. At least I do not think it is true..." After some hesitation, he continued: "Oh, and what I added further are the powdered seeds of a plant the Arabs call kanab. I think that is all..." And with that confession, he fell on the floor.

I do not remember what happened to me afterwards. I awoke late the next morning with a pounding head and congealed blood on my arm.

Matthaeus could hardly stand. We were in no condition to attend classes. When Matthaeus' father discovered why we had missed our studies, he was furious. He forbade us ever again enter the school's 'Gardens of Minerva' where the healing plants were grown. I must admit, however, this cure for pain did, in fact, have its intended effect.

In the following months, I studied under Constantine's disciple, Johannes Saracenus. He was also a convert from the faith of Islam and an immigrant from Tunis, a city on the coast of Ifriqiya. We conversed in Arabic. From him, I learned a lesson that was to become important to me later in life. Johannes related that, as a young man, Constantine had traveled widely throughout the Muslim lands and even as far as India for the purposes of gaining wisdom and engaging in trade. He had begun his life as a merchant specializing in the supply of rare medicinal substances. On one of his many journeys he visited Salerno and found the city to his liking. After a sojourn of two years, he returned to Tunis. There, he devoted himself to the practice of medicine and to further developing his art. Unfortunately, he became the victim of the jealously of other physicians who envied his knowledge. Some accused him of sorcery and lodged a complaint with the city's ruler. Fearing for his life, he left Ifriqiya, carrying with him many of the rare medical manuscripts from his collection. He found refuge in Monte Cassino, where he converted to our faith. The good brothers of Monte Cassino, recognizing the breadth of his medical skill and the value of the manuscripts he donated, sent him to Salernitana to teach. He did so for over ten years. He eventually became a monk himself and devoted the rest of his life to writing.

I will always recall one of the many discussions with Saracenus. We were discussing the use of al-Luban and myrrh for the prevention of corruption in a wound when I asked him to tell me more of his early life.

"My son," he replied, "I will do so after you tell me your own story."

That I did, well into the night. I felt comfortable enough to relate my own father's tale regarding his collegantia and its trade in al-sukkar, which provided me with the funds to study.

"Ahh, trade," he responded wistfully, "that is an art in itself. Like Master Constantine, I too was a merchant before I became a physician. Many of the ingredients we use for cures must be brought from faraway lands at great cost. It was in trade that I learned much. Your father was wise to spend his time with al-sukkar, as its healing properties are well known. There are other substances which have equal if not more benefit. A fortune can be made if one can buy them at their source and bring them here. Now that Christians have conquered the lands of the east, there is great opportunity. You will never become wealthy practicing our medical art. But trade..." he sighed. "That is another matter."

I had little time to think about this. The rigors of my own studies were paramount. From Johannes I learned the value of examining urine and the treatments of excessive body heat. I studied the nature of the eye and how to remove the film which sometimes grows upon it and leads to blindness. From others, I learned how to staunch the flow of blood from a wound by using a hot iron, and then to properly treat the result. For the proper diagnosis of any affliction and the prognoses for the results of treatment, we studied astrological charts. The stars often dictated what we could do and expect. Of course, sometimes illness was the result of sin and punishment by God. In that case, fervent prayer for forgiveness was required. No treatment would otherwise be effective.

The lady Trota was gracious enough to teach me something of childbirth and how to make use of the new instruments designed for the purpose of easing a newborn child from its mother. This great lady, now well into her last years, had focused her studies on the needs of women. She believed that male physicians ignored this. She had written several texts on the subject, the most important of which was De Curis Mulierum, which, of course, I read. She also wrote a treatise on the art of caring for hair and skin. When I inquired why she had devoted attention to this subject, which I thought unrelated to our studies, she explained.

"Thoma, for good health, all people need to feel clean. They should present themselves in the best possible light, both for themselves and for others. God frowns on those who are not good stewards of the bodies He has given them. You already know the six causes of illness we can manipulate to restore the proper temperament of the humors. If you have forgotten, these are: air, food and drink, excretion, exercise, sleep and emotions. Emotions do make a difference. Women in the lands of the infidels understood well how spices and balm improve their fragrance, attractiveness and prevent aging of the face. I believe that following their example will lead to happiness and thus, health. How often have you smelled the vile odors of our Christian sisters and brothers who rarely bathe? How often have you seen visages ravaged by boils and pustules? And teeth, I don't want to even think about teeth. How much better would it be if those persons not only possessed skin clear of blight but carried with them the aroma of flowers? How much better would they feel? How much better would you feel in their presence? The ingredients necessary for this purpose are difficult to obtain. They are, however, available to those who understand their value. Read what I have written and consider it."

Once again, the value of spices was clear. If many women followed Trota's instructions, there might indeed be great demand for the substances she recommended.

I had learned much in my studies and studied even harder for my final examinations. I was proud of my accomplishments and believed myself ready to pursue my quest to discover the fate of my father. Perhaps, I thought, there was a need for physicians in the Holy Land. How to get there was the problem.

III

A.D. 1109–1111
A.H. 502–505
A.M. 4869–4872

My early education ends, and a new life begins

I completed my studies in the spring. Shortly after completing my last examination, I received a visit not from Brother Jehan but, rather, from a black-robed priest. He was about ten years older than me, well-built, with a carefully trimmed beard and neatly cut blond hair. He smiled as he greeted me. I noticed his eyes did not reflect the upward curve of his mouth when he did so.

"Well," he declared, "so you are the one we have been caring for the last five years. It must be a wonder to you to hear me say that! Do you think we would ignore our obligations to your father? My name is Bartolomeo. I am a canon of St. John Lateran in Rome and have other duties as well. We have been paying the extraordinary costs of your study here from amounts we manage on your behalf. Johannes told us you have done well with your studies and, with exceptions, your behavior has reflected well upon the Abbey of

Eynsham. We remain, however, concerned about the strength of your faith. I will let that pass for now. There is still time."

I confess my confusion regarding faith persisted. I had devoted no time to pondering this issue at any length. There had been no time to do so. In any event, I wondered what he meant by his last words. Bartolomeo's statement brought Cardinal de Gaeta's advice to mind. I was to trust no one. I decided to remain silent until I knew more.

Bartolomeo saw the expression of concern on my face but chose not to remark upon it.

"You know that for us to grant your license to treat others, you must devote one more year to serving as an apprentice to a practicing physician. It is time we discussed your future. Oh, and I have a letter for you." Raising his brows, he grinned and said, "Let us find someplace to have wine and discuss matters further."

There was an inn nearby and as we strolled down the hill to Salerno, Bartolomeo related news from Rome and the Holy land. Given the demands of my education, I had paid no thought to the world outside my school. I was ignorant of events and, I admit, cared little about them.

"We have conquered most of the Holy Land," he reported happily. "Baldwin is the King of Jerusalem and the city is open to pilgrims. The lands once belonging to the Turks and to the Fatimid are being divided amongst the noble leaders of our armies.

There is some minor conflict in this regard. Nothing of import. al-Afdal maintains his hold on a few insignificant villages but has not marshaled any serious resistance. God willed it and we have won! Praise be to Him!"

Bartolomeo paused in reflection and then continued quietly.

"Matters are more difficult elsewhere. Almoravid warriors have defeated the armies of Castile and Leon. The Moors have taken several of our cities. We shall, of course, conquer these people as well. It simply requires time and faith to do so. God has commanded that we rid the world of Jews and Moors so that His Son, Lord Jesus, can come again and save us all."

During my studies, I had learned to listen carefully and observe. One cannot properly diagnose a patient's disorder by not doing so. There was something troubling about this smiling monk. I had read nothing in the scriptures supporting his declaration. Further, his reporting of events was too simple, too practiced. He was not relating the whole truth. Of that, I was certain. I resolved to listen and not draw conclusion. Not yet.

We reached the inn, ordered our wine and Bartolomeo then handed me a letter. Its seal was broken, and I suspected it had been read before reaching me. The letter was from Jusuf.

My dearest Thoma,

I pray you receive this message and are in good health and have now passed your examinations. Your uncle Assad and I have received reports of your progress. We are proud of you. There is much we must discuss. Both of us intend to travel to Al-Madinah, which you call Palermo, on the Island of Sicilia so we can meet you in safety. We should arrive in the early summer. Try your best to meet us there. God willing, you will be enabled to do so. Seek the moneylender Ismail, who is known to all. He will instruct you as to our whereabouts. God be with you.

Your loving uncle
Jusuf

Bartolomeo, seeing that I had read the letter, raised his brows and innocently inquired, "Good news?"

I affirmed that it was, indeed, good news and thanked him for delivering it.

"Excellent!" he exclaimed. "I have news for you as well. So you may be awarded your license to practice your newfound art, we have consulted with Johannes and have obtained a position for you in the court of Ruggiero of Sicilia. This is a significant appointment. You will complete an apprenticeship with the doctor, Giovanni Afflacio, who is the personal physician to Ruggiero. He is old and needs assistance. You will love the island. It is beautiful, with a temperate climate. It welcomes all persons whether they be Moors, Greeks, Christian or even Jews. This fact worries us, but such tolerance has attracted the presence of scholars, poets, and artisans from all over the world. Your presence at court will benefit your future. This is a great honor and we know you will accept. Many ships bound for the island leave from our port and finding passage will not be difficult. I have written a letter of introduction for you."

I was certain he had read Jusuf's letter. But what difference did this make?

I finally mustered the courage to ask my own question. "Father, this is wonderful news. I do, however, have a query of my own. You say you have been paying my costs from funds managed by the Church. I received a visit from Cardinal de Gaeta, who asked about this. I promised to tell him if I knew who had control of my trust. I still do not, but does the Holy Father have the information he sought?"

Bartolomeo hesitated for only a moment. "Of course he does. The great Cardinal is the chancellor of the Church. He knows all. Why do you ask?"

"I gave my consent to make use of the funds. I want to ensure that is being done."

"Rest assured your funds are in safe hands, Thomas. They are being used to fulfill God's purpose. If it will make you more comfortable, write a letter to him and I will deliver it myself. Now, let us discuss your future. Do you accept your appointment?"

Given Jusuf's information, I was determined to travel to the island with or without my appointment to the court. However, I did understand the value of gaining such a position and put aside my suspicions of Bartolomeo. I would leave at the earliest opportunity. Of course, my goal to travel to Jerusalem and discover the fate of my father remained paramount. An appointment to the court of Sicilia and meet my uncles was, for the moment, an opportunity I could not resist.

Bartolomeo beckoned me closer. "There is something more," he whispered. This time, he was not smiling.

"For some time, your father provided aid to the Church. He acted under the guidance of the priest, Ogier. That priest made many errors, as did your father. All is different today. We have faithfully discharged our duties to you, but it is time to repay the debt."

What debt, I wondered. How were matters different? Cardinal de Gaeta had disclosed nothing of this. Bartolomeo gave me no opportunity to ask these questions.

"The Regent of the island has established too close a friendship with the Greeks and Moors. This is a danger to those of us of the true faith. There is a Greek, whose name is Christodulus, who has much influence on the governance of Sicilia. We need to know more.

What are his intentions? With whom does he meet? We ask your assistance so we can take appropriate measures to protect our interests. This may discharge some of the debt. You may expect one of us to visit you so you may impart what you discover."

Thanks be to God, I had read my father's chronicle and understood what he was asking of me. Also clear was the ultimate source of the enquiry. I suspected that Bartolomeo was a Frementarius. My father had written about these spies for the Church. If that were so, I believed the Cardinal would have full knowledge. These gatherers of information for the Pope were founded by Desiderius. Cardinal de Gaeta had told me of his own relationship with both Desiderius and Father Ogier. I knew it was not just information they collected. They carried out duties that could never be revealed. I reflected on Bartolomeo's request for a short moment. I had been told to trust no one and was now suspicious. I thought it best if I appeared to agree to provide what information I could obtain. Of course, I had no intention of obtaining anything. Not until I knew more. In any event, I was a physician, not a spy for the Church like my father. Physicians must maintain the privacy of our patients. We all swore to abide by this rule. I would not break my oath.

The priest took his leave from me that afternoon. I wrote a letter to the Cardinal and handed it to Bartolomeo for delivery. Before he left, he had one more demand. "Understand that you must obey the physician Afflacio in all matters, without question. Do not fail in this; Afflacio is carrying out work for God. Your role is to assist him and use your new position to provide the information we seek. That is all."

I returned to my room, but my mind was in turmoil. The opportunity to serve in the court of Sicilia was an honor. But the only reason for my appointment was that the frumentarii believed I would willingly comply with their demands; that I would do all possible to make amends for what they called my father's errors. Bartolomeo assumed I knew what these were and, of course, I did not. After some thought, I decided to ignore all this. It was still a grand prospect. I wanted to meet my uncles and, with the innocence of youth, I put aside my concerns. I would be apprenticed to a famous physician in the court of Sicilia. I sought out Matthaeus to share my news.

"Matthaeus, why don't you join me? You must apprentice with a doctor as well. I am certain a place for you could be made."

"My father will not allow it," he said sadly. "I am to remain here and become his assistant. I will, he tells me, become a teacher here and, someday, become the head of this school. You know him. There is no appeal against his judgment."

"Then perhaps you can visit me on the island when your duties permit."

"I hope I can do just that! God be with you, Thoma. Write to me."

I knew from my own childhood that a major tenet of Islam was the necessity of one's submission to the will of God. God had provided me with many advantages: wealth, education and a mind capable of learning. There was no question that this new opportunity too was a gift from my creator. Despite my suspicions, I would do what He determined. I packed my few belongings and departed the next day.

Sicilia and the future King

Arriving at Palermo's port, I was staggered at the beauty of the city. Vessels, many of them Arab, crowded the port. As in Salerno, the populace was comprised of Normans, Greeks, Arabs and Jews. What surprised me was the fact that most residents were Muslim. They wore brightly colored robes of gazz, with men sporting turbans and the women veils. The streets were wide and clean. The buildings were all in grand condition. Besides churches, there were the minarets of many mosques. The sounds of the call to prayer reverberated through the city five times each day. Outside the walls, there was a large open park called the Jah'nat al-Ard, the 'Terrestrial Paradise'. And that it was. Within were ponds for fish and cages containing colorful birds. Flowers grew everywhere. Workers were busy constructing ponds and streams, all to be connected with pathways. The royal palace dominated the city. The former Muslim rulers had built this edifice before the coming of the Normans. These newcomers had expanded it. Now, flowering arcades connected many of the structures. Some were enclosed by gardens full of fragrant plants. Some of these had delicate white flowers emitting a sweet-spicy fragrance which permeated the air.

I spent the first night at an inn as I had arrived too late to present myself at the palace. The next morning, however, I awoke early, donned my best clothing and organized my satchel of potions and instruments. I wanted to make a good impression and was filled with excitement. This would be my first true employment as a physician. I walked slowly to the palace entrance and presented my credentials and introductory letter to the turbaned guard at the gate. I requested direction to the physician Afflacio. I thought it odd when the guard laughed at my request.

"You seek the good physician," he sneered. "He does not receive visitors at this time of the day. He is rarely in a state to receive anyone. I will have someone ask. Do not be surprised if you must remain here until much later."

For what seemed an interminable time, I waited nervously at the gate. Finally, another guard, also turbaned and wearing a robe of embroidered gold gazz, appeared. He smirked and told me the doctor would see me. "Come with me," he ordered. We walked through many passageways and ultimately reached a grand hall. At the end of this hall was a wooden door. The guard hesitated and then knocked upon it loudly.

"Your Excellency, your visitor is here. Open the door."

I assumed the decrepit old man who appeared and sourly greeted me was a servant. That was not the case. His hair was unkempt, his robe covered with dirt and his teeth, those few he had, were black and rotting. He smelled strongly of wine. This was Afflacio, the physician under whom I would study for a year? I was appalled.

"Come in, come in," he slurred. "I have not slept well; not at my best so early in the day. I am not ready for visitors. You are a visitor? Are you the one I was to expect? Or do you need a cure? Sit over there," he commanded. "Have some wine if any is any left."

Afflacio was unsteady on his feet and I was afraid he would fall as he motioned me to a dirty pile of cushions in the corner of his room. He staggered to those opposite. As he began to speak again, he nodded and then fell sideways, sound asleep. My new master was very intoxicated.

At this point, I had no idea what to do. Should I wake him? Should I let him sleep? I began to have grave concerns about my future.

My meditation was suddenly shattered by a crash as the chamber door opened. A flowing apparition of incredible beauty strode purposefully into the room. She was young and well formed. Her visage was, however, marred by an expression of fury. So angry was she, I escaped her notice.

"Wake up, you filth! How dare you? Your ruler requires attention now!" She paused in her diatribe to look closely at Afflacio, who was snoring loudly. "You are drunk again. You miserable creature; you sorry excuse for a physic. Wake up, I said!"

Getting no response from Afflacio, she turned to me with a glare. "Who are you?" she demanded.

I was uneasy now. I responded as calmly as possible.

"My lady, my name is Thomas. I am a recent graduate of the Salernitan School and have been assigned to the physician Afflacio as an apprentice. I entered his chamber a few moments ago and found him in this state. Do you wish me to leave?"

She stared at me, saying nothing, and then sighed as she calmed herself. "You have passed your examinations?" "

"Yes, my lady, I have. To obtain license to practice my art, I must serve an apprenticeship for one year. I have been recommended to this man and to the court and I have come to present myself. Here is my letter of introduction. I don't know what more to say."

"There is nothing more to say, young man," she declared as she threw the letter on the floor. "A license or a letter from Salerno means nothing to me. This maggot you see here had no license. Were you trained to cure illness? Do not bother to answer that. Come with me."

She did not wait for a response but flowed out of the room, with me following like a puppy, to wherever we were going. We had a short distance to walk. Down the great hall, there was a massive door guarded by two huge warriors. They bowed to the lady and opened it. Reclining in bed was a child, perhaps twelve years of age. His skin was pallid and his blond hair unkempt. He was sweating copiously and whimpering. The room was dark. It stank of decay and excrement.

"This boy will," she said, "God willing, one day be a king. He is my son. His name is Ruggiero, Count of Sicilia and I, Adelaide, am the regent. You will address him as Your Majesty and," she paused, "you will cure him." Turning to my patient, she commanded, "Do as he says. This is your new physician." With those declarations, she left the room as suddenly as she had entered. The door closed with a bang behind her. I had assumed, wrongly, that the Count was a grown man.

The first thing I did was to open the windows of the room to allow light and fresh air to enter the room. Keeping a patient in a dark and airless room is poor practice. That can make his condition, whatever it is, worse. Now that I had light to see, I examined my patient. I noticed first his bed and his clothing were soiled with dark colored urine and feces. No one had bothered to help him relieve himself. Most of what he expelled was foul smelling liquid. When I drew down the bedcover, there was no need to explore matters further. He had two massive suppurating boils on his upper leg. They were oozing a thick white fluid and the skin surrounding them was red. His entire body gave off heat. Next to his bed was a tray with a small knife encrusted with filth and a goblet of rather cloudy wine. It was not difficult to deduce the reason for his discomfort. Someone had attempted to drain the boils with that instrument and, instead of relieving his pain, had caused decay to set in. This putrefaction, I knew, made the body produce more heat than was bearable and unbalance the humors. I wondered what else had been done wrongly.

I called for the guard and demanded a carafe of fresh clean water, several clean rags and new bedcovers. I also asked for a bowl of hot potage and a large flask of good wine. The guard raised his eyebrows but assented to my request.

My patient had said nothing during my brief examination. He looked at me with his soft brown eyes and whimpered softly, "Can you make me better? I hurt everywhere, even my stomach. You must make me better."

I returned his gaze and assured him that soon he would indeed feel better. The water and rags arrived, and I removed his clothing and carefully bathed him. He protested at this treatment, but I ignored his complaints. He finally stopped giving me orders to desist when the feel of the tepid water on his brow relieved some of his discomfort. Even more carefully, I washed the area around his boils. This was painful and he cried aloud. This brought a turbaned guard into the room. I assured him all was well. Thinking of my own safety, I asked this man to stay so no one could later accuse me of causing harm to my noble patient. I prepared a tincture of Af-Yum and wine and helped Ruggiero to drink it slowly. I told him it would make him sleepy. When the tincture had taken effect, I washed the boils themselves with wine and vinegar as I had been taught. Saltwater would have been effective as well. Unfortunately, I had none. I cleaned one of my own sharp knives with wine and then quickly punctured the offending sores. This allowed drainage of more vile liquid and, I prayed, whatever their putrefaction had introduced to this poor young man's body. I concluded that no further bleeding was required and washed the area again and covered it with a clean cloth. I continued to apply cloths, damp with wine and vinegar, to his body. All I could do then was wait and pray.

Ruggiero awoke at midday. He was no longer sweating and had regained some color in his face. "Who are you? Where is Giovanni?" he demanded.

"Your Majesty, I am the physician, Thoma. I have attended you today on the orders of your mother. I do not know the whereabouts of master Afflacio. Are you feeling better?"

"I do not like Giovanni," he replied, ignoring my question. "He is too much in his wine. He made me drink every day from that goblet." He gestured weakly at the tray next to the bed. "He cut me with his knife and hurt me."

Out of curiosity, I sipped some of the wine and found it to have a strange taste. I thought nothing of it, however, and asked the servants to remove it.

"Your Majesty, do you feel any better?" I asked.

"Yes," he admitted. "I am hungry, and my stomach still hurts."

I helped him to eat some of the potage, which was now cold. He devoured it with enthusiasm and then fell fast asleep. I found it strange that his stomach gave him pain and his feces were so filled with water. His urine was dark. The color indicated that his body produced an excessive quantity of black bile. That was not normal. I assumed this was the result of his unbalanced humors. I stayed with him for the rest of the day and the night following. Following normal procedure, I consulted my astrological chart and determined the prognosis was good. Besides keeping both his body and wounds clean and continuing to apply tepid water to his brow, I prayed for his recovery. For good measure, I also recited aloud verses from the Holy Book of Islam. That latter act pleased the guard, who began to look at me with respect. By the next morning, Ruggiero's condition had improved. He was in much better spirits and his body heat had largely dissipated. To provide entertainment, I related my adventures on the road to St Gilles and the encounter with the Cathar bandits.

"Why," he asked, "did you not draw your own weapon to defend yourself?"

"Your Majesty, I had no sword. I have no familiarity with such a weapon, nor do I want such a skill. My father was a master of the staff in battle, but he took an oath to take no one's life. I have taken an oath to do all I can to preserve life, rather than take it."

Ruggiero tool a few moments to consider my response. Whatever conclusions he reached were cast aside. "I know how to use a sword," he declared. "I would have used it with effect. I will become a knight." He paused thoughtfully, "Were you frightened?"

"I was terrified," I admitted. Ruggiero looked at me with some disdain.

"Perhaps it is right you have become a physician. Not everyone is suited for taking arms," he pronounced gravely.

As we talked, the wooden door to his chamber once again opened with a crash. His mother swept into the room in her heavily embroidered gazz robe. She said nothing and smiled as she examined her son. She ignored me.

"My son, you are much improved," she said. "This young physician, I have forgotten his name, has treated you properly." She said this not as a question but as an assertion.

Finally, she turned to me. "It appears you have done well. I hope, for your sake, my son regains his health. You will attend him henceforth. I will have a servant clean Afflacio's room of his filth. You will reside there."

"Thank you, my lady," I responded. "Surely an experienced physician should attend him. I must serve as an apprentice until I am fully qualified."

She glared at me. "Do not question me. You are qualified now. Here, I determine that fact. I have disposed of the maggot and you will replace him until I decide otherwise. When my son is King, he will require all physicians to pass a rigorous test before being granted the right to practice their art. Those that do so without our license will suffer the penalty of death!" She paused for a moment and, almost as an afterthought, declared, "Do not call me 'my lady'. Address me as Madam."

Almost to herself, she muttered, "I never should have listened to Afflacio; I never should have listened to the scum of a priest who recommended him. He might have killed my son. I have lost one and do not intend to lose another."

She left the chamber shaking her head and mumbling.

I become the Court Physician, meet my family, and secure my wealth and future.

And so, without license to practice, I became the personal physician to Ruggiero II, the Count of Sicilia under the regency of his mother, the Countess Adelaide del Vasto. I was frightened at the prospect. I knew only what I had learned at school. One mistake would ruin both my reputation and my life. I did not want to dwell on the fate of Afflacio.

Over the next several days, Ruggiero continued to recover. He regained his color and began to expel his food in a more normal manner. His urine was no longer black. With modest persuasion, I convinced him to walk with me every day in the palace gardens. He was a bright young man with grand ambitions. Even at his young age, he was aware of the significant advantage to trade of Sicilia's position in the center of the Middle Sea. He vigorously defended the island's equal treatment of Muslims, Greeks, Jews and Normans. "We can learn from each other and benefit thereby," he declared. "If we provide a safe home to all faiths and people, we can only profit. We will make this island the center of the world!"

Ruggiero was fluent in all four of Sicilia's official languages: Norman, Latin, Greek, and Arabic. He had devoted study to all three faiths and appeared to appreciate the merits of all. I enjoyed my discussions with him but was impatient to discover whether Jusuf and Assad had arrived. During one of our garden walks a large, black-bearded man interrupted in our talk. Ruggiero appeared to know him well. This portly gentleman was dressed in a fine robe embroidered with gold and, like so many others, wore a large turban. He bowed deeply to Ruggiero.

"Greetings, your majesty," he declared in Arabic. "You appear well. Is it true you are in better health?" Ruggiero nodded his affirmation.

Turning to me, he once again bowed and, continuing in Arabic, introduced himself. "You must be the new physician, Thoma ibn Thomas, with whom our Regent is so enamored. My name is Christodulus. I am the Emir of Palermo and adviser to the Regent. I understand you have replaced the charlatan Afflacio. You are a Muslim?"

I returned his bow and greeting and answered: "Your Excellency, I am who you say but I am a Christian."

"Ah, are you a follower of the Church in Rome or, like me, are you an Eastern Christian?" He paused thoughtfully and thankfully did not grant me an opportunity to respond. "Ignore my question. It makes no difference here. I was born a Muslim but baptized in the Christian faith long ago. We welcome all people on our island. It is enough that, with the grace of God, you have found a cure for young Ruggiero. His elder brother, Simon, died under the so called 'care' of Afflacio. I did my best to warn the Regent that the man either lacked competence or was a spawn of the devil. To my regret, she ignored my counsel. You know the result."

Although I knew Ruggiero had once been blessed with a brother, I certainly did not know he had been under the care of the former physician. I chose to remain silent to give myself time to ponder. Christodulus asked leave of Ruggiero to depart. Before he did so, told me to visit him. This was an order, not a suggestion.

Given Ruggiero's improvement, I no longer resided in his bedroom. Rather, I was now ensconced in Afflacio's former chambers. They had been completely cleaned. On my new bed was a black gazz robe embroidered with fine silver thread and a stark white turban. I assumed this would be my garb henceforth. In those days, I dreamed of recognition, honor, and acclaim. I did not covet wealth. That I had. I failed to realize that the desire for praise was no different from the sin of coveting wealth. It takes time and wisdom to understand this. Some of us never do.

Whoever had cleaned my room had left Afflacio's store of potions and herbs for my use. Many were old or contained substances with which I was unfamiliar. These I threw away. Others were in sound condition and would, I thought, be of use. There was one vile of pale-yellow powder that concerned me. The Arabic script with which it was labeled read 'zarniqa'. I knew this substance was costly. It was used for the treatment of a rare form of pox. In any quantity, or administered over a long period, it was a deadly poison. Why, I wondered, was this substance in Afflacio's possession? To satisfy my curiosity, I wrote to Matthaeus asking that he explore the school records and confirm that Afflacio had, in fact, attended. I also asked him to discover how he had obtained his stores of medicine. Rather than entrusting my letter to anyone at the Palace, I asked permission to go to the city, where I was certain I would find someone to deliver the letter to Salerno. More importantly, this afforded an opportunity to visit the moneylender and discover if my uncles had arrived.

In my new clothes, I felt like a Muslim Qadi. When I passed, people in the street bowed and spoke to me with the greeting of peace. I felt great pride in my new stature. Eventually, I wandered to the port and found a traveler who, for a few coins, agreed to deliver my letter in person. I also inquired into the whereabouts of the money changer and was directed to a small shop close by.

When I introduced myself to Ishmael, he greeted me like a long-lost brother. "Welcome, welcome," he proclaimed; he bowed and ushered me to his offices at the back of the shop. "I have been expecting you. Sit here and tell me what you have been doing on our island. It is not often I have an opportunity to meet such a notable person as yourself. Jusuf speaks highly of you. It is rumored that you have become the personal physician to our young ruler. You are younger than is customary for such an honorable position!"

"Thank you, sir," I said. "What news do you have about my uncles? Do you know their whereabouts?"

"Yes, yes, of course," he replied. "They have arrived from Ifriqiya and are waiting for you. You will find them at the inn across the street, unless they are conducting commerce in the market. Since the capture of the Holy Land, and the closing of the old shipping routes, there is great opportunity here. My own trade has increased substantially. Oh, by the way, I am holding a great deal of coin for you; 10,000 gold dinars. Of course, the palace must be paying you a large fee for your services, so you may not need to draw upon your funds today."

Ishmael's words startled me. It was true I had no need for coin, but neither the Regent nor the Emir had mentioned payment. Obtaining my new position was such an honor that I had completely forgotten to ask what fees I would be paid. I had been foolish. I did not admit this fact to Ishmael, of course. For the sake of courtesy, I briefly related what had happened to me since I came to Sicilia. I was, however, desperate to meet Assad and Jusuf and, thus, brusquer than appropriate. I had given the last of my funds to the courier who was delivering my letter to Matthaeus. Thus, I did request an advance of four Sicilia tari, each equal to about one quarter Dinar, before I departed for the inn. Ishmael raised his eyebrows at such an insignificant request but quickly furnished me the gold coins as I stood to depart. He rose from his desk and bowed.

"Yes, yes, I understand your wish to see your family as soon as possible. Please honor me with a visit when you have time. Bring Jusuf with you. We have much to discuss."

I was excited and made ready to run to the inn. Ishmael called for me to stop.

"You have forgotten the paper which confirms your account. Keep this paper safe. I know you. Others in my trade may not. Anyone possessing the paper can rightly draw upon your funds."

The streets were crowded, and I pushed my way through, almost running to the inn. In the dark main room, there were two men of late middle years. Both wore neatly trimmed beads. One of them, a portly man, was dressed like a prince in a red robe embroidered with decorations of gold and silver. On his head was a turban of the same gaudy color. The other was thin. He wore an elegant, simple black robe. His head was bare and his hair gray. A black-robed priest sat nearby, and several other merchants huddled in conversation. I had no doubt. These two were my uncles.

When I approached, both rose from their seats and warmly embraced me. My uncle Assad spoke first as he wrapped me in his thick arms. He came close to suffocating me with the mass of his great belly.

"My boy, I would have recognized you anywhere," he said. He held me tightly. Tears flowed freely. "You have the appearance of my sister; may Allah bless her. Look at you! Turn around so we may see you fully." Both men examined me thoroughly, appraising my form, my new clothes and my health.

"May Allah be praised," murmured Assad. "You are in excellent condition and, if I may speak for Jusuf, you make us proud."

"Indeed, you do," said Jusuf, who had so far been unable to interject a word over Assad's extravagant welcome. "You cannot imagine how much we have looked forward to this day. We have dreamed of it and prayed we would see you. Sit down and tell us everything. We have received letters, of course. Now we wish to hear your own words. Tell us everything!"

Assad ordered wine and, for much of the day, I related all that had happened to me since my journey from Eynsham. I held nothing back. I found deep comfort in being able to talk so easily, so freely to the only relatives I had.

It was late afternoon when I completed my narrative. Assad complained that his stomach was empty and demanded food from the innkeeper. As we ate, Assad complimented me on my new attire but pointed out that my robe was not in the latest fashion.

"If you are to be respected in your high position, you must dress the part. Tomorrow, I will take you to the market, where we will find the appropriate vestments." I had thought my robe and turban were extraordinary, so I was disappointed when Assad found them lacking. I wanted his approval.

Jusuf ignored Assad's complaints. "Pay no attention to your uncle," he declared. "You are dressed as a court physician should be. We could not be more proud of the man you have become. Let us tell you our own stories so we may all begin from the present and discuss the future."

Well into that evening, Jusuf and Assad brought me up to date on their own affairs and the condition of the Collegantia my father had established with them. Before my father had departed for Jerusalem, and I had been sent to Eynsham, Jusuf had made a home in Merṛakec, a city in al-Maghribiyah which was the center of the gold trade between mines far to the south and Muslim lands. Conditions in Merṛakec, he said, were stable and those of his faith were treated well. Although the ruler did forbid Jews from being outside their homes at night, they were free to engage in both worship and commerce. Jusuf had done well in expanding the gold trade through the Collegantia. So well, in fact, that he had married the daughter of a major trader in that substance. His wife had borne a son about five years younger than me, and two daughters. His son, Elazar, had been sent to Qurtuba in al-Andalus for his education in the city's famous Talmudic school.

"I pray he will join us in commerce upon completion of his studies," said Jusuf. "I wanted to send him to your uncle to be taught the skills of a merchant, but he was steadfast in his refusal. He insisted that understanding our faith was more important. To mollify me, he claimed the friends he would make in Qurtuba would be valuable to our enterprise and, who knows, he may be correct. I did ensure that he learned the art of kalriapayattu so he would be safe on his travels. He writes to me on occasion, so I know he is well. The school is costly, but he does understand his scriptures. I hope he is learning more than this. We will see."

My father had written about kalriapayattu as a means of unarmed defense. Jusuf, himself, was a master. His skill had kept my father alive many times. As it required a close understanding of the human body, I wondered if it might not be useful for me to study this art myself. I asked Jusuf if he could teach me.

"That art takes many years to perfect, Thoma. Your father and I once trained a small band of warriors in a short time, but that was long ago. He took the best of them on his journey to Jerusalem. If we can convince you to join us, perhaps I can impart something of the art. But enough of my story, I can see your uncle is anxious to tell his own." Indeed, Assad was tapping his foot in anticipation of speaking for himself. He was, after all, my true uncle. He called for more wine and a few skewers of broiled lamb.

"I too have a son, Thomas. His name is Abdullah, born in the year you departed for Eynsham. Your grandfather and I have trained him in the arts of commerce, and he has been schooled in an excellent al-Qahirah madrassa. Speaking of your grandfather, he wants to see you before he is too old to impart his wisdom. These days, he spends most of his time in his garden composing poetry and has no one to lecture. He had planned to compose something for you. Unfortunately, he had no time to do so before we left for Sicilia."

"It is good he is well. I do want to see him once again. It has been much too long. What has happened with the Collegantia?" I asked.

Assad answered the question. "When your father left for al-Quds, Jusuf and I continued our commerce. Your father expected us to do that. The absence of the Venetians from al-Iskandariyyah was of benefit. As you know, the armed pilgrims the Franj call 'crucesignati', those who take the cross, never reached Aegyptus. But everything else changed. Trade between Muslim and Christian ports was totally disrupted. All traditional routes are closed. These days, the Venetian, Genoese and Neopolitan fleets dominate the Middle Sea. We cannot trade with most of the Christian ports. When we received word of the massacres in al-Quds we determined it no longer possible to maintain our own sailing fleet. Rowan, our captain, was then fully engaged in transporting warrior pilgrims to the Holy Land, where the killing was still rampant and, to us, that was something we could not in good faith support. Our fleet was important to the welfare of the Collegantia, but we had no choice. Your father was not present, so we decided on his behalf. We sold all interests in the fleet to Rowan. A fair price was agreed but he lacked the coin to pay all at once. Instead, he obtained funds from the ruler of Genoa to settle this matter. Since you, through your father, have an interest, I pray you will agree we have done what is right."

I nodded my head in agreement as, truly, there was no choice. A Jew and a Muslim could not abet those who massacred their people. Assad was relieved that I understood.

"We have been forced to make many changes," Assad continued. "Jusuf maintains his trade in gold, especially with Sicilia. Their coins, the Tari, are in great demand. You understand why, don't you? They are smaller than the Bezant and Dinar and thus more convenient for trade. In exchange, we receive grain and gazz made here. Grain is needed to fill the bellies of the residents of Ifriqiya, especially the Zirid. The gazz is of inferior quality, but merchants here often mark it as coming from Persia and, thus, it has value. This is a tribute to the excellence of the Persian product. Your grandfather, Terryn, claims it is the place of our ancestry. He is proud of the tribute to the land of his origin but appalled at the fraud."

"But what about the trade in al-sukkar?" I asked.

Assad frowned at this question and put his head in his hands. He started to speak but Jusuf interrupted him.

"Your uncle remains distressed about this. I have a copy of your father's narrative but cannot recall if he told you what happened. Did he do so?"

"Yes," I answered, "he wrote there were two mills, one where Assad's wife's family lived in Sharq al Urdun and another in Aegyptus. This second mill was of extraordinary design. It saved both time and labor. The plans for it were stolen by the Venetians who created their own copy in Cipros. I know this substance was the basis for the success of the Collegantia. What happened after my father's departure?"

"You are right. That wonderful substance was the foundation," said Jusuf. "It is of less importance to us today and, I fear, will remain that way. The Venetians have displaced us within Christendom. I told you we no longer have free access to Christian ports. Their mill in Cipros is at full capacity. Our own in Sharq al Urdun has been taken by the Franj. We are still producing al-sukkar in Aegyptus and we can sell it through Sicilia and, often, to al-Andalus. However, the chaos there makes trade difficult. I regret this is the case. Assad is despondent about the loss of his family's mill. It is a sore subject. Everything has changed now that Franj rule the east. Does that answer your question?"

"It does, Uncle," I answered.

It was, however, difficult to empathize with my uncle's distress. The subject of trade was of little interest to me. My own passion was quite different. I could not share this indifference. Commerce was their life. The least I could do was to express curiosity. "So is the Collegantia in poor condition?" I asked.

"Not yet," answered Jusuf. "Our trade in gold, Fustat cloth, gazz and alum is doing well, thanks be to God. Some of my people have developed a new route to al-Hind and we hope to take advantage of it. The future is uncertain." Jusuf hesitated and then continued. "Your father's share in our enterprise is worth at least one hundred thousand gold al-Qahirah Bezants. If he is no longer among the living then his share belongs to you. We hope, God willing, it will be worth more."

I was staggered by this revelation. I knew that my trust already contained fifty thousand Dinars. An additional hundred thousand Bezants was a fortune. The shock must have been reflected by my expression.

"Do not be surprised, Thoma. There is more. Following the wishes of your Father, we have, for many years, sent his share of the profits to Eynsham to be held for you in trust. I have brought an accounting for you. It is about fifty thousand Dinars. Most recently, we deposited ten thousand dinars with Ishmael, as you already know. The balance of this wealth is in the form of trading goods and the value of the al-sukkar mill in Aegyptus. In addition, the makhzans in Bruges and Londres, given by my grandfather as a dowry for my mother, also belong to you, but we have no way to determine their status or value. You are a wealthy man."

I did not know what to say. This was more wealth than anyone required and, truly, I had no need for it. I asked for another flask of wine. My uncle Assad asked for two. It took a few moments for me to make a decision.

"My dear uncles," I said. "I know nothing of trade. I have been trained as a physician. That is my calling. What I desire above all is to discover the fate of my father. I understand you are facing difficulty and I can contribute nothing. Perhaps it would be best if you acquired my father's interests so you and your own sons can benefit from the profit. How can we accomplish this?"

Assad reacted to my question with surprise and began to protest. Jusuf lifted his hand and placed his finger over his mouth to quiet Assad, as some patrons of the inn were now aware of our conversation. After many moments of silent thought, he drank deeply from his cup and responded quietly.

"Thomas, are you certain that you wish this? This is great wealth that you so casually abandon."

I said I well understood my position. It was, I argued, reasonable and fair.

Jusuf was silent for what seemed an eternity as he was deep in thought. "Very well," he finally said. "If you are certain this is the path you wish to follow, I will prepare a detailed account of your interests. You should, of course, retain an adviser to assist in your review."

"I need no adviser; you are my family. If I cannot trust you, who can I trust?" I exclaimed.

Jusuf nodded his head in understanding.

"There is a difficulty," he said. "Your father gave his interest to the Church to hold on your behalf. It was to be given to you in the case of his demise. We have sent reports and coin to Eynsham for years. The existing amount should not be a problem. However, given the present state of affairs, I doubt they would willingly return the interest in our collegantia to the infidels they consider us to be. Laws governing such matters are clear in many places. Canon law, which governs the Church, is unfortunately silent on the subject. The Church can decide what it wishes. In any event, there is no proof your father has died. Perhaps the best solution is for us to form a new enterprise and withdraw our own interests from the old. If we slowly transferred your father's share directly to you, there would be little the Church could do. I am not worried about your father's interests in the mill. The laws of Aegyptus govern that arrangement. The makhzans are a different matter. These were established with royal and ducal charters. They may be empty and we have no way to determine their value. Let us think about this."

Though I had no training in commerce, there was a simple solution.

"You say much of the remaining interests in the Collegantia are in the form of trading goods. I assume these goods are not yet sold. The value you ascribe is based upon their cost, is that not correct?"

Jusuf and Assad both confirmed the correctness of my assumption.

"Then my share, held by the Church, does not include any gain you make when the goods are finally sold. If that is true, repay only my share of this cost to my trust. I have nothing to do with their sale and thus all gain is yours. One day, perhaps, I will deal with the Church to resolve this matter. I am certain you can deal with the ownership of the mill. I will be glad to sign any document you might need. I assume the Church also manages the makhzans through lay persons. That too is something I must settle one day. In the meantime, we are doing nothing wrong. There can be no reason for complaint. Regarding the amounts you sent to Eynsham, these too are held in trust. I have authorized the church to make use of them for the time being."

Assad and Jusuf sat quietly for a few moments.

"Is this truly what you wish?" asked Assad. "I cannot fault your logic. Indeed, your solution is simple but, dear nephew, you are giving control of a great fortune to those you must not trust. Your grandfather would spend hours lecturing you about bad bargains. He might even compose a poem on the subject. This discourse has made me both hungry and thirsty. Jusuf exists on nothing. I need sustenance and so do you. I will order food and more drink so you may consider this solution properly."

I was, in fact, hungry and needed time to consider my position. Our food and drink appeared, and we ate without speaking. I could see that Jusuf was making calculations in his mind. Assad was clearly worried.

When the meal ended, I was the first to speak.

"My dear uncles, the solution I have proposed is right for me. It is fair for you and fair to the Church. There is one thing, however. I would like to withdraw four thousand Tari f my account here and ask you to invest this sum in a venture to trade in medicines. I will prepare a list. You can arrange for their transport here and we can share in the gain equally. I think it will be considerable."

Jusuf responded immediately. "Of course! This is would be a sound venture. I will create a commanda contract. You will provide the funds and we will provide the labor. But dividing the gain into equal shares is not correct. You should receive at least three quarters for the risk you take." Assad nodded his head in agreement.

"No Jusuf, I have read my father's manuscript. The counsel given him by my grandfather was wise. He said a bargain that was unfair to one party would have bad consequence for the other. I want you to have an interest that makes this venture valuable to you. Let us settle on equal shares."

Following much discussion, we finally agreed. I would be entitled to sixty percent of the gain. Jusuf, of course, wanted to reduce this agreement to writing. I promised to prepare a list of the substances I wanted. Assad, now bored, interrupted our discussions.

"Thomas, enough of this. We have missed all your youth. We want you with us. We leave in five days. Come with us. You have no home here. Your skills are needed in al-Qahirah. There is no risk that the Franj will attack us and your grandfather will be forever grateful. He wants to ensure he has imparted his wisdom before he is called to paradise."

I paused briefly to consider this proposal but there was only one answer possible. "I am sorry, my answer is no. My obligations in this place are clear. In any event, I have sworn to discover the fate of my father. I will come to you, just not now."

It was tempting to consider Assad's offer. In Aegyptus I would be with my family and would lack for nothing. My life would be one of ease, providing, of course, no one knew I was baptized as a Christian. In

Sicilia, God had granted me an opportunity to enhance my learning and, I thought, my reputation as a physician. Here, through my own effort, I would achieve fame. In al-Qahirah, others would rightly claim I was merely a person of privilege. Whatever position I achieved would not be earned but granted because of having coin. Most importantly, I had vowed to travel to Jerusalem and that I would do. I returned to the palace in the evening and agreed to meet with Jusuf and Assad every day thereafter to dine and talk.

Now that Ruggiero was well, my duties were few. We spent time in the gardens, and I enlisted his support to encourage the groundskeepers to obtain seeds and plant more medicinal herbs and flowers. Afflacio had kept an acceptable supply of the common herbs but I would need more. There were many that he did not have in his stores. In any event, some were most effective when they were fresh. For example, ordinary poppies grew in abundance in Sicilia. I suggested we also plant the variety from which af-yum is extracted. Ruggiero expressed interest in all the plants I chose. We spent hours discussing their various properties. He was an avid student and a quick learner. His enthusiasm was such that I permitted his involvement in preparing my list of trade goods for Jusuf and Assad. I needed zingiber, al-Luban, Kabbaba and anise. Cardamomum was rare and costly. This too I added to my list. I also wanted a supply of dragon's blood. When I added this to my list, Ruggiero raised his eyebrows in surprise.

"There are dragons?" he asked. "How is the blood obtained? This must be dangerous."

"No, your Majesty, that is the name of a resin which is drawn from a tree growing in Ifriqiya. Some say it comes from a mixture of different plants. There are stories that it is truly the blood of dragons killed by elephants but that is not true. At least I do not think it is true. We use it to treat wounds and ailments of the stomach."

Ruggiero pondered this fact for a few moments. "Make a copy of this list for me. One day, I will ask scholars to collect all knowledge of the physical world and set it down in a book. I will call it 'Ruggiero's book'." I thought his idea had merit. At the time, I thought his dream would be impossible to achieve.

Every evening, I dined with Assad and Jusuf. We reviewed my list of medicines and I gave them authorization to draw up to 4,000 Tari from my account. Jusuf, of course, wrote a document memorializing the commanda contract. It was a comfortable feeling to spend time with my family. When it came time for them to leave my heart was heavy with sadness.

Once again, Assad asked if I were certain I could not come with them. "There are rumors in the market that the days when this country will be welcoming to those of different faiths are numbered. As we speak, there are those who are plotting to retake the island. If this is true, it will not be safe here. Do not ever forget you were raised in my faith. You may have been baptized as a Christian but, to the wrong people, that fact may mean nothing. It is our duty to protect you. Please come with us."

"Dear Uncle, I must decline this offer. I have a secure position on this island. I am not concerned about the future. In any event, I will not be here long; I must go to the Holy Land. I promise to join you when I have done what I must."

Jusuf nodded his head in understanding. Tearfully, he begged me to keep them apprised of my situation. The moneylender Ishmael would always be able to forward my letters. My herbs and medicines, when obtained, would be sent to me in his care as well. Jusuf said they would use the fastest transport. There was one more thing, he said, as he gave me a small fragment of parchment upon which were words in Hebrew. The letters were written in a brilliant blue color; not black as would be common.

"Keep this safe, Thoma," he whispered. "Sew it into your bag or belt. If you are ever in difficulty, show it to one of my faith."

Jusuf and Assad would leave early the following morning. I prayed they would be well until we met again. I walked slowly back to the Palace deep in thought. When I reached the palace gate, the guard was wringing his hands when he saw me approach.

"Sir, we have been looking for you all evening. The Regent demands your immediate presence in her chamber. Her condition is grave. No one knows what to do. Please tell her we did our best to deliver you to her as she commanded."

The guard was obviously more worried by the threat to his position than the condition of the Countess. I immediately ran to her rooms. Her attendants granted me immediate entrance. She was lying in her bed, moaning.

"I am sorry to be late, Highness. Tell me what ails you. What is causing you pain?"

"It is my head," she groaned, pointing at her brow. "I can no longer stand the pain. My head will burst at any moment. Please help me! Don't just stand there asking questions. Do something, you idiot!"

I ignored this tirade. It was how she spoke to everyone. I apologized and asked some further questions.

"Is this the first time your head has hurt you so, or have you suffered this affliction before? I must also ask if you saw a bright light before the pain became severe."

Still holding her head with both hands, she glared at me and whispered viciously, "You fool, yes I saw such a light. Yes, I have had this ache before, but nothing like this. If you value your position, you will do something to aid me. If you cannot do that, find someone who can and get out!"

Thankfully, I recognized her symptoms for what they were. Hippocrates himself had written of this condition. There was a treatment but I needed my medicines.

"Your highness, I know exactly what to do. I will obtain ingredients from my own chamber. Do not worry, I will return soon."

Immediately, I regretted saying that I knew exactly what to do. I did not. I did, however, have a good idea. Ignoring her protests, I left for my own chamber to find the substances for which I had need. I prayed I would remember the lessons of my teachers. Galen had written that white willow bark infused in hot water was an effective remedy. Arabic manuscripts suggested the use of *spira ulmaria,* which is called meadwort. The delicate white flowers of this plant can be infused in hot water and mixed with al-sukkar or honey. If nothing else, the meadwort flower has a delightful fragrance and might calm the Countess. Other scholars recommended a plant called betony or woundwort, which can ease pain and sooth agitation. Finally, there was verbena, the Herb of Grace, given to Lord Jesus to ease his suffering on the cross. I did not recall how to mix these ingredients so, knowing my patient, I infused equal parts of all of them in hot wine, not water. For good measure, I added a small amount of juice from the poppy.

When I returned with my potion, I gave it to the Countess and asked her to drink. She scowled.

"Are you certain this is not poison, that this will relive my pain? For your sake, I hope so."

"Your majesty, this will help you. Smell it and then drink all of it. You will soon find rest." I prayed I was right. The consequence of error was inconceivable.

When she whiffed the scent of the concoction, she smiled grudgingly, tasted it tentatively and then drank the entire goblet without pause. "Do not call me 'Majesty' or 'Highness'. I have told you to call me Madam," she commanded softly as she fell sound asleep.

I do not know whether it was my assurance that she would be relieved of pain or the juice of the poppy, but she slept soundly for the next few hours. I remained by her side praying I had not made an error. To my relief, she finally awoke.

"My pain is gone," she said. "You have performed a miracle. From this time forward you are the Court Physician. I will so order. Now, remove yourself from my chamber so I may rest. Go to the Emir so he may write a decree."

My head, held high, almost exploded with pride as I walked down the corridor to my chamber. I was the Court Physician to the rulers of Sicilia! This was an honor beyond anything I ever dreamed. I silently praised God for my good fortune. In my room, I took a few moments to straighten my robes, adjust my turban and comb the beard which was just beginning to grace my face. Wasting no more time, I proceeded to the chambers of the Emir.

"Welcome, Thoma," said Christodulus and he hugged me. "You have done well. The Regent has sent me word of your success in curing her ailment. She has asked me to appoint you as the royal physician. Sit down. We can discuss everything while I write."

How the Countess had communicated so swiftly with the Emir was a mystery. I had no time to ponder this question, however.

"Thoma, you have managed a significant accomplishment. Our Regent is not easy to please. Sometimes she makes decisions too quickly. More often than not, however, her judgement is unassailable. All of us on this island owe her a great debt. She has kept us free. She has resisted all the impediments that mainland Normans have thrown at her. But I have a question of my own."

With that remark, he casually gave me a letter. It was not from Matthaeus but from his father, Johannes.

"You do not have to read this now, I will tell you the message," he said. When he saw that I was troubled that a private letter to me had been opened and read, he explained. "We are cautious here, Thoma. My people examine everything that enters the palace; do not think we lack trust in you." He paused to ensure I understood and then continued.

"Before I begin, let me thank you for looking into the affairs of our departed Afflacio. Your suspicions, as were mine, have been confirmed. There is no record of his having attended the Salernitana School. Johannes says that if this man represented himself otherwise, he lied. You asked how he obtained the powder of zarniqa. This is, he writes, difficult to obtain. None of the herbalists in Salerno have any stocks of the substance. Johannes wants to know why it was used here." The Emir raised his eyebrows as he sought for me to acknowledge this information.

"So Afflacio was a fraud, your Excellency. I suspected as much. There is no way for me to prove it, but I think he was giving his Majesty poison. The symptoms I witnessed lead me to believe he was being given small amounts of zarniqa, administered over time. Had Afflacio continued, the Regent would have lost another son. I am convinced of that. How did he receive his appointment?"

"That is the heart of the matter, Thoma. In any event, Afflacio will be unable to harm anyone again. We have taken steps to guarantee that. Do you know a priest named Bartolomeo?"

"Yes, I met a priest by that name when I received my appointment as an apprentice to Afflacio. He commanded me to follow the directions of that physician without question."

Now I was frightened. I did my best to keep my visage calm. Besides informing me of my appointment, Bartolomeo had asked me to provide information. I decided to say nothing of this. Fortunately, my simple answer was enough for the Emir.

"Let me tell you some history. Some years ago, a priest named Bartolomeo obtained an audience with the Regent. He presented a letter of introduction from Pope Paschal and offered, on behalf of the Church, to provide a qualified physician to care for her sons. At the time, we only had Muslim physicians here. Against my advice, the Regent decided her sons should be under the care of Christians from the Roman Church. She accepted Bartolomeo's offer. Afflacio appeared shortly thereafter. He brought a stock of medicinal herbs and presented himself well. When her first son died young, it worried me. But the Regent believed this death was the will of God. She did not cast blame on the new physician. She believed he had done all in his power to find a cure for her child's ailment. It was following her son's death, however, that Afflacio began to drink heavily. He was, I believe, drowning his guilt in wine. You know there are those in the Church who prefer this island to not be a haven for what they call infidels. If we had lost both children, the only successor to rule would have been the Duke of Apulia and Calabria. You can guess the consequence."

The Emir paused to ensure I was following his tale.

"That same priest recommended you. That should worry me, but we have witnessed your skill. I have conducted a study of your past and believe you are to be trusted. Johannes thinks highly of you also. That is much in your favor. Be warned there are those in Rome and elsewhere who wish us harm. If anyone approaches you for information or to ask for favors, tell me. If anyone provides you with medicines, I will need to know."

This was a dilemma. Bartolomeo had, indeed, asked me for information. If he were to appear again, it could present a difficulty. I decided not to dwell on this. My new position carried great responsibility, requiring hard work on my part. I spent the next few months tending my herbs, reading texts in the Palace library and attending to the various ailments of high members of the court. Fortunately, most of the complaints I treated were not life threatening. There were minor wounds, painful stomachs and excess body heat. All of these were easily treated. This was fortunate as I was well aware of my own lack of experience. What I knew, I had learned from books. Regardless of this fact, my reputation continued to grow.

In my limited free time, I considered ways to prevent maladies. I had read that the laws of the ancient Persians required all drinking water to be stored in copper vessels. Water remained clean for longer if kept in this way. Drinking tainted or stale water did, I knew, result in stomach pain and other affliction of the bowels, so I recommended that the

Regent make a similar requirement. Presumably I was correct. The incidence of stomach problems decreased once the regulation was in effect.

I cure the Emir, enhance my reputation, greet an old acquaintance and save the City

I remember one incident that became important. The Emir suffered from severe pain in his joints and toes. Often it was difficult to walk. He had, however, learned to live with this condition as it occurred only at certain times. Night was the worst. In any case, he had found no cure. During one of our meetings, he asked me for my opinion. Was there anything he could do? I examined his feet and noticed there were hard crystals evident between his toes. Fortunately, I recognized this condition. It was called 'gout'. I did know a medicine that might help. I prepared an infusion of ground ellaen flowers and hot water. The gardeners hated this plant. It grew in abundance and could overwhelm their careful work. Its roots were poison. The flowers, however, were recommended for this affliction. To the infusion, I added ground colchicum root and a small amount of sukkar. I instructed him to drink this potion every few days. It was not long before he called me to his chambers and told me the condition had abated.

"You are indeed a worker of miracles, Thoma. We made no error in appointing you as the Court

Physician. I thought I would have to live with the pain until God called me. You deserve a reward. Ask and I will deliver it."

"Excellency," I replied humbly. "It is reward enough to know I have aided you. That is my duty."

Of course, I knew that the Emir considered himself to be in my debt. This fact only enhanced the pride I felt.

My sense of importance did not last long. About three months after the departure of Jusuf and Assad, a guard knocked on the door to my chambers.

"Forgive me for disturbing you. You have a visitor who demands to see you at once. He will not give us his name. He says you know him well. He is wearing a black robe and looks like a priest. May I bring him to you?"

I did not recognize the tall, young, blond-headed man who entered. He wore a black robe with an elegant eight-pointed cross emblazoned on the front. He carried himself with dignity. He smiled and raised his brows in anticipation of my recognition. He looked vaguely familiar. My memory failed me. I looked at him quizzically.

"My brother Thoma," he said gleefully. "You do not know me? Your traveling companion? You saved my life! You taught me your language. You remember nothing? Have I changed so much?"

Memories flooded back. "Roland, could it be you? You have changed! You speak Norman! I would not have recognized you. What are you doing here?"

"Thoma, I have changed my life! The good brothers at the priory, where you left me, provided me with a grand education. I have learned your language and others besides. I can read. I can write. I know my sums. Most wondrous of all, I have found a home from which I can find glory in work for God. I have learned my former beliefs were heresy, and everything has changed for me. The priests have taught me much. I owe all of this to you."

I remembered that Roland loved to talk so I said nothing and waited for him to continue.

"You are wondering why I am wearing this robe. I am not a priest, my brother. What I am is close to that. I am a sergeant in the service of God. I have joined the new Order of Saint John in Jerusalem. Our mission is to protect and care for pilgrims who journey to the Holy Land. I have honed my skills with the sword to this end. A few of our Order are armed. Besides our duties to see to the health of the pilgrims, we must also be ready to defend the Holy Land from our enemies. I will be traveling to Jerusalem soon. One day, I will become a knight. Who would have thought this was possible?"

It took me a few moments to absorb this news. I never expected to see Roland again. To see him now and learn of his new calling was surprising. His mention of the Order of St John prompted a vague memory.

"Roland, I am happy to see you. Indeed, it has been a long time. To hear you address me in my language brings me joy. I can understand you! Wasn't Brother Jehan also a lay brother of the Order of St. John? Have you seen him?"

"Of course, Thoma. He is one of our leaders. He has watched over me from the beginning. I owe my life to him as well. I almost forgot; he sends you his love and blessings and a message. But tell me about yourself. I understand you have become the Court Physician to the so-called rulers of this place. You must have done well at your school to achieve such a high honor. Do you treat their illness? Could you have treated the wound given to the Cathar? Please tell me everything."

My suspicions were aroused now. That Jehan would send me his love was inconceivable. I poured Roland a cup of wine and gave him a short history of my years at school and my time here in Sicilia. I shared nothing of substance. Instead I asked him questions. He had not changed; every query I made prompted a long discourse. St Gilles had not taught him the art of listening. Frustrated with his incessant ramblings, I told him I had duties to which I must attend and asked if he was staying long in the city.

"Oh no, Thoma, I am to board a vessel for Salerno tonight. I only wanted to see you once again and deliver the message from Brother Jehan."

"Roland, what is the message?"

"Thank you for reminding me, my dear lost friend. I have been so excited to talk to you that I might have forgotten. Brother Jehan has asked for your report. You are to give it to me, and I will take it to him myself. I do not know what this report entails. He was certain you had followed the direction of Father Bartolomeo in this matter and would be ready."

I took a long drink from my cup. I needed a few moments to collect my thoughts. I had not forgotten Bartolomeo's demand. Unfortunately, I had not considered what to do if it was ever brought to my attention. I decided to be forthright in my response.

"Roland, please convey my best wishes to Brother Jehan. I have not made the report he asked. By my oath as a physician, I cannot disclose any information about my patients without their consent. There is nothing occurring here that should concern the Church. If there are questions he wishes to ask, I can arrange for him to meet the Emir and he can ask himself. I regret you have traveled this far to no avail. I cannot tell you how happy your visit has made me. To see how you have changed; to learn of your progress is a delight. If you can stay longer, please do. I would enjoy talking to you again."

Roland frowned sadly at this. "Thoma, Brother Jehan will be unhappy," he said. "I have learned it is wise to obey him. The consequence of not doing so can be severe. He always gets what he wants. Tell me something I can say to him. You are my friend. I do not want any harm to befall you."

"I am sorry," I replied. "There is nothing to report. I enjoy a high position here and cannot betray the trust placed in me. Brother Jehan must know that."

Roland frowned. He said nothing at all for a few moments. "Thoma, I will tell him your report is not ready; you have had no time to prepare it. Conditions here are calm. All is well. We are leaving for the Holy Land in a few days so, perhaps, he will be engaged in other more important matters and will ignore this failure. I wish I might stay with you longer. There is much upon which we could converse, but I cannot do so now. I will be resident in Jerusalem, so if you travel to that city, find me at the Hospice of St. John. I pray we will meet again."

And with that final discourse, Roland left my chamber. I put the matter behind me as I had duties to which I needed to attend.

For the next few months, I duly devoted my life to my work as the Court Physician. Ever since I had cured the Emir of the gout, my services were constantly in demand. Often, my patients offered gold coin and precious jewels in exchange for cures. I did not accept these gifts as I lacked for nothing. I was already wealthy. My self-importance grew. My pride knew no bounds and, I admit, I sought further recognition and fame. My sole concern was that the herbs and medicines requested from Jusuf and Assad had not arrived. I visited Ishmael many times. He had heard nothing. I assumed it was simply a matter of time before they appeared. On one of those visits, Ishmael asked if I were keeping my letter of credit safe. I had forgotten about it. I remembered putting it in the pocket of my robe on my first visit and assumed I had placed it somewhere in my chambers. When I returned to my room, I searched everywhere. I found nothing. I searched again and again, more franticly each time without success. Was it possible I had dropped it? No one would dare take anything from my chamber. I could only assume it was lost. When I told Ishmael of this, he frowned, sadly shaking his head in disappointment.

"Thoma, I begged you to keep the letter safe. Anyone possessing it can draw upon your funds. Not from me, of course. I know you. There are others who do not. They would be correct to honor the letter and then seek reimbursement from me. I would have no choice but to honor such a request. Let me think about what to do. Do you need funds today? If so, I will advance what you need."

I had no need for coin but was now troubled. I deeply regretted my lack of attention to this matter but was certain Ishmael would find a solution. There was nothing else to do. My worry was soon put behind me. The following week was a horror.

There was no time to ponder my own problems as we were all faced with a new difficulty. I had just completed my duties and was returning to my chamber to rest when the Emir himself appeared in the hallway.

"Thoma, we have a grave problem. I need your help. I have assembled physicians from the city in the hall of the Regent and we require your presence."

"What is the problem, Excellency?"

"About two weeks ago, a trading vessel from Tunis arrived in the port. One of the passengers, a Christian, was ill with an affliction no one had ever seen. He said he felt hot, was coughing, had difficulty breathing and had excess discharge from his nose. Upon his arrival, a rash spread over his entire body. The physician who examined him was not alarmed about the rash and applied ointments to relieve his discomfort. He did not think the condition to be serious. However, it became worse. Within a few days, this man was dead. The physician assumed this was an act of God and arranged for his burial. A week later the physician himself suffered from the same ailment. There must be twenty or thirty others, all Christian, who have an identical condition. Every day, more are falling ill. We must find a cure before this pestilence afflicts everyone in Palermo. Hurry, come with me. Everyone is waiting for you."

The Regent's chamber was crowded. There were probably five or six elderly men dressed in the robes of physicians. Two priests were there as well. The Regent herself sat upon the dais, as did her son. The rest of those in attendance were members of the court and common people from the town. They were waiting for me and I felt myself in a cold sweat. Never had my position as the Court Physician put me in such a situation. I had no idea what to do or say. I swallowed hard and did my best to calm myself. The crowd was silent, waiting for me to speak. It was evident that they expected me to have answers and I still did not even know the questions. My palms became wet with fear. Thinking as fast as possible, I summoned the courage to address them:

"Your Majesty," I began, looking at Ruggiero, "please tell me the purpose of this meeting; how can I be of aid?"

"Do not waste time, Thoma," said the Regent. "The Emir has already told you what is happening. Before he died, the man who brought this affliction to us said he came here to see you. Why is that?"

She hesitated and then continued: "Answer me later. What is important now is to stop this sickness before all of us die. These physicians from the city tell me there is nothing they can do. They have not seen this condition before. I have no patience for those who do nothing. Our people are dying. You are the Court Physician. You will know what to do. Tell them," she commanded.

As I attempted to collect my thoughts, I looked more carefully at my audience. It was then I realized that all the physicians were Christian. There were no

Muslims. Most were smirking as they waited for me to answer. They were, I thought, hoping for my rapid downfall. I needed time to think.

"Madam, I must examine a few of the patients. The Emir has indeed explained their symptoms. I need to see myself if I am to provide wise counsel. Would that be possible now?"

"He is wasting our time," shouted one of the older physicians. "This young man has just passed his examinations. The school he attended promotes texts written by infidels. He has no experience. He cannot know what to do. We have spent our lives studying the art of medicine and have already examined the patients. What can he add?"

Ignoring this interruption and the murmuring of the crowd, the Regent motioned for her guards to escort me to the grounds outside the palace, where several patients lay moaning on cots. It did not take long to discover that all of them exhibited the same conditions. Their bodies were hot, their breathing labored, and their eyes inflamed. Most had small white pustules inside their mouths. A flat red rash covered all their bodies. I began to panic as I realized what this was. The Christians were correct. There was no cure. I took more time than necessary as I was desperately trying to remember my lessons at school. God be thanked, I recalled the work of the famous Persian physician al-Razi. He had written a manuscript called 'Kitab al-Jadari wa al-Hasba' which described this very condition. He wrote about two almost identical possibilities. One condition was less serious than the other, but both could lead to death. They could be differentiated by two facts: the existence of severe pain in the back and the degree to which the patient experienced nausea. The patients I examined said they only had mild discomfort in that area, and all felt ill in their stomachs. I was convinced I was dealing with al-hasba.

Al-Razi had found no cure for this. Al-hasba was, he wrote, a condition of the blood. Anyone afflicted with this illness would either live or die according to the will of God. Through contact, it would spread rapidly through a population. It had to be contained immediately. Why, I wondered, did it only seem to affect Christians? As I completed my examinations, I recalled a famous quote from one of his texts:

'The physician, even if he has doubts, must always make the patient believe that he will recover. The state of the body is linked to the state of the mind.'

That recollection gave me an idea of what to do. Praying to God I was correct, I returned to the Regent's chamber and addressed Ruggiero directly.

"Excellency, we face an enemy the Muslims call al-hasba. It is serious but we can deal with it. First, separate the afflicted from those in good health. Next, the priests here should pray with each of them and assure them of God's grace. It is important that all have faith in their recovery. Then, our physicians should draw blood as is the usual practice. For a few days, the patients should not eat anything solid. Water, lots of it, and broth will be sufficient. To alleviate their discomfort, wrap their skin in cloth which has been soaked in a mixture in equal parts of Af-Yum, the juice of cucumber, bangha and al-sukkar. I have stores of these medicines in the palace. You should know that even with this treatment, not all will live as the condition may be too far advanced. Those who treat the patients should cover their mouth and nose with a veil. If these instructions are followed and God wills it, we will defeat this enemy."

I completed my instructions and the crowd immediately began to talk amongst themselves. This talk turned to argument. One priest shouted over the hubbub.

"Why has this malady affected Christians, but no one else? What you propose may be right for those not of our faith. What makes you think it is right for us? Your so-called cure relies on the words of infidels. Physicians of the true faith have prayed on this matter. Have you? Are you even a Christian? It is a punishment from God."

Others in the chamber began to talk amongst themselves, vigorously nodding their heads in agreement. Encouraged by this support, he began to shout.

"Nonbelievers have corrupted our people. God has visited this affliction upon us for betraying Him. We must pray for forgiveness. We must rid ourselves of the infidels who infest our city. There is no cure! You are questioning the work of our Lord."

This outburst caused pandemonium in the chamber. While I waited for quiet, I thought as quickly as I could. The first of these questions was good despite the way it was asked. The logical answer was that the patients had all been those who had no direct contact with the Jews and Muslims in the city. How to respond to the rest of his diatribe was not evident. I was considering how to respond when the Regent did this for me.

"Silence," she shouted. "The Court Physician has given you instruction. Do as he demands. There is no time for argument or further discussion." With that declaration, she left the chamber, motioning to me to follow her.

When we reached her private quarters, she looked at me with her piercing hazel eyes that reminded me of those of a hunting falcon.

"For your sake, I hope you are correct."

I swallowed hard and tried to respond succinctly: "You know well I have not been a physician long; but all I have learned convinces me that I have given sound advice. Some of the afflicted will surely die. For many this will pass in time. What we must do is keep al-hasba from spreading elsewhere."

She nodded her head and sat, deep in thought, without speaking. My nerves almost got the better of me as I waited for her to speak again. Finally, she raised her brows and asked softly.

"Why was the first man with this complaint traveling to see you? There was a shipment of herbs and other medicines on the ship addressed to you in care of a Jew in the city. What are you not telling me?"

"I do not know why anyone from Tunis would have reason to seek me. I know no one in that city. Regarding the shipment, I requested those medicines to enhance my stores here. We are growing plants in the palace garden and Afflacio had many herbs in his chamber, but our stocks are low, and I need more. His Majesty, your son, helped me to prepare my list. I did think to sell some of what I bought to physicians in the city and am hoping to profit thereby."

She looked at me directly. "That man was one of the few remaining Christians in Tunis. He told us, shortly after he first became ill, that an acquaintance from Salerno kindly arranged passage for him on that vessel and instructed him to find you. You say you do not know anyone in that city, so how could that be? Who then sent your medicines from Tunis?"

Now I was worried. I think she noticed my legs beginning to tremble. My heart was racing. "Madam, I swear before God that I do not know this man or anyone else in Tunis. I asked my uncles to acquire the medicines and send them to me. Why they chose Tunis from where to transport them, I do not know. Please believe me."

"Whose God do you swear before? Your uncle is a Muslim and his partner a Jew. Is that not true?" I nodded my head in agreement. The Countess waited for my response. I had none. After a few moments of silence, she said, "I will accept your word – for now. Others may not. You had no permission to bring medicine to this island, did you? That is an offense under our laws."

Following a moment of silence to ensure I understood her words, she continued, "Let us deal with our current problem. We may have more to discuss. Leave me. Attend to your duties."

I think my legs were still shaking as I left her. She had made serious allegations. I had not thought to seek consent for my trade. I was a physician, not a man of commerce. It never occurred to me to ask. The only thing I could do was discover if my instructions were being followed. They were. Those who had fallen ill were being collected in a space outside the palace. This process would take at least another day. Meanwhile, servants, keeping their distance, threw reed mats for sleeping in their midst. I prayed it would not rain as I had not ordered tents to be constructed. In any event, I wanted them all in fresh air and separated from each other. Several priests, their faces covered with veils, went among the patients praying and reassuring them they would live if God so willed.

Several of the physicians engaged in bloodletting. Others prepared and applied the ointment I recommended. With everyone carrying out my directions, there was nothing more for me to do. I retired to my own chambers and drank several glasses of wine to calm my nerves. This had been a very bad day.

It took two weeks for the illness to stop its course. Five patients died but the rest recovered fully. None were scarred from their rash, so I knew my thinking was correct. The affliction had not spread to any new patients. The Christian physicians grudgingly agreed my advice had been correct, and, for a time, my prestige was enhanced. I could once again lift my head high and enjoy my position. Some in the city began to address me as the 'Protector of Palermo'. I was achieving the fame I coveted. Neither the Emir nor the Regent mentioned anything more about Tunis. I assumed that matter was closed. Once again, I was wrong.

I lose all

I was engrossed in reading a text in my chamber when a guard announced another visitor, a priest he said. A priest? This was not good, I thought. It was not. My visitor was the once cheerful Bartolomeo. This time he was not smiling. He closed the door behind him.

"I am here for your report. You have no reason for further delay."

Given my new position, I had no intention of responding politely. He insulted me with both his terse statement and lack of greeting. My blood boiled.

"Well met, Father," I retorted coldly. "You should address me properly. The report you so rudely demand does not exist, nor will it. I am busy, so if that is all, you may leave, and God be with you."

"No, Thomas, may God be with you. You should pray for His aid. You do not understand your situation. Did not you vow to provide us information in exchange for your position here? You have broken that vow. Your betrayal has consequence so, perhaps, we should discuss this further. There are matters that have come to our attention which may make your life complicated here."

With that remark, and without my consent, he settled himself on one of my cushions and casually waved a letter at me. "You may be missing this."

With a shock of recognition, I saw what he held was my letter of credit with Ishmael. It was only then I recalled an event occurring during my dash to the inn to meet my uncles. As I ran, a turbaned, veiled man, bumped into me from behind. He apologized profusely. He had not been paying attention to his route, he said. He politely brushed my robe, bowed and apologized again. I was in such a hurry that it took me a few moments to realize he had spoken in

Norman, not Arabic or Greek. I thought nothing of it at the time and only recalled the encounter now. I was speechless.

"I see you know what this is," he pronounced as he returned it to his satchel. "I wonder what the Regent would think. Why would you have so much coin? Ten thousand gold Dinars? A princely sum, is it not? Where did it come from? The Church will not be pleased either. You do not yet have the right to your inheritance. It is held in trust until we have proof of your father's death. Until then, your funds belong to the Church to be used for your benefit or, as you agreed, as we otherwise see fit. That you received rights to these funds without consent of the Church is proof of theft, is it not? Of course, this may be a payment for services to be rendered. I wonder which?"

There was no response possible. If the source of my coin was from my trust, I could be rightly accused of theft. If, on the other hand, it was a payment for services, how would I explain that? I said nothing. Bartolomeo raised his brows and smirked.

"I see you do not answer. Are you admitting guilt?" He did not wait for me to reply.

"There is more, of course. We understand in your conversation with the infidels you claim as relatives, you discussed a plot to purloin the remaining funds from the trust. One of our members was sitting nearby at the inn. He listened to the entirety of your discussion. I have a copy of his testimony here. He swears before God it is true and correct. Among other things, you agreed that deducting profits from your share of trade would not harm the Church. Is this not true?"

"No profit on the goods had been earned," I said. "How could my share be calculated when goods have not been sold?"

"Ah, you do not deny the report, then," said the still smirking Bartolomeo. "I think it best you accompany me to Rome where you can answer all our questions. We have ways to ensure you tell the truth. Is that what you want? Or, perhaps, we should speak to the Emir and you can explain how you intended to avoid tax on your so-called earnings. And that reminds me," he paused. "There is the matter of your herbs, brought here without license. Our loyal physicians have examined these substances. Some are most questionable. What were you bringing to this city?"

I sat stunned as if from a blow to my head. Any explanation would be countered by fact. My world began to crumble.

"Thomas, you underestimate what we can do to those who break their oaths or are traitors to our faith. We were too lenient in the past. Now we do not tolerate disobedience. We face too many dangers." Bartolomeo settled himself further in my cushions and asked for a cup of wine. I gave it to him to take time to settle my mind. It was difficult to keep my hands from shaking.

"The enemies of our Lord are everywhere" he continued. "Now that we have recaptured Jerusalem, we must purge the world of the Moors and all others who threaten our faith. I tried to explain this to you before. The Regent has been foolishly tolerant of the infidels living here. They must be converted or removed. Even the Greeks here are a problem. Our Pope, Paschal, commanded their Patriarch to accept his dominion, but his demand has been ignored. We must cleanse Sicilia of evil. It is too close to our own lands and, of course, the will of God must be carried out." He took a long drink from his cup and waved for more.

"As we are alone, I will disclose another matter. We sent Afflacio to assist in ridding this island of heirs to their first ruler. He was told to achieve that objective in whatever manner he chose. Without direct heirs, power would be transferred to someone faithful to our interests. He succeeded with respect to the eldest son. Thanks to your interference, your lack of obedience and his own failings, he failed to deal with the second. You reported nothing of this. Some believe you should never have been sent here; that we should never have assumed you would be faithful in your duty. They think you may be traitor to the Church or, worse, an infidel yourself. It is unfortunate that our emissary from Tunis did not reach you before he died. We granted him absolution for his sins in exchange for his services. He failed in his duty but, at least, his presence has caused some strife between those of our true faith and the infidels. I wonder if the Regent has questioned you about this. Has she asked why that man was seeking you? Do you have a ready response?"

I was shocked. I had been the intended carrier of al-hasba. My role as Court Physician would have enabled al-hasba to spread silently throughout the palace and that illness might have killed me as well. Bartolomeo saw my expression and smiled.

"I see you understand, my boy. It would be best if you did as we ask. It is the only path you can take. I will return in two days to receive the information we have demanded. Do not fail us this time."

With that remark, he rose from the cushion, casually put down his cup and left without any parting words. He did not even look at me. Thankfully, he gave me no time to stand as my shaking knees might have failed me. My mind swirled. I understood his threats and there was no way to counter them. Everything I had done to establish and enhance my reputation was being turned to dung. Bartolomeo had relieved me of my funds and inheritance. With a few words, he could destroy my future. I did not sleep that night. Over and over again, I relived the meeting and desperately tried to think of some course of action that would save me. I would not betray my oath as a physician. That had been made before God. I may have been confused about my own faith, but I knew the consequence of making a false oath. I could not betray the trust granted to me by the Regent, the Emir and young Ruggiero. There would be no report. But the consequence of my failure to deliver it would be devastating. I considered an appeal to Cardinal de Gaeta but realized this too would be a risk. I had never received a response to the letter I sent him. I had been a fool to entrust it to Bartolomeo. After all, the Cardinal was chancellor of the Church. He must be aware of all this. I thought I could trust him. He told me I might be in danger. Could I have been wrong? Confessing matters to the Emir carried the same danger. The Cardinal was correct in one thing. I could trust no one.

The next morning brought no relief. All I could think about was how easily the gifts I had received from God – my wealth, education and nascent fame – could be destroyed. My subsequent visits to the infirm in the Palace were perfunctory. Thanks be to God, no one was seriously ill. My mind was too much in turmoil to have been any use. There was no solution to my problem except one. I had to leave my life here behind.

In those days, I did not need to formally request audience with the Emir. He readily received me when I entered his chamber unannounced.

"Excellency, I beg for a favor. It seems my grandfather in al-Qahirah is gravely ill. I must travel to see him. I will not be gone long. May I depart on the next available vessel? Will you grant me leave to do so?"

I lied. What other choice did I have? The Emir looked at me suspiciously. I prayed he would not see how nervous I was. His response was measured.

"Ahh, now I understand. That is why you were visited by the priest. He was delivering this news. We have been wondering about that. Of course, you may leave. Family always comes first. You have been of great service to us and to me personally. We will miss you, so return to us as soon as possible. Is there anything I can do to assist?"

There was much he could do but I could not admit I lacked funds for this fictitious journey. I remained silent. The Emir, seeing my hesitation, called for one of his assistants and whispered to him. A few words were exchanged, and the assistant immediately left the chamber. Christodulus then turned to me.

"Thoma, one of our own vessels is leaving for Tunis on the coast of Ifriqiya in the morning. You will board as an important passenger. There will be no cost. This is the least I can do for you. I regret we have no means of transporting you directly to Aegyptus. You will easily find onward transport to Iskandariyyah from the port. From there you can find passage to al-Qahirah."

My mind was not clear enough to wonder how he knew where my grandfather resided. I realized that by arranging for me to travel in this way, he would be assured I was making the trip I requested. He was no fool.

"Do you have sufficient coin for your journey?" he asked. "I still owe you a reward for curing my affliction. It seems we have not paid for your services in any event."

Again, I hesitated to respond. If I said I did not and it was later shown that I possessed thousands of Dinars, the Emir would consider me not only be a thief but a liar. Thus, I merely responded in the affirmative. I claimed I had enough funds and could collect my fees when I returned. I thanked him profusely for arranging my passage to Tunis and turned to leave.

"Thoma, there is one matter on which your aid would be helpful. We think it may be in our interest to establish control of the coast of Ifriqiya to better strengthen our position in the Middle Sea. I would appreciate receiving all the information you can obtain about the current situation in Tunis. We also need to understand why the Christian infected with al-hasba wanted to see you. In exchange, we will, how shall I say, forget about the irregularities in your shipment of medicines. I will hold your goods until your return. We can resolve the taxes due then. Godspeed on your journey and God save your grandfather."

With those parting words, I was dismissed from the Emir's chambers. I left feeling guilt for my lie; ashamed that I had so grossly misled this friend. Free passage to Tunis was a great help. The only coin I possessed was four gold Tari. I did not know how I would pay to secure passage beyond, but that was the least of my concerns. Somehow, I needed to avoid Bartolomeo and his associates until I was safely on board the Emir's ship. A means of doing so occurred to me. Given his aversion to nonbelievers, there was a place Bartolomeo would not seek me out. I went to my own chamber and packed a satchel with some of my medicines and instruments. Donning a simple brown robe, I left the palace in the evening hoping no one would recognize me in the dark. Thanks be to God, Ishmael the money changer had not closed his shop.

"Ishmael, you asked that I visit you when I had time to do so. As you know, my duties have been great. It is only now I can free myself."

"Of course, of course," he responded eagerly. "Will you share a flask of wine with me? I would enjoy hearing your stories and telling you my own. We must become better acquainted with each other. You have achieved great fame here and I am honored by your presence. Have you found your letter of credit? Is there anything I can do for you?"

I told him I was still looking for the letter and counseled him not to worry. To gain time, I related a tale of my journey to Salerno and experience at the school. When I grew tired of my own talk, I asked him to tell me how he had met Jusuf. As I expected that question prompted a lengthy discourse on Ishmael's history. Ishmael ordered food to be brought to us. We drank more wine and talked well into the night. By the time we completed our dialogue, it had grown dark. I asked to stay in his shop until daybreak. Everyone knew walking alone in the empty nighttime streets was not prudent. As I had hoped, he readily agreed.

I escape Sicilia and face a new danger

Early the following morning, I walked to the docks. It was easy to find the vessel bound for Tunis. It was a well-used merchant sailing cog with a single sail. This one had a stern castle which sheltered the single rudder and a small cabin where a passenger could rest. Presumably, it would be useful for defense against pirates. I noticed there were two archers and three or four men at arms on board to protect the cargo.

The captain, a man of middle years by the name of Demetrious, greeted me warmly in Greek, a language with which I was acquainted. He knew to expect me and provided a resting space in the castle itself. Depending on the wind and condition of the sea, our voyage to Tunis would take two days and nights. We cast off from the dock soon after my arrival. I sighed with relief as we left Palermo behind.

The first day of our travel, God blessed us with mild winds and calm seas. That was common at this time of year. Because my stomach was calm, I spent my time at sea lost in thought. Everything I had desired had been bestowed upon me in Sicilia. I had been respected and honored by the island's rulers and even some of the populace of Palermo. I had achieved recognition well beyond my expectations. I had become proud of my own skills as a physician. Wealth, I had taken for granted. What God has given, He can take away and that, most certainly, had transpired. Everything I had gained or possessed was gone. What had I done wrong to deserve such a fate? Had my failure to always attend mass offended God? Was my confusion about my faith an unforgivable sin? My eyes filled with tears as I bemoaned the injustice of it all. Worse, perhaps, was the dawning realization that my future was bleak. How could I join my family in Aegyptus as a supplicant? How could I hide what others would see as apostasy? Other than my training as a physician, I had nothing to offer. My four small coins, my clothing, my satchel and a few medicines were all I possessed.

My fall into the depths of despair was interrupted by Demetrious, who joined me at the rail of the ship. I prayed he would not notice my red eyes. It took my mind off my own woes to listen to his stories. He and his crew were Greek Christians from Constantinopolis. Until a year ago, the Pisans engaged him to carry cargo to the Holy Land. Unfortunately, receiving payment for his services was a constant problem. Often, he had to beg for recompense. Even then, it was slow to be delivered. He and the crew had concluded that the dangers involved, coupled with their irregular earnings, were reason enough to abandon their employment. Fortunately, the Emir had retained them to carry cargo to Tunis. This was a much easier voyage and there had been no problem with collecting the fees owed to them. The slaves used to pull the oars had no choice in the matter.

"Are there not risks in the route from Sicilia to Tunis?" I asked.

"Of course, there is always a risk. At this time of year, the seas are usually calm, but storms can fall upon us at any time. Part of our journey is at night and the dark always carries its own threat. Do not worry, we have made this voyage many times and are not concerned. In any event, our cargo is grain. On our return voyage to Sicilia, we will be carrying Qutun cloth from Aegyptus as well as gold to be minted into Tari. This is somewhat more dangerous, but we have armed ourselves accordingly. In any event, there is no war between Sicilia and Ifriqiya, so trading vessels like ours are constantly sailing between the ports of Palermo and Tunis and no one has reported any difficulty as of late. Of course, in this part of the Middle Sea, there is no danger from slavers either. It is different further west. Those who trade in slaves and steal from merchant ships we call 'peirates' in my language. Thanks be to God, we have never been assaulted. Your stay with us will, God willing, be both comfortable and peaceful."

"I pray that will be true," I said. "During your employment with Pisa, did you ever encounter a ship's captain named Rowan?" I asked.

"I never met him in person, but I knew him by reputation. He possessed his own small fleet and was a master navigator. He was respected by all of us. On many occasions, he led the way and never failed to discover the shortest and safest routes to the Holy Land and back. He knew the Middle Sea well. How is it you know this man?"

"Long ago, I sailed with him," I answered. I chose not to disclose anything further and changed the subject. "You speak of him in the past, Captain. Is he no longer living?"

"He was when we entered into the service of the Emir. It was rumored he was wealthy. I think he once had close relations with the Fatimid. Some said he made his fortune by supplying arms to them. For some reason, he avoided the port of Amalfi."

I hoped Rowan was still alive. He would be an old man by now. We conversed well into the evening and the captain regaled me with tales of his adventures on the routes to the Holy Land. For a short time, I was able to forget my problems. When it grew dark, I retired to my mat in the castle and, with the aid of the gentle rocking of the ship, I fell sound asleep.

I awoke to the sound of screams. In a panic, I attempted to open the castle door, but I could not. Something was blocking it. I heard the sound of shouting men, running feet and splashes in the ocean. When I was able to push the door open, I found that it was obstructed by a body, resting in a spreading pool of blood. An arrow protruded from his left eye. The sun had just begun to lift above the horizon, and, in the early morning haze, I saw a scene of horror. Turbaned men were slicing their way through our remaining men at arms. One brigand lay moaning on the deck. The unarmed crew had been herded to the prow of the ship and they were quaking with fear. Our captain, Demetrious, was gallantly fending off two attacking swordsmen. He did not last long. When he raised his sword arm, a spear point suddenly thrust through his chest from behind. He cried aloud and fell. As I turned to escape into the castle, one of the attackers saw me.

"Halt," he shouted in Arabic. "In the name of Allah, if you value your life, remain where you are. If you move, you will die."

I had nothing with which to defend myself and had no choice but to obey. I am not certain how I mustered the courage to think, much less speak forcefully.

"What is this?" I bellowed in Arabic. "I am the physician Thoma Ibn Thoma, traveling to Madhya. This is my crew. If you interfere with us, you will answer to the ruler." Madhya was the capital of this part of Ifriqiya. I had no idea who the Zirid ruler was. I hoped no one would ask.

In Greek, which I prayed our attackers would not understand, I shouted to the crew, "Do as I command and we all may be saved. Bow to me and show your understanding."

Thanks be to God, they understood my words. Acting as one, the crew bowed to my order.

"We do not care who you are," shouted an attacker. "This vessel has come from the lands of the infidel and we claim it. Our master will determine your fate. I am certain you and the crew are destined for a new life in the desert, as servants to the Banu Hilal. You may find these nomads to be hard masters but, if you do as we say, and Allah wills it, you might live."

The peirates suddenly became silent as an elderly, white-bearded man jumped over the ship rail from his own vessel with a vigor that belied his age. He apparently was their leader. The man who had shouted at me whispered to him while he pointed to the wounded peirate lying on the deck.

"You," roared the leader. "You claim you are a physician? Cure my son." He beckoned to me to go down to the deck.

Summoning all the dignity and courage I could muster, I walked down the castle steps onto the deck and examined the wounded pierate. The unfortunate fellow was moaning in agony as he lolled in a pool of spreading blood. The source of his pain was evident. He had suffered a deep cut in his upper abdomen. Some of his glistening intestine hung loose from the site of the wound. Most often, an injury of this kind led to a slow and agonizing death. I peered at him closely. His bowels were still intact. The sword had sliced cleanly through his skin. It did not appear to have done any other damage.

"Sayyid, if Allah wills it, I can save your son. You, in turn, must do something for me. You may keep this vessel and its cargo. You have won that through conquest. But the crew must be freed and sent to Tunis."

The leader scowled. "You bargain with me? I am Khalid el-Idrisi. You dare to barter for the life of my son?"

"With respect, I am bargaining for the life of the crew. I will, with the help of Allah, cure your son."

"Then do so, physician," he answered. "I will do what is right. If you fail, I swear I will likewise do what is just. I cannot be clearer."

"Very well," I responded. "Bring me my satchel, a sponge and a bucket of water from the sea. I need vinegar as well."

While I waited, I pressed firmly on the lower part of his abdomen to reduce the bleeding. When the seawater, sponge and vinegar were delivered, I washed the area as gently as possible. Using the sponge, which I had soaked in wine, I pushed the bowels back into their original position. What needed to be done next would, I knew, result in even more pain. From my satchel I took a small spoon of dried 'sharab alshuwkran' and combined that with a small amount of vinegar. I knew it was dangerous to have someone with a wound of this kind drink anything. In this case, I had no choice. The sharab alshuwkran itself was dangerous. Too much would kill my patient. I prayed I had made my potion correctly. Over the protests of his father, I mixed this with a cup of wine and forced him to drink. It was not long before he fell asleep. I could then do what was necessary. Using a fine thread and a small square needle, I sewed his bowels back into their casing. I cleaned the wound again and, using a cloth, removed as much of the blood as possible. I then applied a salve and closed the wound, leaving a single small opening to allow further drainage. This procedure was difficult. I had to concentrate hard to prevent my body from shaking. I had never performed something like this on a living person. For good measure, I recited aloud the verse from the Surah Ash-shu in the Holy Book of Islam.

'Remove the harm O Lord of mankind and heal this ailment; you are the one who heals and there is no healing except Yours with a healing which does not leave any illness behind.'

"Sayyid, I am finished. His fate is in the hands of Allah. He is not to be moved. I want him to be kept warm until he wakes. This wound must be carefully cleaned with a cloth soaked in wine and vinegar after each call to prayer."

Khalid looked at his son and then turned to me. "You are a Muslim?" he asked softly.

I swallowed hard and told him, yes, of course, I was of the faith. Silently, I prayed God would forgive my lie, if it was a lie.

He nodded slowly and steadily looked at me.

"My son's fate will be determined by Allah. If he lives, I will grant your request. The crew will be freed. You, however, will stay with us. We have need for a physician. If he dies, then so will you and all the crew. The Holy Quran teaches us that revenge is to be avoided; that forgiveness is blessed by Allah. But this is my son. Your fate will be the same as his."

Khalid's son woke in the afternoon. He moaned in pain. Thanks be to God, he was alive. I continued to gently wash his wound and drain some of the blood. The sea was calm, and we recommenced our voyage in the evening. Khalid took the helm of our cog to monitor his son's progress. He ordered both ships to sail close together and our own crew to continue their duties. With the peirates' ship alongside, our progress was slow. On the morning of the second day, we spied the coast of Ifriqiya and eventually entered a small walled harbor.

By the time we arrived at port, my patient was complaining of hunger. He was angry at being forced to remain prone on the deck. This was a good sign. I inspected his wound and my handiwork. There was no sign of rot. His body was not hot to the touch. His urine was of the normal color. I reported my findings to Khalid and suggested that my patient be carried in a hammock to his home so he could continue to rest. For another few days, he was to drink broth and eat nothing else.

We had landed in a small city called Safaqus, which was about one day and a half's sail from Tunis. In ancient times, this place had been an important Roman trading town. Later it was the seat of a Christian bishop. Now the Zirid controlled the city. So far, they had avoided conflict with the Banu Hilal. These nomad raiders had been dispatched by the Fatimid in Aegyptus to punish the Zirid for converting to what they thought were the false Sunni beliefs of the Turks and vowing allegiance to the Caliph in Baghdad. The city was governed by a council of elders and this body provided slaves and grain to the Banu Hilal in exchange for peace.

Khalid was delighted with the improvement of his son's condition. I saw him smile for the first time as his son was taken f the deck.

"Tell your crew they are free. We will provide provisions. They will walk along the coast to the city of Sousse. There they may find passage on a ship bound for Sicilia. Their journey will take them at least two days. I suggest they walk by night and hide during the day to avoid difficulty. You will stay here and attend my son. We will go now to the Great Mosque to pray for my son's recovery."

I translated Khalid's words for the crew, and, with one exception, they were visibly relieved. Some even smiled and thanked me for their salvation. It had not yet occurred to them that their walk to Sousse would be full of danger. They only cared that they had not become slaves. That would be the worst possible fate. One man stood apart from the others. He politely asked to speak to me alone. I had paid little attention to him on our voyage. His body was thin, but his build was wiry and quite strong. Although he looked much like his Greek companions, he was somehow different. I recalled that the crew treated him with disdain. They had avoided him whenever possible and he kept to himself. I beckoned for him to approach me.

"Hakim," he addressed me formally in surprisingly fluent Arabic. "I wish to stay with you. The Greeks will make certain I do not return to Sicilia alive. They suspect correctly that I am a Muslim. They hate me for that. They accuse me of being responsible for what has happened. My true name is Sukman Ibn Artuq."

With this introduction, he leaned even closer to me and whispered, "I am what you call a Nazri Ismaili." He looked at me carefully to see if I understood. I did not. I simply nodded my head, hoping he would continue. Sukman took my lack of response for understanding.

"I have been praying for a means to escape these Greeks. If you permit me to remain, I swear I will protect you until I can find a way to return to my people. I am familiar with the lands of the Turks. I have traveled everywhere in al-Shaam and Palestine. You will find me useful. My service will be at no cost."

I looked cautiously at Sukman. There was no way to judge his honesty but, I thought, it would be useful to have a knowledgeable companion if I were ever to complete my journey to the Holy Land. How he would protect me and from what I did not know. I knew there were two branches of Islam: Sunni, who followed leaders chosen for their ability; and the Shiites, who believed only a direct descendent of the Prophet (may his name be blessed) had ultimate authority. The Fatimid rulers of Aegyptus as well as many of the Muslim physicians whose works I had studied were of the latter persuasion. My own grandfather and uncle were Shiite. The Turks were Sunni. Much like the Greek and Roman churches, the two branches of Islam worshiped in slightly different ways and held slightly different beliefs. Thus, being accompanied by a Shiite in areas dominated by their enemies, the Sunni, might not be prudent. I hesitated for a few moments and then turned to him.

"Swear before Allah you will do as you say, and I will permit you to stay with me." Sukman made such an oath and knelt on the deck in a sign of fealty. For better or worse, I told him to rise and accepted his proposal. I now had my first retainer.

I become a peirate physician and befriend an Assassin

The Greek crew was released and sent on their way. With modest persuasion, Khalid agreed that Sukman could remain with me. Together we walked to the Grand Mosque. Along the way, Khalid stopped and looked at me.

"Hakim, if that is what you are, it appears you saved my son's life. It remains to be seen, for how long. I do not yet trust you. You have already lied to me once."

"Lied?" I asked innocently. "Lied?"

I prayed he was not referring to my declaration of faith.

"Who is the ruler of Madhya?" he asked softly. "You said you were called to him."

I hung my head and admitted that I did not know. I began to fabricate an explanation. Khalid cut me short.

"I do not care where you were going or the reason for your voyage. Just save my son and you will be rewarded. If he dies, so will you and your new companion. We will go to the mosque and pray."

The Grand Mosque was an imposing edifice in the center of the city. It had a high minaret and was beautifully decorated with script. Before entering, we removed our shoes and washed our hands and faces.

Thanks be to God, I recalled the ritual of Muslim prayer. It was a relief to fall into the rhythm and chants I remembered from childhood. We stood erect, facing the Holy City of Mecca, with our heads down and arms folded to recite the beginning of the service.

Allaahu Akbar. God is the most great
I bear witness that there are no gods but Allah
I bear witness that Muhammed is the Messenger of
Allah
Come to prayer.
Come to felicity. Prayer is better than sleep. Our
prayers are now ready.
Allaahu Akbar.
There is no deity save Allah.

As I had discovered in my attendance at mass in St Mathew's Cathedral in Salerno, the ritual was comforting. Chanting prayers to our common God with the other worshipers made it impossible to dwell upon the tribulations of the past days. I felt at peace. When we eventually left the mosque, my mind was clear. Sukman seemed to feel the same. I had noticed that during prayer he grimaced in disgust as he folded his arms. I wondered why. He did not speak until we reached the residence of Khalid.

We entered a walled compound through a strong gate. Two guards protected the entrance. The home was not large but was a virtual fortress. Sukman and I were led to our chamber, which appeared comfortable enough compared with our quarters while at sea. Slaves made a simple meal and Khalid's servants led us to the baths, where we were able to clean our entire bodies and were given new clothing. Khalid appeared when we were clean and well fed. He motioned for us to accompany him to his son's room.

My patient's color had returned and, when we entered, was complaining loudly to another servant.

"I am through with this gruel; all I have had is liquid slime! I need meat. My wound will not kill me, starvation will."

"Quiet, my son! Stop complaining," ordered Khalid. "This is the physician who saved you at sea. His name is Hakim Thoma. Greet him with respect."

Khalid's son became quiet. "Forgive me, Father." Turning to me, he asked with some diffidence, "Hakim, thank you; but must I continue to only drink liquid? When can I rise from this bed?"

"Are you in pain?" I asked.

"Of course, I am in pain. What have you done to my wound? Why is it bound with these threads? Why do the servants keep washing me? It hurts every time they do that. My gut feels as if it will burst."

I examined him thoroughly. He was young and recovering much faster than I expected. His wound was clean. I saw no sign of rot. Perhaps my visit to the mosque had been of benefit.

"You are doing well," I told him. "If you are careful, you may begin eating lamb stew. Eat little at first and we will see how you are doing. I want you to remain in your bed for another day and then you must walk. My assistant here will help you to do that. Your condition was serious. Most often a wound of this kind is mortal. Thanks be to Allah, I believe you will recover if you follow my direction. You asked about the threads. These are to keep your belly together. I will remove them later. When I have done that, you will forever be scarred. All who see it will know you suffered a grave wound in battle and triumphed over death. You should be proud of your scar. It is a sign of bravery."

That pleased him. A shadow of a smile marked his face and he thanked me. I prayed he would recover from my very first attempt to repair a living body. If he did not, my fate was certain.

IV

A.D. 1112–1114
A.H. 505–508
A.M. 4872–4874

Sukman and I spent the next two weeks caring for our patient. I instructed Sukman in how to best assist in the daily cleansing and walking routine. He was not happy with this chore but followed my orders without question. We were not permitted to leave Khalid's home except to attend worship in the mosque. Otherwise we were treated well. The food was palatable, and we bathed every day. Our patient's condition improved until he was able to walk without assistance and live an almost normal life. His wound became, as I had promised, only a thin red line on his abdomen. I was proud of my art. Khalid, who we had not seen for some time, finally visited our room.

"It seems you have fully cured my son. I promised to reward you. That must wait. We have need for you in this place. There is no one to care for those who are ill or have suffered wounds. My position here is secure because it is only through my efforts that Safaqus can secure tribute for the Banu Halal. The desert tribe needs the grain and slaves we provide in exchange for peace. The city council supports our efforts but there are other shipmasters that could, if given the chance, do the same. If I make your services as a physician available to the city, then no one will dare attempt to displace me."

"But how long do you demand we remain here?" I asked.

"Until I no longer need you," he replied angrily. "Do as I demand, and all will be well."

It appeared we had no choice, at least for the moment. Thus began our days of servitude in the city of Safaqus. Every day or two Sukman and I visited a new patient in the town. On each occasion, we were accompanied by Khalid's surly guards, presumably to ensure we did not escape. There were the usual imbalances in the humors, an occasional broken bone requiring attention, and ailments of digestion. Our patients were grateful for our visits and, all things considered, we were treated well. Sukman was a fast learner and soon could treat minor ailments himself. Surprisingly, he was well acquainted with some of the medicines we used. I asked him about where he had gained his knowledge.

"Hakim, I thought you understood. I am a fida'i. I trust you now but say nothing of this to anyone. We are trained in the use of many potions. Of course, we do not use them to cure anything except the troubles of life itself. I watched you put Khalid's son to sleep with Sharab alshuwkran. I wondered about that. Such a substance can be used for other purposes, with which I am more familiar."

I began to have concerns about my new assistant. "Sukman, I must ask, what is a fida'i?"

Sukman looked at me strangely. "Surely you know of us, the Hashashiyin? I tried to tell you who I was when we first met. I thought you understood."

"No, Sukman, I understood you were a Shiite like the Fatimid but nothing else. Perhaps you should tell me more."

Sukman's Tale

"I am a Shiite but most certainly not like the Fatimid, may Allah's wrath be upon them. Have you no understanding of my faith? I know you are a Muslim as we attend prayer together. To whom do you owe allegiance? Do you follow the Caliph in Baghdad or the pretender in al-Qahirah?"

This was a good question. I was uncertain how to respond. I knew there was deadly conflict between the Shiite Fatimid and the Sunni Turks. But Sukman said he was a believer in the Ismaili Shia. What was an Ismaili? That there were also two branches of Shiite was a surprise to me. I decided to be vague in my answer.

"Sukman, I was born in al-Qahirah under the Fatimid. I have been among the Franj for many years. That is where I learned the art of medicine. I lack education in many matters of faith. Please do tell me your story."

Sukman paused to consider this. He furrowed his brows in thought and then answered.

"Perhaps then I can help you understand the true faith. You have been kind to me. So far, you have not betrayed my trust, but I have concerns for your soul if you do not have allegiance to the true Caliph. Let me tell you some of my story and we will discuss matters of faith later. I was born in the mountains of Persia, not far from the lands of al-Shaam, the area the Franj call Levante. My father died when I was young and, truly, he was a hero. He aided the young Caliph, al-Hadi, to escape the Fatimid in Iskandariyyah. I am certain you know al-Hadi's father, Nizar, was a direct descendant of Ali, whom the Prophet (may his name be blessed) had chosen as his successor. Nizar was the true Caliph-Imam. The Fatimid under the rule of al-Afdal – I beg Allah to destroy him – refused to accept this fact. They committed the unforgivable crime of executing Nizar. Can you believe that? Do you know what they did? They buried him alive. May they be forever cursed! They placed a usurper named al-Must'ali on the throne. Forever after we, the Nizari, have been mortal enemies of the Must'ili Ismaili. We do not speak of the Sunni Turks who reject the true descendant of the Prophet (May peace be upon Him). Both they and the Must'ali are heretics!"

Sukman was turning red in the face as he spoke. "Our captor Khalid is a Sunni," he scowled. "He has allegiance to the Zirid who rule this place. He is our enemy. Did you not notice how he folds his arms during prayer? We keep them at our side."

I could see Sukman was preparing to continue this diatribe so, hoping to calm him, I begged him to tell me more of himself.

"Yes, forgive me, I was telling you my own story. You need to understand something further. To defend our position as exiles, we built a strong fortress in the mountains of Persia. From there, my people sought to expand knowledge of the true faith to the lands of al-Shaam. In the early days, we had no proper army to confront either the Turks or the Fatimid who ruled this land. Imam Hadi concluded it would be easiest to achieve our goals not through the means of traditional warfare, but by carefully lulling our opponents into submission. By removing the leadership of our opponents, we create fear amongst the heretics and other enemies. If you remove the head of a snake, what danger is the tail? A small, well-trained band could accomplish this. Hassan-i-Sabbah (May he be blessed with good health) was chosen to form such a group. He called them Hashashiyin, those who are dedicated to the foundation of the faith."

"Then you were part of this group?" I asked.

"Yes. I was indentured at the age of ten years and trained as a fida'i. That is what we call our warriors. I cannot disclose all that I learned. I am proficient in swordsmanship, archery and other martial arts. I studied potions and the means to deliver them secretly. That is why I recognized sharab alshuwkran. It is an effective poison. In any event, I was a good student. I learned how best to infiltrate an enemy camp without detection and move silently at night. There are those who claim that we, the fida'yin, are given substances which give us courage. That is not true. If our acts are acceptable to Allah, then our reward will be in paradise. That is sufficient for anyone, don't you think?"

Sukman paused for a few moments as he considered what he should say next.

"Hakim, the foes of the Nizari Ismaili are the foes of Allah. It is my duty and sacred obligation to obey the dictates of the true Imam and protect the community of believers, even if it means the sacrifice of my own life. Do you understand?"

Although I nodded my head in the affirmative, this revelation gave me great concern. Had I made a grave error in choosing my new companion? He had promised to protect me. Now I knew that was not an idle oath. What if he were to discover I was not a true Muslim? What if he found that my father had carried out duties for the Fatimid? What if he knew my grandfather and uncle were Shiite but not Ismaili? I did not permit my face to reflect my concern. I did, however, have a question and changed the subject.

"Sukman, how is it you came to be employed by the Greeks. Surely you have no reason to have done that?"

Sukman scowled. "I was not employed by them. My service was not my choice! Let me tell you the rest of my tale.

I completed my training and was sent to the city of Aleppo in al-Shaam. There, I was given many tasks. Most of these I accomplished alone. It was on my last assignment that everything went wrong. The city of Tripoli in al-Shaam had been besieged by the Franj for almost seven years. In the end, some of the city's elders betrayed their own people by telling the invading force how the city was supplied with food. The populace was starving. They could not hold out on their own. The Turk leaders had escaped the city to seek help from Baghdad but failed in their mission. The evil al-Afdal, may he be punished and never see paradise, saw an opportunity. He realized that he could retake the city for the Fatimid. He dispatched a fleet to aid in the defense and secure the city for himself. Of course, we did not want him to succeed. Believe me, we had no quarrel with the Franj. Those Infidels were not a threat to us and, often, our aims have been the same. My task was to remove the leader of al-Afdal's forces should they arrive so the Fatimid would fail in their mission. Do you understand?"

I did, at least partially. Both the Turks and the Fatimid were a threat to the Nizari. Under the rule of the Franj, Tripoli would be ripe for infiltration and conversion. Many of the Franj wished only to gain wealth and power. Often, they fought amongst themselves for the spoils of conquest. Disputes between the Muslims were of little concern to them. I was not certain how Sukman could carry out his task.

"Sukman, how would you 'remove', as you say, the Fatimid leader?"

"Hakim, my task was to send their leader to Allah. I was ordered to perform this task in public where all could see. My act was to be with upmost violence to create fear amongst the Fatimid. They are cowards. They would take to their ships and return to Aegyptus. The Franj would prevail. I would lose my own life in carrying out this mission and my reward would be in paradise. I had no opportunity to accomplish anything. The Franj took the city and sacked it before al Afdal's fleet arrived. When they did, all became chaos. I had disguised myself as an unarmed sailor so I could be unnoticed on the docks when the Fatimid fleet arrived. That was my misfortune. When the Franj attacked the city, supply and war vessels entered the harbor. I, along with others, was captured and enslaved. We replaced those of the crew of these vessels who either left their employ or had died on the inbound voyage. It was the will of Allah that my new master was Captain Demetrious. I was bound to him until you rescued me from servitude. I will forever be in your debt."

I did not sleep well that night.   Who had I befriended?

We Escape from Servitude

We had little time to engage in further discussion during the next few weeks.   There were constant demands for our services. One of these presented a danger. It was early in the morning when Khalid burst into our rooms with a new demand.

"You must come with me at once. It is distasteful, but there is a worshiper of the cross, we call them Nazarene, in the city, and he must be saved. He has provided services to me that I wish to retain. I do not want him to die, at least not yet. His name is Alexios."

Accompanied by our usual guards, Sukman and I were led through the narrow streets to a modest dwelling near the Great Mosque. There we met our patient. There was no mistaking that the man was ill. His name was Greek, so I spoke to him in that language.   He was quite weak, and he had some difficulty in understanding me. Christians in this part of the world spoke an odd dialect of Roman as well as heavily accented Arabic.   It took some effort to discover he had lost a great deal of weight in a short period. He was urinating frequently and was constantly thirsty. His right leg had begun to turn black. Thanks be to God, this condition had been the focus of one of the most obscure questions in my examinations. It was a question I failed to answer correctly. That is why I remembered it. Aretaeus of Cappadocia, the famed ancient physician, had written of this rare affliction. He called it 'diabetes' in his language. It was, without exception, a sentence of death. I needed to confirm my suspicion. Although Sukman found it disgusting, I tasted his urine. As expected, it was sweet. The Persian Ibn Sina had proposed a treatment using lupin beans and the seeds of fenugreek and roots of the zedoary plant which, he claimed, would lessen the excretion of sweetness in the urine. I had none of these. I knew it was only a matter of time before this patient met his maker. There was nothing I could do.

For the first time, I decided to tell my patient the plain truth.

"Sir, it would be best if you call for your priest so you may prepare to join God in heaven. Pray that Lord Jesus saves your soul and gives you comfort." I had spoken in Norman assuming Sukman would not understand my words. I was mistaken. Sukman looked at me strangely.

"Hakim, why are you telling this man to pray this way? He will not be saved. He is an infidel. They worship three gods, don't you know."

"Sukman, his people are Ahi-al Kitab, people of the book, just like the Jews. It will do no harm if he prays and has some hope of entering paradise. Those who are ill always benefit from having hope and trust in their maker. Our duty is to provide him some comfort."

This seemed to mollify Sukman. Just as he began to respond, a black-robed priest interrupted us. We had been so focused on our patient that we had not seen him enter the room. He spoke angrily.

"Why are you here?" he asked in Greek. "You have told this pious man there is nothing that can be done and that he will die. You are questioning the power of our Lord Jesus to save him? How dare you? Leave us at once!" He shook his head and mumbled, "Thanks be to God you did not give him any of your infidel medicines."

I swallowed my pride and remained silent. I motioned to Sukman that we should leave. As we turned, the priest asked again, "Who sent you here?"

Now I was angry myself. "His friend Khalid sent us. I am a physician of the Salernitana School. What business is it of yours?"

The priest's face turned red. "Friend? Khalid is no friend! That thief has kept Alexios under his thumb for years. This poor man is merely a merchant doing his best to survive. Yes, he has made some errors in the past but that is no excuse. God will forgive him. Your master Khalid forced him to divulge information about ships leaving Sicilia. You know the reason why." The priest paused for a moment. His face screwed into a frown of recognition.

"You claim you are a physician of the Salernitana School? We have been looking for a man of that kind. The one we seek has committed crimes against the Church. What is your name?"

Sukman looked at me quizzically. There was only one answer I could give.

"I doubt anyone is looking for me. We will leave now, and may God save the soul of Alexios. You will not." I turned away, grabbed Sukman by the arm and departed the house as fast as I could.

As we walked back to Khalid's home, Sukman leaned close to me and whispered.

"Hakim, are the Nazarene looking for you? Have you committed a crime? I will not judge you. I just need to understand."

"Sukman, I must escape this place. I was wrongly accused of breaching the laws of Sicilia and those of the Christians. Some in their Church wish me harm. I am not safe here. There is the fact too that Khalid will be angry with us for not being able to cure Alexios. I will understand if you no longer wish to keep my company."

"Hakim, I owe you my life and I pledged to protect you. Perhaps it would be best if I were to remove our captor Khalid so we may leave in peace. I too must return home. That is my own obligation. We will travel together."

I knew what Sukman meant by 'remove' and that I could not condone. I begged him not to take such a step. "There must be another way. Let us leave at night while the household is sleeping. If we are quiet and are careful in walking the streets, perhaps we can be far enough away when our absence is discovered that we will be safe."

"What about the guards, Hakim? There is always one at the gate and one wandering outside the walls. I have seen both at night. Perhaps I can deal with that?"

"Let us pray that Allah shows us the way, Sukman," I murmured.

We decided to make our attempt that night. Khalid had been angry that we failed to cure Alexios, but he had no time to consider punishment as he had duties of his own outside the city. He departed for the next few days, presumably to seek additional victims for his trade, and had left us alone with our guards. There was no time to lose. Sukman took more than his share of our meal and, I noticed, an entire loaf of bread. In our room, he placed the food in my satchel, added a goatskin of water and tucked a jeweled dagger into his belt.

"Where did you obtain such a weapon?" I asked in surprise.

"I borrowed it from the chamber of our captor. It is always best to be prepared," he said. "I have other matters to which I will attend; meet me at the gate when you hear the next call to prayer."

At the appointed time, I went to the gate and prayed that all was well. Khalid opened it from the outside and whispered that I should remain silent. I almost tripped over the man lying in the street. My boots sloshed through a fresh pool of blood. I bent down to see if there was still life in the body. Sukman placed his hand on my chest to stop me. "He has gone to Allah, Hakim. Do not waste your effort," he said flatly.

"What have you done?" I hissed in horror.

"What would you have me do, Hakim? Were you planning to beg him to free us? Were you thinking idle conversation would help us escape? Perhaps you could have given him something to help him sleep. Oh, but you do not have all your medicines. I have done what was necessary and, in any event, this man was a Sunni. Let us be gone before his demise is discovered. There is another by the wall." Sukman pointed to another body. "Watch your feet and do not step on him."

I sighed in resignation and, together, we walked silently through the deserted streets. It was dawn when we left the city through the western gate. There were guards at the gate and I whispered my concern to Sukman that they might impede our exit. Sukman ignored me.

"How do we reach the road to Merṛakec?" he asked the guards. "We have a long journey ahead of us and may Allah bless you for providing us direction."

Both guards looked at us with indifference and casually pointed the way to the old Roman road. "You have a long journey indeed. A caravan left for that place a short time ago. If you walk quickly, you can join them. It is safer that way."

Sukman thanked them profusely and we headed west. When we reached the sea, we turned south, circled the city and then headed east. My heart was still racing from recent events but I realized Sukman had made a good judgment. He wanted to ensure that the followers that Khalid would surely send to search for us began in the wrong direction. I had already told our captor I had family in Meṛṛakec so, perhaps, he would be fooled. It took some time for me to calm myself. My calling was to preserve life, not take it. My boots were still wet and sticky from stepping on the blood left by Sukman's solution to our captivity. What now lay ahead? There was no turning back.

We traveled for a considerable distance that night. Far enough, I hoped, to keep us from capture. The sea was on our left and we stayed as close as possible to the road that wound around the coast. I wondered how we would survive. We had no coin, little food and no friends. Neither of us knew anything of the lands through which we would travel. The only certainty was we were heading in the direction of Iskandariyyah. That place of refuge was very distant.

None of this concerned Sukman. The further we traveled from Safaqus, the happier he became. That he had caused the death of two men clearly did not weigh on his conscience. That we were free was, for him, sufficient and he praised our common God for deliverance. That is, until we had eaten all our food by the second day. Then his mood began to change, as did my own.

"We need to join a merchant caravan," he said. "It will be safer to travel in that way and, who knows, perhaps we can even ride. If we stay on this road, perhaps we will find one when evening falls."

"And then what?" I answered sullenly. "We cannot pay for the privilege of joining such a group. We have no goods to trade."

"Ah, Hakim, be calm. You are a healer and I am your assistant. Everyone needs a physician. That is our trade. The problem is not that. Any caravan we meet here will be friends of the Fatimid. I will find it difficult to tolerate such an association, but I am hungry, and we do what Allah wills."

Indeed, as the sun began to set, we saw the fires of a camp near the road. Sukman silently climbed the nearest dirt hill and crept close to it. There must have been about twenty merchants, together with several camels and at least five sword carrying guards. Praying that our judgment was sound, we walked into the camp. Before I could say anything, Sukman loudly proclaimed our presence.

"As salaam aleykum, Peace be upon you, my brothers, we seek shelter. My name is Abu Hassan. I have the honored privilege of being the chief assistant to the great Hakim Thoma ibn Thoma standing here to my left. We have had a hard journey. Thieves accosted us on the road and took all we possess. Hakim Thoma is traveling to Atrabulus where he will see a Jew who keeps his accounts so if you want, we can pay for all costs required for your companionship."

"Abu Hassan? What Jew?" I whispered. "I know no one in Atrabulus, nor do you."

"That is a matter for another day, Hakim. Keep quiet."

We continued to stand just outside the camp while the men discussed what they had just heard. Because they were camped next to a freshwater spring, custom and law required them to grant us refuge. Nothing, however, obligated them to permit us to join their caravan for an onward journey. An elderly man with a flowing white beard approached us.

"May peace be upon you. I, Sheikh Ahmed ibn al-Khattab, am the leader of these merchants. You are physicians? If so, you may travel with us. We may have need for your services on the road. We ourselves are traveling to Atrabulus. Our journey will take at least two weeks. If we do make use of your skills, there will be no fees. You may share our food and water in exchange."

We were not offered the opportunity to ride any of the camels which, as my uncle had reported, were most unpleasant and foul-smelling beasts. These animals reluctantly carried the trade goods of our companions. Instead, we walked. We passed through the oasis city of Gabes without stopping and continued through the settlement of al-Hamma which, at the time, was a trading center for the Banu Hilal nomads. A group of pilgrims bound for the Holy Cities of Medina and Mecca joined us there. A small number of archers protected them. This added to our own capability for defense. The lands through which we passed, always near the sea, were marked by tall date palm trees and flourishing groves of Zeituun. The desert was never far away.

We were about two days from our destination when the fiends from hell descended upon us. It was always dangerous to travel the coastal roads, but we believed our group to be safe from thieves. We had armed guards and our new archers to protect us. That was a false assumption. They came at dawn, when we had just departed one of the many oases where fresh water was available. There must have been twenty camel riders, shrieking as they charged our vulnerable group. We were unprepared for the onslaught. Several of our guards were cut down before they even drew their weapons. The archers too were not ready. They fumbled in their packs for arrows. One ran away screaming in fear. In a matter of moments, we would all either be dead or captured and enslaved. Sukman was the first to react. He grabbed a bow from an archer nearby and notched an arrow. I have never seen anything so quickly done. He aimed and shot. His target was riding a white camel and wore a headdress of gold. It took only an instant for Sukman's arrow to strike this man in the chest. He fell off the camel, blood flowing freely from his body. His companions halted their charge at once. One of their members dismounted and took Sukman's victim in his arms. He looked at the others, threw the body on the white camel's back and waived for his companions to leave. "You have killed our prince! We will have vengeance," he angrily shouted as he and the others turned to ride south into the desert.

"Cowards," Sukman retorted. "Come back and we will send you to Allah, all of you!" Casually, he notched another arrow and shot it squarely into the throat of the man who had shouted. "You will cry 'vengeance' no more," he declared with a wicked chuckle. He casually returned the bow to its previous owner, who was still trembling in fear.

I was so stunned by what had just happened that it took me a few moments to recover my breath.

"Sukman, you have saved us all. May you be blessed!" In my relief, I had forgotten to call him by his new name. I hoped no one else had heard me.

"Have I not told you about cutting the head of a snake? These thieves without leaders have no courage. They need to be given direction and, now, there is no one to do that."

Sheikh Ahmed joined us then. He had drawn his own sword but was visibly shaking.

"Thanks be to Allah, and thanks be to you, my dear Abu Hassan. There were too many of them. Without you, we would have lost our goods and our lives. We are in your debt."

"It is nothing," Sukman responded calmly. "Let us pray they do not return."

"Abu Hassan," I said. "We have no time for discussion. Others may need our help. Let us do what we must."

We spent the rest of the morning treating those injured by the raiders. I had enough gazz thread to close most of their wounds. I had nothing to relieve their pain. There was no wine, so Sukman and I did our best to wash the injuries with seawater before we closed them. Our companions did have some honey, which we used to cover the most serious of the wounds. This, I knew, could keep rot from setting in. One of our guards had been struck in the head. He was unconscious but he was still alive. Upon examination, I could see the white matter within his broken skull. There was nothing to do. It took a few more moments for him to die. Beside him was the sack carried by his camel. It had been cut in two and its glistening contents were spilt on the dirt. It was filled with gold powder. Sukman and I looked at each other in wonder.

"Now you know what we carry," said Sheikh Ahmed as he shook his head in sorrow. "Someone in Gabes told the Banu Hilal about us. They were sent by the Caliph to punish the Zirid. Instead, they have despoiled this land. They care not who they attack and rob. I will report this to the authorities but there is nothing they can do. The gold we carry is for the Fatimid treasury, so they can rebuild their fleet. The Franj are preparing to invade Aegyptus. When we return, I will take more guards with us."

"You carry much gold?" asked Sukman innocently.

"Enough. Some of it is ours. We have sold glazed tile and pots to merchants in Tunis. The pay us in gold dust. The rest is tribute we carry for the Caliph."

I was amazed. "Gold for pots," I exclaimed. "How can this be?"

"You are a physician and know nothing of trade. The infidels of Pisa love our glazing. They will pay ten times its cost to decorate their home and churches. I do not ask why. It is enough that this is true. Enough of this. We will continue our journey. We are expected in Atrabulus soon. Soldiers of the Fatimid will meet us to collect what we bring. It will take us longer now that we have wounded among us."

With that remark, Sheikh Ahmed ordered the gold to be repacked and our small caravan to proceed along the road. Sukman had said nothing. As we began to walk again, he whispered to me.

"Hakim, these people are carrying a great quantity of gold. We cannot permit it to fall into possession of the Fatimid. That is not in the interest of my people. If they cannot resist the Franj, that will be to our benefit. I know you do not share my beliefs though, Allah willing, you will someday, but we must work together to discover a solution."

Traveling slowly, we reached Atrabulus in the late afternoon of the third day. All our patients had survived the journey and were relieved to reach their destination. Sheikh Ahmed was particularly delighted and thanked us again. He insisted that we go together to the al-Naqah Mosque to offer thanks for our salvation. This mosque, sometimes called the Camel Mosque, is a wonder to behold. It was larger than any I had ever visited. Sheikh Ahmed told us the tale of how it came to be. It seems that over five hundred years previously, Caliph Umar had captured the city for Islam. The populous, seeking amnesty, had offered him a camel loaded with coins as payment. This camel reached the site of what would be the al-Naqah Mosque, knelt in the sand and refused to move. Caliph Umar took this as a sign from Allah. On the spot, he swore to use the coin to pay for a grand mosque to be built there. That is how this mosque came to be. Inside, there are thirty-six columns, all of which were taken from ancient Roman temples. We washed ourselves outside and prayed together in the hall.

The expected Fatimid soldiers had not yet arrived. Sheikh Ahmed worried about this as, he told us, the quantity of gold was large. His solution was to store it at his residence in the city. He asked us to stay with him for a few days. He trusted us, he said, and would enjoy our company. Having nowhere else to go and given that our plans were uncertain, we agreed. A few days of rest and access to baths to cleanse ourselves from the dirt of travel would do us no harm.

Although made of mud, as were most of the buildings in Atrabulus, Ahmed's residence was grand. High compound walls shielded a delightful garden full of fragrant flowers and bubbling fountains. Our chamber was comfortable and, for the first time in weeks, we were able to enjoy complete nights of sleep. Although we prayed together at the mosque, we did not discuss our faith. Sukman wanted to avoid that subject at all costs. Khalid had an extensive network of informants, who kept him apprised of commercial developments, and that was what he most wanted to discuss. I was happy with this as there was little I could disclose about myself. I was in constant fear. Sukman must not discover that my relatives resided in Aegyptus and were bound to the Fatimid. It was impossible to disclose anything of my background or faith. Both Sukman and I had a great deal to hide. I had told Sheikh Ahmed I had been called to al-Qahirah to consult with a physician in that city and translate some old medical texts he had discovered. This was the first time that Sukman had heard this fabrication. He wisely made no comment. Both of us were improving our skills in deception.

We had been in Ahmed's residence for about a week when he came to us one morning.

"The soldiers I was expecting will not be coming. I have received a letter instructing me to send the gold onward to Iskandariyyah by ship without further delay. There is a vessel in the harbor whose captain has worked with me before. His seamanship is competent, but I cannot trust him. You told me you were going to Aegyptus. Such a journey will be much easier by sea. If I pay for your passage, could you escort my cargo to ensure it is delivered?"

This request presented a quandary. If I could reach Iskandariyyah I could contact my uncles and relieve my current poverty. I could not do that in the company of Sukman. Upon reflection, I realized that my pride would not permit me to seek aid from my family in my current circumstances. How could I explain the disaster in Sicilia and the loss of my share in the Collegantia? Of course, my primary goal was to reach Jerusalem. I had promised to make that journey before I rejoined my family. I could explain nothing of this to Sukman.

Thanks be to God, he too had a dilemma. We had time to talk quietly; Sheikh Khalid had been interrupted in his conversation with us by a messenger.

"I cannot go to Iskandariyyah," he whispered. "I must return to my people. I cannot be an accomplice in transmitting this gold to our enemies. What shall we do?"

I thought for a few moments and reminded Sukman of his words to me on the road. "We must do as Allah wills. We have no coin and neither of us can stay in this place. Let us agree to Sheikh Khalid's request and trust Allah to lead us rightly."

Sukman nodded his head in agreement. "You are right. Sometimes Allah asks us to think for ourselves. We will find a way."

We thanked Sheikh Khalid for his proposal and agreed to accompany his shipment. The next morning, he escorted us to the docks, where a vessel awaited us. My first impression was that this so-called vessel was a floating disaster. It was what is called a quarib, a seagoing barge propelled by banks of oars, not sail. Capable of carrying heavy loads, it was entirely uncovered except for a cramped shack at the bow. It looked well used. Its old, unpainted timbers were cracked in places. Seeing our concern at the nature of our transport, Sheikh Khalid turned to us.

"Don't let its condition deceive you. It has made many voyages between this city and Iskandariyyah. Travel will be slow, but you will not depend upon the wind. Despite its appearance, it is strongly built. In any event, at this time of year, the seas are calm. You will be safe. Besides transporting our gold, they are carrying a cargo of silphium. This plant cures all sorts of maladies. It is highly prized by physicians in Aegyptus." Khalid bent down to whisper, "it is mostly valued for its use to induce women to make love. It is valuable! We grow it here. Its odor is sweet so you will comfortable if you lie upon it. The captain is experienced. He knows these waters well and expects you. I have given him a letter to the officials in Aegyptus so your role is acknowledged, and asked that you be granted what privileges you desire. There is food and water on board, and you are the only passengers. Have a safe journey and, once again, thank you for all you have done."

With that remark, he handed me two Gold al-Qahirah Bezant. He gave me no time to refuse this gift and walked away.

I become a peirate

We boarded the quarib with some trepidation. Besides the captain, twenty slaves worked the oars, with four sword-bearing seamen to manage them. The slaves were chained to their benches. They looked at us sullenly and I saw that, beneath their sunburned skin, most of them were Franj. There was one old white-bearded man and some of the others did not look well. Our voyage to Iskandariyyah would take almost two weeks and my heart went out to these poor souls who would be rowing us to that city. Their condition could have been worse, but this was truly an evil servitude. The captain greeted us and showed where to place our meager possessions and sleep. At least we would be covered. Everyone else was in the open. I prayed there would be no rain. We slowly rowed from the harbor and turned east.

During the day, all twenty oars were in service. Our captain was indifferent to the exhaustion of the slaves. He drove them without mercy. When I expressed concern regarding the condition of these men, the captain was quick to respond.

"These are Nazarene infidels," he said, as if this was enough answer. Seeing that his response was not acceptable to me, he continued, "I paid good coin for them. These Franj were captured on the field of battle. No one paid their ransom. We have given them the opportunity to convert to the true faith. None have accepted, so their condition is one of their own choosing, is that not so? At least they are fed better than would be the case with the Banu Hilal. The Franj do the same to our people. Don't waste your concern."

I did not find the captain's explanation comforting. I could only guess at the depths of misery into which these men had fallen. Silently, I prayed God for their deliverance. Sukman, of course, was oblivious to these matters. He wondered why our rowing was so slow.

Each night we stopped at small ports to refresh our water and food supplies. We bathed at every opportunity. The slaves were not so fortunate. It was indeed a slow, and increasingly odiferous journey. After what seemed weeks at sea, our captain informed us we would reach Iskandariyyah in two more days. Sukman and I engaged in many discussions as to how we would escape our predicament. Sukman suggested that he could remove the seamen, free the slaves and force the captain to take us to a friendlier destination. I thought this course of action, besides causing more death, was too great a risk. There had to be another way. I spent a sleepless night, pondering alternatives. After much thought, a course of action occurred to me.

"Sukman, do you trust me?" I queried. He responded affirmatively. "Then give me your dagger and prepare to experience some modest pain. Do not cry out!" Sukman looked at me quizzically, with just a touch of fear. After a moment of hesitation, he did as I asked.

I took the dagger from his hand, motioned to him to remain silent and made four small incisions in his legs. All of these began to bleed copiously. Sukman looked at me with an expression of both horror and pain but maintained his silence. I had a small quantity of powdered turmeric in my bag. This herb, especially when combined with Kabbaba , can cure ailments of the stomach and redness in an injury to the skin. It is also a wonderful yellow dye. I bound the small wounds I had inflicted on Sukman with white cloth and then roughly painted the bandages with a mixture of this powder and seawater. I told Sukman that his visage should reflect pain and concern. Otherwise he was to say nothing.

"That will be easy to do," he responded. "Your craft is painful! What are you doing?"

I told him to have faith and called the captain to our tiny abode.

"Captain, I do not want anyone to know this. My companion here is ill." I lifted Sukman's robe so the captain could see the mottled yellow bandages which were weeping red blood.

"This is the bleeding sickness," I whispered urgently. "It can be fatal and will spread quickly to others. We cannot bring this to Iskandariyyah. Thousands will die. We must find another port, perhaps Askalon where there will be physicians who can aid me. We are all in danger now. We cannot let this illness loose in a large city. Can your vessel sail to Askalon?"

The captain was horrified. I had guessed he would have no knowledge of my fabricated illness and I was right. He begged me to find a cure and keep Sukman away from him and his crew. He was not worried about the slaves. They were easy to replace. Although he had never sailed so far up the coast of the Levante, he claimed he could find the way if there was no other choice. I assured him there was not. The prevailing winds blew from the north but, as we were powered by oars, we could make proper headway. Others, I lied, had made this voyage and survived. Because we all believed that Askalon remained under Fatimid control, the captain knew it would provide a safe refuge. I was not certain of that. At least it was far from Iskandariyyah.

I apologized to Sukman, who I required to remain in our shelter. Visitors were forbidden and Sukman was not happy with playing his new role as a dying patient.

"Hakim, your plan achieved our objective, but I am its victim. It would have been better if I had carried out my own proposal. Have you seen how the crew treats the slaves? These heretics do not deserve to live. To lie in this place for many days is unpleasant to say the least. Next time, think of something else!"

During the following week at sea, Sukman and I continued to debate our course of action. Sukman claimed that if the Franj had not already conquered Askalon, it would be a stronghold of the Fatimid and we would be no better off than before. Worse, he said, would be if our golden cargo fell into the control of his enemies. That would be a disaster. We had no way to determine the truth, so we did nothing. "Allah will guide us," I promised.

When we came in sight of the city, we spied several small fishing vessels plying their trade off the coast. I asked that we come close to one of them so I might ask about the situation in the city. The fisherman happily explained that Askalon remained under control of the Fatimid. There had been a great battle with the Franj in which the forces of al-Afdal had been defeated. Traitors from the city had told the Franj everything they wanted to know about the location and strength of al-Afdal's army, but the Franj had never followed up on their victory. The city remained free and was now the home of many refugees from Jerusalem as well as a large contingent of Fatimid troops. This was not what we had hoped to hear. Of course, we could not share our disappointment. An idea occurred to me. I called the captain.

"Captain, we cannot land in this place either. Allah would never forgive us if we spread illness to the poor refugees. We must continue up the coast to the next port. It is called Jaffa, I think, and is close by. The Franj may control the port but do not worry. I have friends amongst the infidels who will help us. You will be safe," I lied. The captain looked at me skeptically but could not argue. After consulting his crew, he agreed. It would take another day of travel. Our slaves, knowing nothing of all this, looked on in anger and exhaustion as they were ordered to take to their oars once again. If they understood how close to freedom they were, they would have had a different reaction.

Sukman looked at me askance. "Hakim, who do you know in the port of Jaffa? Never mind, I already know the answer. Can you pretend to be a Franj? It will serve the interests of my people if we place our cargo in their hands. I will not be at risk if you can convince them you are one with them. We have no quarrel with the Franj. After all, they do make use of the services we provide. Before I forget, remind me to tell you about the horse."

I remained silent, wondering what any of this had to do with a horse. Sukman misinterpreted my hesitation. He thought I was afraid of further pretense. He was wrong. Here I was, a Christian pretending to be a Muslim who would now pretend again to be a Christian. At best, this was confusing.

Sukman looked at me with sympathy. "I know this will be hard for you. There is no choice. Allah will forgive you. Can you do this? You speak their language as if you were one of them; I have heard you. There is no other way."

There was no option but to agree. I hoped I could regain fluency in the Norman language. For too long, I had only spoken in Arabic. To protect ourselves and our precious cargo, I decided we should moor some distance from the port itself. There were many small fishing vessels passing by and I used one of my coins to arrange passage on one of them for the short distance to the harbor and back.

We landed at the dock and two soldiers, accompanied by their leader wearing a white robe with a red cross sewn upon it, hurried to meet us. Someone had noticed our arrival and my transfer to the fishing boat. By this time, I had grown an unkempt beard and wore the clothing of an Arab. The leader did not recognize me, but I immediately knew who he was. My head spun as I realized that my deceptions were becoming even more complicated.

As I expected, the leader gave me no time to say anything.

"What are you doing here?" he demanded officiously. "This is a Christian city! Do you have a letter of free passage from King Baldwin? Of course not! Order your vessel to the dock. We will inspect your cargo. You and your infidel crew will stay with us. We will treat you according to the laws, but you will be placed in custody. If you fail to comply, we will order a warship to take the necessary action." He was going to continue his diatribe. I interrupted him.

"Roland, do you not know me?"

Roland opened his mouth in shock and recognition.

It took a few moments for Roland to absorb what I had said. Then he embraced me; his arms had grown strong.

"Praise be to God. It is you, my beloved friend. We thought you were dead. Where have you been? We looked for you for many months and sought word of you everywhere. There was a report you had been seen somewhere on the coast of Ifriqiya, but we heard no more about that. Why are you here? Why are you dressed like a Saracen? I must tell Brother Jehan. He is here in the city. He still speaks of you in anger. Perhaps you can make amends. Our order of the Knights of Saint John has been blessed by the Pope. I myself have fought many battles but, after Askalon, I have put down my sword and have devoted myself to the care of unfortunate pilgrims. One day, I might even become a priest. I must tell you everything!"

I paid little attention to his jabbering. He had not changed! But now I was in shock. Brother Jehan, here? I had thought I was free of him. I could not remain in this place. How could I explain any of this to Sukman? There was no time to think.

I pulled Roland away from the soldiers who accompanied him and whispered conspiratorially, "My mission is secret. Listen carefully. Tell no one. My assistant and I have commandeered a Saracen vessel; the one you see waiting in the harbor. It is carrying Christian slaves who must be freed. This vessel is also carrying a great quantity of gold which I think would be of benefit to your order. The ship's captain and crew believe my assistant has a terrible illness and that is why I came to the dock alone. You will need to keep silent until everyone is safe. Let me return and I will direct them to land at the dock." I paused for just a moment and then said, "Roland, they think I am one of their faith. Let us keep my true beliefs between ourselves."

Roland raised his eyebrows and nodded his head in understanding. "I will keep your secret, my dear friend. Your mission is important, is it not? Of course, it is. I must call for some armed assistance, of course. It most likely will not be necessary for me to explain anything regarding the cargo. However, I will need to inform my superiors after it is unloaded. You must understand it is my duty to disclose your presence to Brother Jehan. But that can wait as well." Roland paused, tilted his head and pressed his lips together. "You are posing as an infidel, dear friend? Are you not concerned for your soul? Will God understand why you are carrying out this deception?" Roland answered his own question. "Of course, of course, you are carrying out duties for the Church. How did I fail to see that?"

I assured Roland that God would indeed understand. At least I hoped He would. I silently prayed that Roland would keep quiet for the present. If he failed me, I was unsure of the consequences.

The fishing boat was waiting to carry me back to our quarib. Sukman was impatient.

"Did the Franj accept your story? Will they accept our landing at the dock?" he whispered.

"Yes, they did," I answered. "We are free to enter the port. One of the officials knows me from my days in the school for physicians. He is a member of the Order of Saint John."

"Excellent, Hakim. We will be safe. My people enjoy a sound relationship with the Order. They can be trusted more than the other Franj. Tell the captain he should row to the docks."

"There is a difficulty, Sukman. I promised to give our gold to the Order. I had no choice."

Sukman pondered this for a few moments and then, with a wicked smile, answered. "That is not a problem,

Hakim. They pay for our services in gold, so this will come back to my people over time. It will do no harm if I take some credit for helping bring this cargo to the Franj."

I was surprised at this revelation. For what purpose did the Order engage the Hashashiyin? There was no time to pursue this question. I decided to ask later.

When I told our captain that we could land at the dock, he grinned in delight. Now, he said, we would be free from the danger of Sukman's bleeding sickness. As we approached the dock, however, his breathing quickened, and his face fell as he saw we would be met by a contingent of soldiers. I calmly told him not to worry; that all would be well. I should have felt remorse for my lie, but I did not. He had chosen his path and knew well its risks. No sooner had we tied our vessel to the dock than the soldiers leaped aboard. The crew and the captain were unarmed. Although they cried in protest, they had no choice but to submit to being placed in chains. Some of the soldiers came to capture Sukman in the same way. I waved them away, explaining that he was my assistant. The slaves were freed from their bondage. All of them knelt weeping on the dock in a prayer of thanksgiving. I doubt that all of them were Christians. If they were not, they had enough sense to pretend to be so.

At least twenty heavy sacks of gold dust were unloaded onto the dock. This precious cargo had been destined for the mints in Aegyptus to be turned to coin. Now it was in the possession of the Franj. Roland's eyes widened as he saw just how much gold we had delivered. I briefly regretted that Sukman and I had not kept at least a small quantity for ourselves but, for both of us, outright theft would have been a sin.

I briefly introduced Sukman to Roland. I did not want to engage in any further discussion, so I encouraged Roland to remove the gold from the docks and promised we would meet later. I had no intention of doing so. I needed to escape from his presence before he began any long rambling discourse or asked further questions. I knew he would have to tell Brother Jehan everything. It was only a matter of time. Sukman and I needed to leave the city as soon as possible. Sukman narrowed his eyes in obvious wonder at my haste but said nothing.

Taking Sukman aside, I whispered, "We must leave this place immediately. It is dangerous for both of us. Where we can we go?"

"Yes Hakim, we must go to the city of Sur. The Franj call that place Tyre. It is not far; four to five days if we walk along the coast. Why must we depart so quickly? You have a friend here it seems, and I have no concerns for the reasons I have told you. We have enriched the Order. They will praise us for this. Let us find a bath where we can clean ourselves and an inn where we can eat proper food."

"No, Sukman, I will explain later. Believe me, I am in danger. Please trust me on this."

"Very well," he responded grudgingly. "But I do not understand. If you insist, we can begin our journey now. I hope Sur remains held by of those of our faith. We should be safe there until we can find a way to Dimashq, the city the Franj call Damascus, where my own people hold sway. If we meet Franj on the road, you can claim to be one of them and say I am just a simple assistant."

Such a journey in these turbulent times would be difficult. I still had possession of my dwindling stock of medicines; nothing else. How would we survive over the next few days? I shared my concern: "Sukman, we have only one coin left to purchase food. Perhaps I can trade my skills as a physician for sustenance, but it will require good fortune and may not be easy."

Sukman tilted his head and grinned. "Hakim, I told you it is always wise to be prepared." It was then I noticed that he too had a small satchel. "What is that?" I asked, pointing at his new acquisition.

Sukman laughed. "I borrowed this from our captain after we docked. He will have no further use for it. In any event, he is a Sunni, so I will be forgiven this small transgression. It contains a few more gold coins, which will resolve our difficulty, I believe," he said with a smile.

I nodded in affirmation, thanking God I had such a friend. We began to walk towards the city gates. We were not questioned as we departed. As we had done before, we turned south, making certain we were noticed. Then we circled the city and began our long journey north to Sur. We walked until darkness fell and found an inn catering to pilgrims. The inn itself was almost full but, with Sukman's coin, we were able to secure a room. That night, we ate a simple potage and, for the first time in months, I ordered a cup of wine. Sukman raised his brows in surprise. He began to berate me for this sacrilege. I waved my hands, asking for patience. I had worried about the steps I would take to finally tell the truth. I could no longer retain my secrets; not with Sukman.

"Sukman, for many days we have trusted each other. I owe you a great debt and have learned to value your friendship. What I am going to say may forever taint your view of me and, perhaps, destroy all that has passed between us. I can no longer deceive you and will accept the consequence of your judgment."

Sukman opened his mouth to protest. Again, I raised my palm and motioned him to silence. Over the next hours, I told him my story; all of it. He listened gravely and did not interrupt. When I had finished, Sukman put his head between his hands and sat in thought for a long time.

Finally, he looked at me piercingly. "Have you renounced Islam? You have prayed with me in the mosque. Each time we recite the words of our faith and you have always done so. Have you ever affirmed your Nazarene faith? Are you an apostate?"

It took me a moment to consider his question. "No, Sukman, I have never renounced Islam. I was never asked to do that. As a child I was baptized. At least I think I was. No one has ever since asked me to affirm my belief in the Christian faith."

Sukman smiled. "I am no Qadi, but I can find no fault. Each time we prayed, you affirmed there is no god but Allah and that Mohammed is His messenger. I have heard you say this many times. With me, you have never by deed or word denied any basic tenet of our faith. The Nazarene may see this differently. To me, you are a Muslim. Of course, you are ignorant of the Nizari faith. If we remain together, that can be corrected. From what you have told me, I understand we may be in danger from those of your faith. It may be prudent to change our plans. In the meantime, I beg you to avoid drinking wine."

He saw my relief. I had told so many lies that I was certain my disclosure would destroy everything. But Sukman accepted me for what I was. I wondered if God would be as understanding. My Christian brothers would certainly not be. At the very least, we could continue our journey north.

V

A.D. 1115
A.H. 509
A.M. 4875

We never completed our journey to Sur. Sukman, after considering our plans in light of my own tale, decided the best course would be to proceed directly to Dimashq. He was confident we would be safe there. Using some of the 'borrowed' coins, we purchased two old but serviceable horses from a merchant. We also acquired new clothing to present a proper appearance as a Hakim and his assistant. We hoped that any crucesignati, which is what the armed pilgrims were called, would leave us in peace if we presented ourselves as physicians. Traveling to Dimashq required us to follow an old Roman road and cross both the river Jordan and a high mountain range. Sukman said it would take about six days to reach our destination if there was no snow in the mountains. In spite of the discomfort, I thanked our common God for the horses.

There were few travelers along the road. Sometimes, we met groups of wandering nomads grazing their sheep. We always asked for news. There was little. No Franj had been seen. Often, in the desert heat, I saw what I thought were small lakes, but Sukman told me these were only illusions. It was not until we had crossed the River Jordan and the mountains that the air became cooler and we learned more. The small town of Ahri'at was a strategic station on the caravan route between Dimashq and Medina. All those of the Muslim faith were obligated to make a pilgrimage to that city and to the Holy City of Mecca. Ahri'at had been conquered by the Franj several years ago, but they had long since withdrawn. Once, it supported a large Jewish population. There were a few Jews living there still, but most of the town was in the hands of Muslims. Among the earthen homes and buildings, we found a shabby inn for pilgrims. It was from an old man there that we learned of recent events.

"Where have you been?" he said. "You do not know what has happened? You do not know of the atrocity committed? Do you not know we will drive out the infidels?"

We admitted our ignorance, explaining we had been traveling. Our journey had been difficult, and we had heard no news. We were returning to Dimashq.

The old man puffed his cheeks and shook his head at our ignorance. He smiled and drew himself up straight, in anticipation of regaling us with a tale.

"Then let me tell you. Last year, our Sultan in Baghdad dispatched Emir Mawdud, may he rest in peace, to raise an army for battle against what the Franj call the Kingdom of Jerusalem. He was greeted in Dimashq by that city's ruler, the Atabeg Tughtigin, who professed to be greatly honored by the visit. He was, may Allah punish him, only pretending. What happened next was all the evidence anyone needs of his betrayal. No, it was worse than betrayal, as I will tell you. You see, every day the Emir and Tughtigin walked to the mosque, where they prayed together. They always left at the same time. One day, however, after they competed their devotions, Tughtigin left a moment earlier. He left the Emir to walk alone. You can guess what happened next?"

"What happened?" demanded Sukman, who was losing patience with this story. "We have told you we know nothing of events in Dimashq. Who was Mawdud?"

The old man looked at us with surprise. "You do not know the Emir? Where have you been? You are ignorant indeed!"

Sukman gazed at our narrator wrathfully. "How many times did we tell you? We have been absent for a long time."

The old man sighed in exasperation and continued. "He was the Sultan's favorite leader of the army. He fought the Franj for years. Just two years ago he almost succeeded in driving out the infidels at the battle of al-Sannabra. He was a clever man. During the battle, he feigned retreat to draw the crucesignati into the waiting arms of his army. He killed most of them. After that great victory, the Emir raided the towns controlled by the Franj, may they be cursed forever! Our Sultan ordered him to Dimashq to raise an even stronger army and finish the infidels once and for all."

I interrupted the tale. "You were telling us of events in Dimashq," I reminded him.

"Oh yes, that is what I was relating. Be patient, and I will tell you." The old man was reveling in his ability to entertain us with a long tale. "A large crowd surrounded the courtyard of the mosque. From out of the crowd a beggar approached the Emir seeking alms. Or so it appeared. In an instant, the beggar, a Hashishi, may they be cursed, stabbed him deep in the belly. The Emir staggered as far as the north gate and then collapsed. His companions called for a physician, who bound the wound. It was too late. He died there in agony. Can you imagine such a crime? Tughtigin blamed this deed on his enemy, Prince Ridwan of Aleppo, and his friends the Ismaili. Everyone believes that is a lie. Tughtigin is the master, the Atabeg, of Dimashq. He too makes use of the Hashishiyyin when it serves his purpose. This could not have happened without his knowledge and consent. Nothing does in that city!"

"Then what happened?" I asked. Sukman remained sullenly quiet. He was turning red in anger. This man was blatantly insulting those of his faith! I nudged him in the ribs to remind him of our position and motioned to him to remain silent.

"Well, you can guess. The Sultan was furious. This act of evil was a personal insult. He decided to bring the city under his control and rid himself of both Tughtigin and, I am certain, Prince Ridwan. Both have rejected his authority. He also intends to rid this land of the Franj and the Ismaili heretics. They have done nothing but produce chaos and steal from us. They make a bad situation worse. He has raised a powerful army and has declared jih'ad against the Franj. A traveler told us an army led by the Emir Bursuqi has entered the country and is marching to Dimashq. If that is your destination, be warned!"

Sukman and I needed to talk alone. The old man was clearly ready to share his opinions and continue our dialogue. But we had heard enough. I feared Sukman would voice his opinion and that would be disastrous. I apologetically turned to the old man.

"Thank you, sir, for your warning. You have given us greater understanding of what has happened. Please accept our gratitude. Given this news, we must continue our travels if we are to avoid the conflict to come. May Allah be with you."

We left the inn immediately and found a place to talk without being overheard.

"Hakim, if this story is true, I must contact my brothers. My people are in danger."

"Sukman," I responded calmly, "first we need to discover if the tale is indeed true. Let us find someone else to question."

I knew with whom we should speak; someone who would have an impartial view of events. A solution occurred to me. I recalled the parchment given to me by Jusuf. It was, I prayed, still secure in my bag. Without warning to Sukman, I asked the next passerby where a money changer would be found in Ahri'at. Sukman raised his eyebrows at this but did not comment. There was one nearby, we were told. We would see his sign outside the shop.

'Sukman, trust me on this. A money changer will possess the best information and, I believe, will confide in me."

As we had learned, the shop was a few hundred paces from the inn. I entered and asked for the proprietor.

"Sir," I said in Norman, "my name is Thomas. My adopted uncle is one of your faith. I need to send a message to him in al-Qahirah. It is a matter of urgency. Can you help us?"

He answered in Arabic. 'My comprehension of the language of the Franj is poor, young man. I think you have asked if I can send a message to al-Misr. Is that right?"

"Yes, my uncle's name is Jusuf Ben Abulafia. He is an important merchant in that country. He may be there or in Merṛakec." I cut open the hiding place in my bag and gave him the parchment I had saved for so long and almost forgotten.

The money changer took my parchment and examined it suspiciously. Twice, he read the blue Hebrew characters slowly to himself. He pursed his lips and looked at me carefully. For a long while, he said nothing. He rose from his seat, walked to the front of the shop and closed the door. Finally, he spoke.

"You know what this says?" he asked softly.

"I do not," I replied. "I only know my uncle said to show it to one of his faith if I were ever to find myself in need of help."

"It is a directive from Rabbi Ephraim, the highest legal authority in al-Misr. He is the head of the Jews, what we call the 'rais-al-Yahud', in that place. I know this is real. It is written with an exceedingly rare ink. This ink is made from a stone we call lazaward, which comes from lands far to the east. It says the bearer of this letter is trusted and must be provided any aid he demands. Costs, it affirms, will be reimbursed by the Jewish community in al-Misr. He swears this before God. I am your servant. My name is Elhanan. How can I assist you?"

Both Sukman and I were astonished. I had not expected this to be so easy. I made a silent prayer of thanks for my uncle's foresight.

Briefly, I told him of the news we had received at the inn and asked if it were true.

"Indeed, your informant was correct. The Sultan's army is large and composed of his best warriors. Emir Bursuqi is one of his most trusted generals. Those of us who remain here are worried. Our relations with the Turks are not good. We have worked well with the current ruler of Dimashq and do not want change. There is no difficulty with the Ismaili. They leave us in peace to conduct our trade. The Franj are a different matter. When they last sacked this city, they killed most of my people. It is said the Franj King Baldwin is tolerant of us. But we have no way to confirm this."

"Elhanan, what do your people think will happen?" I said in surprise.

"If King Baldwin does not know of the Sultan's plans, the Turks will take Dimashq. The Regent of Antioch is attempting to stop them, but he will need support from the King to prevail. If he does not receive aid, the Turks will achieve their goals. Once they do, they will try to enlist all the cities in al Shaam to revolt against the Franj and drive them from this land. You know what happened the last time the Turks declared war?"

We signaled our ignorance.

"The ruler of Aleppo, Prince Ridwan, would not admit entry to Mawdud. The city then refused to provide provisions promised to the Turks. Ridwan and the city's merchants feared the Sultan wished to take the city for himself. They were right. Of course, he did. When Mawdud was rebuffed, his troops took revenge by devastating the lands around the city. No one has forgotten that. My people fear it will happen again. If I am correct, we will once again be forced to seek safety. Our commerce will be destroyed. Does that answer your question?"

Sukman and I looked at each other. We had the same thought, and I had another question.

"Yes, it does, Elhanan. What do you know of King Baldwin?"

"They say the King is an honorable man. Those in my profession have done well with his troops and the administrators within his kingdom. All use our services to send coin to their homelands. It has been to our benefit that he has married the Countess Adelaide of Sicilia. We enjoy a strong position in her country. Their ruler, Ruggiero, has been a great support to us."

I was shocked. "Baldwin has married Adelaide?" I said in surprise. "When did that happen? Is she in Jerusalem? Did you say Ruggiero is the sole ruler of Sicilia?"

Sukman remembered my own story and was equally stunned. He thought more quickly than I and did not give the money changer time to respond.

"Kind sir, I am the assistant to Thomas. I too have a question. Do you have means to send a message to the King or his wife?"

"Not at present," he said. "I can arrange for delivery of a letter to Sicilia. I do not have a correspondent in

Jerusalem. We have reports of a small force of Franj encamped about a day's journey south. If you could reach them, they would know what to do. I can provide directions."

I was still in shock at the news. Ruggiero ruler of Sicilia? The Countess the wife of Baldwin? This was either good fortune or disaster. Sukman gave me no time to ponder.

"Hakim, we must try to find the Franj now. If we delay, it will be too late."

I had to agree. Our news was urgent. My fate was in the hands of God. It was too late in the day to leave for the camp of the crucesignati, so Elhanan invited us to sleep in his shop that night. I took time to write a letter to both Jusuf and Ruggiero. In my letter to Jusuf, I briefly described all that had happened to me. I assured him of my good health and safety and promised I would resolve all matters soon. When my tasks were complete, I would come to Aegyptus to see him, my uncle Assad and my grandfather. The letter to Ruggiero was more difficult to compose. I wanted him to know I had not left his service without cause. I decided that truth was called for and, thus, wrote as much of my own tale as was possible in a short missive. I prayed for his good health and promised I would present myself to either his mother or him as soon as possible.

Elhanan said it would take many days for my letters to arrive, but he was confident it could be done. The following morning, he asked if there was anything further he could do for me; did we need coin for our journey? We needed nothing. We had to move on.

We warn of war

Following the directions we had been given, we came upon the camp in about two hours. Foolishly, the Franj had encamped at an oasis surrounded by low hills. Of course, they needed a source of water, but they had not chosen a defensible position. When we dismounted, Sukman and I could come close without being seen. I was afraid we would be taken for the enemy so, from a distance, I shouted in Norman.

"God be with you. I am Thomas Woodward of England and I need to speak with your commander. May we come close?"

All of the small group drew their swords and looked in our direction. They were surprised by our presence.

"We come in peace. I am one of you. We have urgent news," I bellowed.

A crucesignatus, who by his armor must have been the commander, shouted back.

"If you come in peace, put down your weapons and walk slowly towards us."

"We have no weapons, your Grace," I replied, as we walked slowly down to the camp.

The commander was a youth with the beginnings of a beard. He was nervous but greeted us with great formality, introducing himself grandly as Pons, the Count of Tripoli. He was nonplused when he realized this name or title meant nothing to me.

I decided it was time I lied again. I introduced myself as Thomas of Eynsham, the court physician to the Kingdom of Sicilia. Sukman, I said, was my faithful assistant. The Church had dispatched us on a secret mission to Damascus. We had learned news which must be relayed to King Baldwin with great haste. My credentials, I exclaimed grandly, could be verified by a member of the Order of Saint John in Jerusalem named Roland. There was, I said, no time to lose. Our information was a matter of urgency.

Pons was easily impressed. We learned later that this was his first scouting mission. He yearned for praise from his superiors and had searched for a means to distinguish himself.

"I will send a rider immediately to seek audience with the King," he said. "Can you tell me the message, or do you have a sealed letter?"

"There is no time for a letter," I retorted gruffly. "Just have your messenger tell the King we have learned that a massive army of Turks, thirty thousand men or more, has entered the Levante. They are bound for Damascus. The Emir intends to raise additional troops when he seizes the city and disposes of its rulers. He will then raise even more troops from Aleppo and elsewhere and attack Jerusalem. King

Baldwin must march now. If he does so, he can surprise the Turks and drive them back to Baghdad."

The Count's face paled with shock. He pondered my words for a few moments. I guessed he was considering how best to use this information for his own benefit. As I hoped, he came to the expected decision.

"I will present this news myself," he declared, solemnly. "It is too important to entrust to one of my troops. Only I have sufficient credentials to gain audience with the King. If I ride hard, I can be in Jerusalem tomorrow."

I had correctly assumed Pons would see this as an opportunity to display his valor and value to the King. Neither Sukman nor I cared at all about enhancing our own reputations. Our goal was to stop the Turks. The Count did care. Would he verify my own position with Roland? I prayed he would not. That would only result in further delay. Time was short.

Pons called for his horse and made ready to ride. He ordered Sukman and me to stay in camp until he returned and, of course, we readily agreed. He appointed one of his troops as temporary commander and ordered him to remain vigilant for enemy Saracens.

There was nothing more Sukman and I could do but wait for Pons's return. I had just found a place to sit under a palm tree near the water when Sukman, who had been roaming the camp, knelt in the dirt in front of me and whispered, "Hakim, these people have no sense. They have made their camp below the hills surrounding us. They do not even post troops above. You saw how easy it was to surprise them. Can you imagine if we had been a party of Turks? We would have annihilated them. They need to move into the hills. We are near the Kings Road to Dimashq. It is certain there will be roving bands of the enemy nearby. If the money changer knew of the Franj presence, so will others. Can we do something?"

"I do not think anyone will pay attention to us, but I will try my best," I answered.

No one did. I spoke to the new commander. As he had no orders to move the camp, he refused to do so. He feared the Count would rebuke him for taking such an action in his absence without authorization. He did agree to post a guard on the west facing hill at night. Sukman shook his head in disgust.

"Hakim, tonight will be too late. The Turks will not attack at night. They will do so at dusk or dawn. It would be wise if we ourselves climbed the hill to the east so we can provide some advance warning should they appear from that direction. I will borrow a sword and lance to be safe."

Sukman quietly removed the chosen weapons from a pile near the water. No one noticed this. We climbed the low eastern hill and, just as we reached the top, Sukman's worry became reality. Not fifty paces from us, three Turks, all on horseback and in full chain mail, were riding towards us. One of the horsemen reacted swiftly. He removed his short bow from his back and notched an arrow. Sukman pushed me to the ground just as the missile passed over my head. One instant of delay would have ended my life. Sukman did not hesitate. At almost twenty paces, he threw the lance: not at the archer but at his horse. The horse fell at once, casting its rider in the dust. The two other Turks drew their curved swords and charged Sukman. Just as they reached him, Sukman bent low and, in rapid sequence, cut the legs of their mounts, which fell with their riders. The screaming of the wounded horses and cries of the Turks caught the attention of the crucesignati below. But even if they collected their weapons immediately, it would take time to reach us.

By now two of the Turks had recovered from their fall. They ran towards Sukman. One, shrieking in agony, was pinned underneath his horse. Sukman, faster than I had ever seen anyone move, gracefully danced between the two and delivered mortal blows with his sword. He swiftly turned to the wounded Turk and neatly separated his head from his body. Without hesitation, he dispatched the wounded horses and then calmly cleaned his blade. I gasped at the sight. I had never seen a battlefield, but it must be like this. Pools of dark blood stained the sand everywhere. As if by magic, multitudes of flies descended upon the human and equine carcasses and began feasting upon the newly spilled blood. The killing field smelled of copper and excrement. I had done nothing. I had been paralyzed by fear. My mouth gaped open in horror. The crucesignati who had arrived at the hilltop shared my shock. One of them, upon seeing the devastation, bent over and retched. Sukman raised his eyebrows at this and shook his head. "These Franj are warriors?" he mumbled. "May Allah protect us!"

Seeing my expression, he whispered to me. "Hakim, I am sorry about the horses. They were noble animals. I had no choice. I will ask Allah for forgiveness." He had tears in his eyes.

I shook my head in disbelief. Sukman was indifferent to the human lives he had so swiftly taken. He was in sorrow for the horses. I was uncertain if I could ever understand this man. Our troops, who had been so late to give us support, all expressed their gratitude to Sukman for his swift action. He had saved all, or at least some, of their lives. Sukman dismissed their praise and thanks.

"It is nothing," he said flatly. "It would be wise to post a guard up here at all times." With that remark, he took me by the arm and led me back to the camp. I was still in shock and had said nothing. I simply stared into the distance, shaking in fear and overwhelmed by what had just happened.

Sukman hung his head and pleaded, "Hakim, will you forgive me for killing the horses? The others were only Turks."

I looked at him sadly and shook my head. "Of course, my friend, you had no choice," I mumbled.

We meet my greatest enemy and embark on a secret mission

The next and following mornings, Sukman and I climbed the hills surrounding the camp. On the final day, we had just reached the summit of the hill to the west when we spied five riders approaching us. They were not Turks. Three of them wore white robes marked with a bright red cross over their mail shirts. One rider was unarmed. The other was in full armor. As they approached, we saw that one of the riders was Pons. I recognized the unarmed rider at once. Roland, it appeared, was going to plague me once again. I looked at the others, and one of them brought fear to my heart as I realized who he was.

We climbed down from the hill to the camp to await the arrival of our new visitors. I did not know what to do. I was unable to think clearly, so great was my anxiety. I made a silent prayer for guidance. Sukman, as was his habit, looked to me for direction.

"That is the man I have told you about. The lay brother who threatened me in Sicilia. The man who has looked for me for so long. I do not think he has come here to thank me."

"Do not worry, Hakim, if he becomes a problem for us, I will resolve it. We must stop the Turks. That is all that matters."

Sukman's reassurance only gave me greater fear. I did my best to calm myself and think. We stood away from the gathering crowd.

The riders dismounted. Our temporary commander and his troops all talked at once, describing what had happened on the hill and pointing in my direction. Pons and the others listened attentively. He motioned for us to come forward. I think he was planning to thank us for saving his troops. He had no time to do so.

The unarmed rider ran to me and engulfed me in his arms. "My dear friend, I could not believe it was you! Where have you been? Is your news true? I looked for you after you delivered the treasure. Do you know how much that was? I have been worried and prayed for you. Your companion from the boat is with you, I see. Look who is with me; your old friend, Brother Jehan. He has missed you as well. Do you see him? The one in the white robe of St John. Come, let us go to him."

Brother Jehan's limp had become more pronounced and his skin was pale. I wondered if he was ill. He was looking at me with malevolence. Presenting his artificial smile, he spoke.

"Quiet, Roland," he ordered. "Remain silent!" He turned to me.

"Well Thomas, my boy, what a surprise," he said coldly. "I have searched for you everywhere since our discussion many years ago, when you failed us so badly. I told you our reach was long. I see you have befriended an infidel. You have much to atone and answer for. What do you have to say for yourself?"

Jehan's tone was enough to quell my fear. It made me angry.

"I see you are in ill health and have grown older," I retorted. "I am no longer a boy. Is this the way you greet those who have provided great service to you?"

"What service? You think all is forgiven by bringing us gold and killing a few Turks? You failed to perform the one service we ever asked of you," he said angrily. "You owe us everything! Answer me, why have you hidden?"

"I have hidden nothing," I answered angrily. "Both Count Ruggiero of Sicilia and his mother, Queen Adelaide of Jerusalem, have been informed of all pertinent matters."

Although this was true, I had omitted an important detail. I had indeed informed them, but they could not yet have received my letters. Why, I wondered, did he hate me so much? Yes, I had ignored his demand for information in Sicilia. Yes, I had run from Bartolomeo, but what other harm had I caused? After all, the Church possessed the funds in my trust and had ruined my position at court. I owed them nothing.

There was no time to dwell on this speculation. What we had to say was much more important.

"My companion and I have brought news of a new army of Turks approaching Damascus. They must be stopped, or you and the people of the Holy City will be in grave danger. Have you advised the King of this news? Is he marshaling his own forces?"

Jehan looked at me, surprised that I answered in this way. For a moment, he was unsure how to respond. The fully armored rider stepped forward and motioned for Jehan to be silent. He pushed Jehan away and came close to me. This man, who I had not noticed before, was in his middle years. He had a well-trimmed white beard. His elaborate armor was glistening, and he carried himself with authority.

He first addressed Jehan and then turned to me. "Silence, Jehan. There will be time enough to address whatever dispute you have with this man. Now is not the time." Jehan turned red with anger but bowed and returned to the crowd.

"I am Raymond du Puy, the deputy Grand Master of the Order of Saint John," he announced gravely. "We received your news and have acted on it. We have heard the same from the Regent of Antioch, who sent spies to discover the movements of the Turks. The King's army has left Jerusalem and is marching towards Damascus as we speak. Tell me what more you have learned."

I briefly recounted the tales we had heard. Raymond listened silently, nodding his head as he did so.

"What you have said confirms the rumors we have heard regarding Sultan Mohammed's plans. You are correct. There is no time to waste. You say you travel to Damascus? That is dangerous for you, is it not?"

I explained that, given my position as a physician and my appearance, I had no fear of the Saracens. Jehan began to interrupt but Raymond stopped him once again. Looking towards the sky, he paused for a few moments, deep in thought. I wondered if he was praying for guidance.

Eventually, he stared at me directly. "You will proceed at once to Damascus. There, gain audience with the Atabeg Tughtigin and deliver a message." He handed me a sealed parchment. "Guard this with your life," he commanded.

"May ask its contents?" I asked.

"Suffice it to say that many of the infidel princes share our fear of the Sultan. The time is ripe for us all to resist a common enemy. We need a response from Tughtigin urgently. The young man here says he knows you well. He will accompany you and return with whatever message you receive from Tughtigin."

Roland raised his brows in surprise and smiled broadly in delight. He rushed forward to embrace me.

"My dear friend, this would be an honor. Once again, we will ride together. Just like we did so long ago! You can tell me of your adventures, and I will relate my own. We have so much to talk about!"

I could not think of anything worse. Sukman looked at me quizzically but remained silent. I turned to Roland.

"Roland, do you speak the language of the Saracen?" I asked.

"No, Thomas; God will protect me. Do not concern yourself with my safety. It is enough that I travel with you on this most important mission. I will not be a hindrance."

I shook my head and addressed both Raymond and Roland.

"Master, we can deliver your message, but it will not be possible for my old friend here to accompany us. Any Saracens we meet will know he is not one of them. His presence would put our entire endeavor at risk. If I may be so bold, I think it best that Roland wait here in this camp and we will bring Tughtigin's response to him. We would not know where to find you. We will return on the King's Road and we can find the way to this camp. That would be the most prudent course."

Roland's face fell. It only took him a few moments, however, to realize he would still have an important role. Thankfully, he said nothing. Jehan, however, was visibly shaking in anger. He could no longer contain himself.

"Master, I protest," he roared. "This man is an apostate! He has betrayed us before and will do so again! Look at him; he is traveling with an infidel, an idolater. You cannot trust him in this! I do not report to you. I will appeal to the Grand Master and my own people."

I gripped Sukman's arm to keep him calm. He was going to intervene and that would not be helpful. I was about to respond myself when Raymond turned towards Jehan and spoke.

"Jehan, I have heard enough from you. You have given your oath to obey your superiors and this decision is mine. If you have difficulty with my decision, do speak to the Grand Master, or anyone else you choose, when we return. I will not defer what needs to be done. I do not care if Thomas here is a Christian or a Muslim or a Greek for that matter. What I know is he is not a Turk. Unless you wish to go to Damascus yourself there is no choice but to use what resources God has presented to us." Turning to me, Raymond looked at me with his piercing eyes.

"Thomas, do you swear before God you will deliver my message to Tughtigin?"

"I so swear," I said quietly. "My companion will do so as well."

"There is no need. It is enough for me," said Raymond. "Go now."

I nodded in assent and motioned for Sukman to follow me. Jehan then stepped close to me and whispered balefully.

"I will not forget this. We will meet again, and I swear you will pay for your sins."

I ignored him. We mounted our horses and rode for Dimashq.

We precipitate an unusual alliance

Riding swiftly, we reached the walls of Dimashq in two days. As we rode, Sukman assured me he had friends in the city that could help us gain audience with the Atabeg. There were, he said, sound relations between his Ismaili brothers and the local prince. "Who do you think sent Mawdud to his reward in heaven?" he asked. "Tughtigin is in our debt, I believe."

The city of Dimashq is huge. Surrounded by high ramparts, the minarets of the Great Mosque tower over the city. It is, I am told, one of the largest places of worship in the world. Sukman told me that some adherents of his faith believe that Lord Jesus will appear there at the end of days. We approached the southeastern gate, Bab Kisan, where Saint Paul had made his escape from the city so long ago.

As I had come to expect, Sukman's judgment was correct. He addressed the guard there in a language foreign to me; Persian, I later learned. Thanks be to God, the guard responded in the same language, thus acknowledging that he too was an Ismaili. Sukman asked further questions and received what must have been an acceptable response. Whatever it was made

Sukman very happy. We passed through the gate and Sukman turned left through a warren of narrow streets. He seemed to know exactly where to go. I could not contain myself.

"Sukman, how did you know to speak to the guard in that language?"

Sukman shook his head at my ignorance. "Hakim, we have ways to recognize a brother. You do not need to know more."

"Well, whatever news you received has made you happy. You seem to know where you are going. I am indeed ignorant. What has happened?"

"Hakim, we have the best of news and, yes, I know exactly where I am going. We are blessed! Our leader, the chief da'i of al-Shaam, is here. I can find him. His name is Abu Tahir al-Sa'igh. He will help us. I am certain of that. My brother at the gate has directed me to his place of residence, near the gate of orchards. We will arrive in moments."

"This is wonderful news; but what is a da'i?

"The leader of all the Isma'ili and the Hashashiyin fida'yin. Everyone thinks he is simply a wealthy gold merchant. Our leaders almost always have another profession. He keeps his true role secret. He was one of my teachers and I have performed valuable service to him. He knows me well. Providing that he forgives me for being captured so long ago, he will ensure we gain audience with the Atabeg."

So now I would meet the chief of the assassins. It was worrying that Sukman required forgiveness. What sin had he committed? We had no choice but move forward and trust the benevolence of God. It was too late to do anything else.

We eventually reached a large, three-story building surrounded by its own wall. Sukman spoke to the sentinel, who granted us entrance a courtyard full of flowering plants and fruit trees. Seated on a bench near the central fountain was an old, long-bearded man, dressed in robes of embroidered blue gazz. He turned towards us and immediately recognized Sukman.

"What do we have here? Is it you, Sukman ib'n Artuq? We thought you were dead. Who is this man with you?"

Sukman responded in Persian. He must have told his whole story, as his discourse took a long time. Several times, he pointed to me. I heard him speak my name, Thoma, but, otherwise, I had no idea what he was saying. Finally, he stopped and waited for Abu Tahir to speak. That did not happen quickly. We stood in silence for an uncomfortably long time.

Abu Tahir scowled. "You let the Franj capture you alive," he said, angrily, in Arabic. "You should have taken your own life and entered paradise. Did you learn nothing when I was your teacher?"

Sukman frowned at this. He hung his head in shame and said nothing.

The da'i then smiled broadly and laughed. He stood and wrapped Sukman in his arms. "My dear young man, I thank Allah you did not follow the rule. I am certain it was not possible. I have missed you. A few years ago, one of our brothers failed in his task in Aleppo. He had been assigned to remove a leader of that city. Unfortunately, he did not perform his duty correctly. The population turned against us and we lost many of our people. I only escaped by a miracle. There are not many fida'yin left. We have need of you! I have need of you! You were one of my best pupils! Come, let us sit together and you can tell me everything." Hesitating and then pointing to me, he asked, "And who is your companion here? You have not properly introduced him."

Sukman proceeded, in Persian, to relate the story of our meeting and all that happened after. The da'i listened carefully, nodding his head in understanding as Sukman talked. Finally, he turned to me and spoke in Arabic.

"My dear Thoma; that is your name is it not? We thank you for rescuing our brother from the Greeks and befriending him as you have done. Friendship is a valuable thing. It is a gift from Allah. Sukman tells me you are a Muslim who has not been properly instructed. I can help. My title, da'i should tell you that I am a da'wah, one who invites persons to faith. You can call me 'Moallim', teacher. I will be happy to assist your learning and we have need of physicians here. Have you found a place to stay?"

"Moallim," I replied. "I am grateful for your offer, but Sukman and I have sworn to deliver a letter from King Baldwin to the Atabeg and return with his response. Can you help us?"

Abu Tahir sighed. "Tell me more," he said.

"Sultan Mohammed has sent a great army to seize Dimashq and then Jerusalem. He intends to drive out the Franj and regain his control over al-Shaam. We have warned the Franj and they too are sending an army to meet him. The Franj seek an alliance with the Atabeg and the princes of al-Shaam to prevent this. Sukman tells me the Turks are your enemies as well. Is that not so?"

"Indeed, it is. We have received similar news. If Baldwin has made such an offer, we must inform Tughtigin at once. We will go to the palace. I am always welcome there. He will listen to me."

Before we left to see the Atabeg, Abu Tahir insisted that Sukman and I wash ourselves thoroughly from the grime and dirt we had accumulated on our journey. As we walked to his hammam, he asked me another question.

"Thoma, I have been thinking about what Sukman has told me. I knew that a large shipment of gold was delivered to the Franj and understand that you and Sukman were responsible. Is it correct you have an uncle in al-Misr named Assad, who has a Jewish partner? Would that partner be named Jusuf, and does he reside in Meṛṛakec?"

"Yes, Moallim," I answered.

"It is a small world, Thoma. Your uncle has been a supplier of gold to me for many years. His enterprise brings it from Ifriqiya. Although we have never met, I have learned to trust him. He has never failed me. You may find it amusing that the Franj gave me a large part of the gold dust you and Sukman separated from the Fatimid so it could be converted into coins. There is no way to do that in Jaffa. Without the knowledge of the Franj, I have sent it to your uncle. I asked him to arrange the necessary work. The coins he will send to me will bear the image of the Christian cross. Such an image is forbidden, but gold is gold. It will eventually be paid to us for our services in any event. Isn't it a strange world?"

Indeed, it was, I thought. In the Holy Land, the Christians hated the Muslims; the Muslims hated the Christians. The Shia despised the Sunni and the Western Christians despised the Greeks, each calling the other infidel. Everyone cooperated with and made use of the Jews. Often, all of them worked together and ignored their differences, but cooperation was always temporary. And, at the end of the day, even though they all worshiped the same God, they were in ignorance of each other's faith. It was most certainly a strange, small world. What held it together was avarice. Even then, the holders of commercial power

– be they Venetians or Neopolitans or the Turk princes of the Levante – vied with one another for coin and power. I thanked God I was a physician!

When we reached the hammam and cast aside our clothes, I noticed a brick with which Sukman began to wash himself as we entered the warm water. It smelled of perfume. When I asked about this, Sukman was astonished at my question.

"Hakim, this is 'sabun'. In civilized places, we use this to clean ourselves. They do not use this in Sicilia?"

I admitted that this was the first time I had encountered this substance. It was, indeed, a marvelous thing. It removed dirt easily and left the skin soft and fragrant. I thought it would be much better to wash a wound with this brick than to use only water, wine or vinegar, if it also prevented decay. Sukman told me it was made from the boiled oil of olives, wood ash and ground seashells. The wealthy added lavender and other perfumes. It took weeks to make.

When we had finished our bath, Abu Tahir brought us new clothing so our appearance before Tughtigin would be acceptable.

The Atabeg's palace was near the northwest corner of the city, not far from Abu Tahir's home. The palace, called Qal'at Dimashq, was enclosed by its own wall and protected by fourteen massive towers. Although I knew nothing about matters of war, it seemed to me that the palace would be easily defended from any attacking force. We were granted entrance immediately. A guard escorted us to the audience chamber and announced our presence.

Tughtigin recognized Abu Tahir at once. After the customary salutations and questions about health, Sukman and I were introduced. The Atabeg raised his brows when he was told that I had been the Royal Physician to the ruler of Sicilia. That was an exaggeration, of course; I was once the Court Physician, but 'Royal' sounded more important. The Atabeg asked many questions. He did not ask the reason for our appearance. I was anxious to deliver my parchment. However, it would not have been polite to discuss business at the beginning of conversation.

Eventually, Tughtigin asked me directly if I had a message for him. Relieved to get to the heart of the matter, I answered in the affirmative and gave him the sealed parchment. He took it, broke the seal and attempted to read it. He took a long time to do so and I realized he was having difficulty. In frustration, he gave the letter to one of his counselors and asked him to read it aloud.

The message confirmed that Sultan Mohammed had sent a large army to Surya and was even now approaching Damascus. King Baldwin wished an alliance with the Atabeg to confront this army and drive it back. The interests of the Atabeg and the Princes of Surya were, said the message, the same as those of the Kingdom of Jerusalem. King Baldwin admitted that previous alliances had been broken and admitted that Tughtigin might have suspicions about his sincerity. Baldwin swore that this time he would be faithful; this time, the danger facing both was too great. The message stated that if Tughtigin agreed, he should send word with its bearers. The armies of the Franj and those of the Atabeg would meet in the north.

When the message had been read aloud, all the counselors and others in the room began to shout and argue amongst themselves. Tughtigin motioned them to silence and stroked his beard, deep in thought. After what seemed a long time, he glared directly at me. His stare was frightening. As I returned his gaze, I noticed his left eye was milky white.

"You received this parchment from Baldwin?" he asked.

"No, Excellency, it was given to us by the Master of the Order of Saint John," I replied.

"How can I trust these Franj? You know what happened in Aleppo when the Franj Emir Tancred imposed his demands for coin and demanded a cross be placed upon the tower of the mosque? We have attempted alliance before. The Franj have pillaged our cities and towns ever since they arrived in our lands. They merely wish to enrich themselves. Even Emperor Alexios has offered to assist us in expelling this scum. That came to nothing, of course. What can we expect from infidels?"

"Excellency, what happened when the Turks came to rescue Aleppo? You know well what they did. Who is the greater danger?" asked Abu Tahir. "My people have enjoyed a sound relationship with the Order of Saint John and, so far, they have honored their words. I believe the Princes of Aleppo, Antioch and Tripoli will join their forces with yours. None of them want the Sultan to once again appoint his own rulers to their lands. If what we hear is correct, the Sultan's army will be here in a matter of days."

One of the counselors then voiced his objection. "Abu Tahir has forgotten how the so-called King, Baldwin, has insulted the Atabeg. Upon learning Mawdud had been killed, he sent a message saying any nation that kills its own leader in the house of prayer should be annihilated. Is not that true? Why should we believe his sincerity now?"

The Atabeg nodded his head as he remembered the insult. "I must think about this. Leave me. I will call you back when I have made my decision."

During the discussion, I had been thinking. To my mind, there was no question that it would be in no one's interest for the Turks to take Damascus. If they were to do so, the entire region would be thrown into chaos. It was in disorder now. It could be much worse. My own training led me to consider something else. There was something wrong with the Atabeg's eye.

"Excellency, before you leave, may I ask a question?"

Tughtigin motioned for me to continue.

"If I may be so bold to mention it, you seem to have a problem with your eye. Am I mistaken?"

"You are not," he said tersely. "My vision has become poor lately. It is like looking through fog. It is especially difficult at night. My physicians here say it is a sign of age. There is nothing they can do. Why do you ask?"

It was time I contributed something to this situation. I knew that quick action was needed if the Turks were to be stopped. Tughtigin's first response had not led me to believe he would respond favorably to Baldwin's request. Perhaps, I thought, my training would be of use. I knew what the problem was and knew its solution. Whether or not I could resolve it was another matter. I decided to be bold. I had nothing to lose.

"Excellency, I can help you. If you permit me to do so, perhaps you can then see the situation more clearly and reach a decision that will benefit all."

Both Abu Tahir and Sukman nodded their heads in agreement. The others in the room were at a loss for words.

"Tell me more," ordered the Atabeg.

I proceeded to do so. A great Arab physician who had once resided in al-Misr, named al-Mawsilli, had written of this condition in his treatise on conditions of the eye. I had studied it in school. Although I had never practiced it, he had described the procedure to remedy this affliction. I did not admit my own lack of experience to the Atabeg and promised I would cure him. The procedure would, I said, be uncomfortable but it would produce the desired result. There was no reason for him to suffer from this condition any longer. I repeated my opinion that, if he could see more clearly, he would reach the correct decision.

Tughtigin absorbed this information and advice and, once again, stroked his beard in thought. Finally, he answered.

"For your sake, I pray you are correct. You may do what you say. If I can see again, perhaps I will make a better decision. If you cannot, that is another matter. What do you need?"

I told him I needed a tube of glass as thin as possible and then I would ask him to sit quietly in a comfortable position. Tughtigin ordered one of his servants to fetch a glassmaker. When the artisan arrived, he ordered him to make the instrument I required. While we waited, all of us were served juice made from something called 'sharab'. This refreshing drink was made by combining leymun and al-sukkar. It was delicious.

Late in the afternoon, my instrument arrived. It had been made as I ordered. I asked the Atabeg to sit on a cushion and knelt before him. My racing heart and shaking hand belied my outward calm and confidence. The room became silent. No one noticed the tremors. I prayed God for aid and tried to remember the instructions of Mawsilli. While I did so, I took many deep breaths. When my hands were still, I spoke to the Atabeg.

"This will just take a moment, Excellency. Try your best to compose yourself. Do not close your eye and hold a Quran with both of your hands." With that request, I used my glass tube to gently move the white film over the lens of his eye to the side. He dared not raise his hands to stop me without dropping the Holy Quran, and that would have been a sin. The film was crystalline hard. Should I break it? Mawsilli had written this was dangerous. Perhaps, I thought, it would be best to leave it in the new position. As I considered this, my hand moved slightly, and the film broke into pieces. There was only one solution. I removed some broken pieces by applying suction to the tube. I could not remove them all so, once again, I prayed. Tughtigin, who had remained motionless while I worked, suddenly shouted.

"I can see! I do not understand what you have done! Everything is clearer. You have performed a miracle!"

The others in the room were not only surprised but delighted. Everyone talked at once. The Atabeg smiled and looked everywhere. Finally, he turned to me.

"Hakim, you have done as you promised. How can I repay you? Ask anything and it shall be granted."

"Excellency, that you can see clearly is reward enough," I replied. "Perhaps, now, you will come to the correct decision regarding alliance with Baldwin."

He did not respond. Rather, he turned to his military commander and ordered him to raise the army and to send messengers to Aleppo, Antioch and Tripoli. He then called for his scribe and, rather than dictating a message, asked for parchment and ink and wrote it himself. When he had finished, he gave me the parchment.

"Go to Baldwin and deliver this," he said. "Before you go, I will pay you for your service. You may not refuse my offer. Tell me what you desire."

I thought for a few moments and remembered the teaching of the lady Trota so long ago. "Sabun," I said. "One hundred pieces of sabun. That will be payment enough."

Tughtigin looked at me quizzically. Then he began to laugh out loud. So did everyone else.

"Sabun? Sabun?" he chortled. "You must be very unclean! You want sabun, I'll give you two hundred pieces. No, make it three hundred. I'll fill a ship with it. You will never be unwashed again," he laughed. "You are joking, of course?"

I assured him I was not. I said I would ask Abu Tahir to send it to my uncle Assad in al-Misr with a request to forward this wonderful product to Count Ruggiero in Sicilia as a gift. Perhaps, I said, beneficial trade would result.

The Atabeg realized that I was serious. He understood it would be wise to develop relations with Ruggiero. His mother, after all, was King Baldwin's wife. He promised that the sabun would be delivered immediately.

Tughtigin commanded Sukman and me to depart at once to deliver his message to Baldwin. He would, he said, give us two of his fastest horses for our journey. Abu Tahir, who I realized had been absent from the room during my procedure, called both of us aside.

"Sukman, guard your friend here with your life. I have just learned that a brother has been retained by a Franj to remove him. This was not sanctioned by me. I must find who agreed to this. It will take time. I will do all in my power to do so. Take care!"

Sukman was shocked at this news. Without hesitation, he swore to protect me. There was only one Franj that could have done this: Jehan. If I lived, I swore to confront him and denounce his actions to the Queen and the Master of the Order of Saint John.

Death on the King's Highway

Sukman and I mounted our horses and set out for the crucesignati camp that afternoon. We rode all night, stopping only to rest our horses and permit them to graze. During this tedious ride, I once again developed sores on my behind. These were uncomfortable but reminded me of a story I had not yet heard.

"Sukman, you asked me long ago to remind you to tell me the story of a horse. Do you remember?"

"Of course," he exclaimed. "I had forgotten to tell you. There is a lesson in the tale worth remembering. al-Afdal, the ruler of the Fatimid, may Allah curse his name, tried many times to drive out the Franj. He and his son, Sharaf, lost many battles in their attempt. They tried one last time. The chosen commander was the governor of Beirut and was probably the best leader of all. He had proven himself in battle and was both courageous and prudent. He suffered from a single flaw. Can you guess what it was?"

"No, I cannot," I answered. "Tell me more."

"This commander, I have forgotten his name, was very superstitious. He did not believe the will of Allah alone governs our fate. He consulted a soothsayer who told him he would die from a fall from his horse. As a result, he ordered all the paving stones covering the streets of Beirut to be removed so his horse would not stumble. We, the fida'yin, knew of his fear. Anyone who does not trust his steed will be unsteady in their saddle. Of course, we did not wish the Fatimid to prevail. The solution was simple. At the beginning of the final battle, one of my brothers purposefully startled the commander's charger. It reared and the commander fell as expected. It was then simple to remove him. When his troops realized he was dead, they fled the field. They all believed the soothsayer was right and, thus, lost hope. That was the end of the

Fatimid attempt. Do you see how easy it is to win a battle with only one simple act? I tell you this as I have seen your discomfort on your own mount. I do not wish you to suffer the same fate by accident!"

Early the next morning, we stopped to refresh both our horses and ourselves in the shade of a cluster of palm trees near the road. We had just recommenced our journey when a group of mounted knights rode towards us. One was in armor. The others wore vests of chain mail. Their legs were unprotected below the skirts of their hauberks and above their chausses. All of them carried small shields and long lances. At about one hundred paces, they came to a stop. There were four of them. I noticed their armor was in poor condition. Their tunics were stained with dirt. Sukman slowly removed his bow and concealed it behind his back.

"Peace be with you," I shouted. "We are not Turks; we come in peace."

"We do not, Saracen," shouted one of the warriors. "We do not care if you are Turk or anything else. All Saracens are infidels and idolaters. You are forbidden to use this road. This is a time of war. Go back to wherever you have come from."

They edged closer. I tried to speak to them again.

"We are carrying an urgent message to the King. We have no time to waste. We beg you to allow us to continue our journey."

"If you have such a message, give it to me and then leave this road. Our orders are clear. No Saracens are permitted here. We will deliver the message you claim to possess."

The King's army must be close, I thought. These knights were a scouting party sent to make certain the army's movements were not betrayed too early. Sukman and I had been entrusted with delivering the Atabeg's message to Roland and that is what we would do. The camp could not be far. I would not entrust it to these people. They looked more like bandits than honorable crucesignati. I might be wrong about this but could not risk an error of judgement.

"No," I replied, with as much authority as I could muster. "We too have our orders. The message must be delivered by our hands. I ask once again that you stand aside and permit us to proceed. The King will not be happy if you delay us any longer."

"You lie," the warrior shouted. "You are spies sent by the Sultan. Go back or pay the consequence."

When we did not move, the speaker motioned to one of the knights. He spoke in a language I did not recognize. The horseman to whom he had spoken was in full armor. He leveled his lance and charged. As he did, he cried "Deus Vult"; God wills it!

Sukman muttered a prayer and, once again, shot the horse of the knight charging us. With a crash of iron, the knight fell from his now wounded horse and lay motionless in the dirt.

Sukman did not hesitate. Crying aloud for Allah's forgiveness and attesting to His greatness, Sukman swung himself on his horse and drew his curved sword. The stallions given to us by the Atabeg were small but swift and nimble. Our adversaries were mounted on steeds called destriers. These are massive, strong and slow. They did not have a chance. Swift as lightning, Sukman, low in his saddle, gracefully wove his horse through and around the remaining knights. Using his curved sword, he sliced neatly through the unprotected space below their waists. These were mortal wounds. The knights screamed in agony as their blood poured onto the ground. Mercifully, it took little time for them all to die. Sukman returned to me, dismounted and, as he had done before, asked that I forgive him for killing the horse. That he could take a human life so casually yet be so regretful for killing an animal was still a wonder.

To this day, I have not forgiven myself for what happened next. I had forgotten the fallen knight in full armor. So had Sukman. We both believed that, lying stunned on the ground, he was no longer capable of doing us harm. The two of us were gazing at the carnage resulting from Sukman's attack. Sukman began to speak. As he opened his mouth to do so, nothing came out except a wail of pain. I looked down and saw the point of a sword jutting from his chest. He had been stabbed from behind by the once fallen knight. There had been no warning. The knight, having accomplished his purpose, fell back to the earth. I grabbed his sword, kicked him in his helmet and took Sukman in my arms.

There was no hope. It was easy to see that Sukman's wound was mortal. He would die quickly. There was nothing I could do. From his expression, I knew Sukman was aware of this. He tried desperately to speak.

"My dear friend," he murmured. "Tell the Teacher I died performing my duty."

Tears welled in my eyes. This was my fault. I had not thought to look at our first assailant. I had made an assumption regarding his condition and assumptions without fact are always an error. Sukman looked at me. His eyes were beginning to glaze over. He made a valiant effort to speak through the blood running from his mouth.

"Do not grieve for me. I will enter paradise. Someday, Allah willing, so will you. I will greet you there, my brother. Allahu Akbar." With those words, he took his final breath and died in my arms.

I wept for a long time, holding him as would a mother with child. He had died protecting me; a man who pretended to be one of his faith. Apart from Matthaeus during my residence at school, Sukman was the single true friend I ever had. We had shared much together. And I had learned from him. How could our common God permit this to happen to His devoted servant? I realized that if I was to truly honor Sukman, I had to complete our mission. My eyes wet with tears, I recited the words of the Muslim prayer for the dead.

O Allah, forgive your servant Sukman Ibn Artuq and elevate his station among those who are guided. Send him along the path of those who came before, and forgive us and him, O Lord of the worlds. Enlarge for him his grave and shed light upon him in it.

I buried him near the palm trees. The armored knight, who had been lying quietly all this time, made an attempt to rise. Given the weight of his iron, this was difficult. He moaned in pain as he tried to remove his helmet. I betrayed my oath as a physician and ignored him. In any event, he had not suffered a mortal wound. Someone else would find him. I had no time to waste. I mounted my horse and rode to the camp.

The hills surrounding the oasis were now occupied by soldiers. I shouted that I had a message to deliver and rode directly into the camp. Roland beamed when he saw me.

"My friend, I am happy to see you! You were gone longer than I had expected. Where is your companion? Did he stay in Damascus? What answer do you bring? Is it good news?" He hesitated as he looked at me. "I see by your face that the news is bad. Your eyes are wet. The army is close. I will report to them at once!"

He was going to go on in his interminable way. I held up my palm to quiet him.

"Roland, I do have bad news. It is not what you think. The Atabeg will support the King. I have brought a message from him. He is marshaling his own troops as we speak. Here it is. Send this now with someone you trust. I can answer your questions later."

"You are right as always, my friend. I will take this myself. Rest here and wait for my return." He paused. "Did you see the scouts I sent to search for Turk spies?" he asked.

"I saw them," I answered flatly. "Did you not tell them we might be coming to you?"

"Of course not," he replied. "Your mission was secret. Why do you ask?"

"It is not important," I sighed. "I suggest we waste no further time. Deliver the message to the King. That is what is important."

Roland, thankfully, did not comment further on the tears in my eyes. He agreed and, without further talk, mounted his own horse and rode south.

I become a pilgrim

What to do now? I pondered this question all night in the camp of the crucesignati. I was truly alone; a target for a skilled assassin with no one to protect me. Although I had no proof, I was convinced that Jehan had ordered my death. I could think of no reason for this. To make matters even worse, I had no coin and, other than the talkative Roland, no friends. But I had sworn to go to Jerusalem to discover the fate of my father and that I would do at all costs. Sukman had lost his life so that I could achieve that goal and, for that, I was responsible. I was so near yet so far.

Before all had gone to sleep, I engaged in the idle conversations of the young soldiers, who, I learned had just arrived in the Holy Land. I paid little attention. I needed time to think. Many of them were gleefully anticipating the great battles to come as this, they declared, would provide an opportunity to prove their valor on the field of arms and show their devotion to God. Almost all of them dreamed of becoming rich from the spoils of war and ransom of captives. I felt sorrow for them. They had yet to learn of the horrors of battle. Of course, if Baldwin and Tughtigin's plans failed, they would soon have their lesson.

A few had engaged in actual combat. These veterans spoke little. They spent the time sharpening their weapons. I did talk briefly with an older man wearing the robe of the Order of St John. His name was Robert. He asked me a few questions to which I gave fabricated answers. I had a question of my own.

"Robert, what is the purpose of your order? Is it true you are a monk?"

"I am not a monk," he said. "We are known as the Knights Hospitaller. Our order has always cared for pilgrims at our hospice in Jerusalem. When the Pope confirmed our role two years ago, we expanded our services to provide them with an armed escort. We even protect the Greeks and the Rum. Some of us have been trained in the arts of war and we have sworn allegiance to our master, Raymond du Puy. I myself am only a man at arms but, in the Order, I can become a knight. Nowhere else would someone like me have such a chance."

The words 'hospice' and 'pilgrim' gave me an idea. The assassin, if there was one, would have knowledge of my intention to return to the camp. I was not safe here. Jehan would assume I would avoid the city of Jerusalem, where he had influence and allies. In any event, he knew that Roland would seek me out and could be easily persuaded to disclose my plans. The solution was obvious. I would become a pilgrim, enter the Holy City and make my way to Queen Adelaide to seek refuge and aid. I was certain I could convince that strong woman to forgive me for my precipitate departure from Sicilia. I could think of nothing better. All I could do is place my fate in the hands of God.

Early the next morning, I left the Atabeg's fine horse with Robert, asking that he give it to Roland if he returned. I was, I declared, going to Tyre, where I had other duties to perform. Robert said he would honor my request and wished me Godspeed.

I walked west for two days until I found a band of ragged pilgrims heading south along the banks of the River Jordan. They were all Rum; Greek Christians from Arminiya and Suriya. Many of them spoke the language of our Lord Jesus, Aramaic. The Arminiyan had all come from the region of Cilicia. I did not speak the language of these people, but some spoke Greek. I spoke enough of the tongue to communicate. I was, I declared, a physician from Tricia far to the north, and asked to join their pilgrimage to the Holy City. None of them were familiar with the land west of Constantinopolis so they did not question me. They were delighted that I was a physician and welcomed me to their group. Together, we walked to Jerusalem.

We moved slowly. Along the way, I treated several minor ailments which did not need any of my remaining stock of herbs. Many of them suffered from sores to their feet resulting from the poor condition of their boots. They had walked a long distance. Although we spoke only in the simplest way, I discovered that these were sincere people. They had engaged in pilgrimage not for glory or riches. They simply desired to show their devotion. They hoped for salvation, of course, but most believed that traveling to the Holy City where Lord Jesus was crucified and rose from the dead was an obligation and tribute to God. None of them spoke badly of the Muslims, although some believed Islam to be a religion of idolaters. I do not know how they came to that conclusion. Perhaps they had heard that Muslims venerated the sacred black stone set into the corner of the Kaaba at the Grand Mosque of Mecca. That, of course, was no idol. The

Saracens, they said, merely needed further education to amend their beliefs. Many had friends among the Jews and believed it was just a matter of time before they too finally understood that Lord Jesus was, indeed, their messiah. Jesus Himself, they argued, was a Jew. No one complained about their sore feet. Some were convinced that such mortification showed the extent of their penance. "Lord Jesus suffered for us, we can do the same for Him," they said. I began to greatly admire these dedicated servants of God.

In about two weeks, we arrived at the small city of Ariha that the Jews call Yeriho. It is, I am told, one of the oldest cities on earth and is mentioned many times in scriptures. I recalled from my father's letter it was also the place which had first supplied al-sukkar to the Collegantia and made its fortune. It was also the birthplace of my aunt. We rested in Ariha for two days, washed the dust from our clothes and faces and otherwise made ourselves presentable. I seized the opportunity to visit the mill of Tawahin, about which my father had written. As my uncle told me, it was now owned by Franj. Cane was growing in abundance along the river and the mill was in full production. Cartloads of al-sukkar, the sweet salt, were being dispatched to the port of Accra. The mill was earning a great deal of coin, I thought. I did not linger. I was eager to reach nearby Jerusalem. The horse given me by the Atabeg could have reached the Holy City in a day. It took us another week at our sluggish pace.

Like other pilgrims, our band arrived at St. David's Gate and peacefully passed through. I was certain no one would recognize me. I had permitted my beard to grow and my clothing was ragged. Upon reflection, I realized my best course of action would be to find Roland. It was a risk, but I had few alternatives. The best place to begin my search would be the hospice controlled by the Order of Saint John. Wandering through the warren of filthy lanes, I asked for directions and was told the hospice was just south of the Church of the Holy Sepulcher in an area of the city known as Muristan. Part of the church itself had been rebuilt at great expense by Emperor Constantine many years ago. Now, much of it remained in ruins.

It was not difficult to find the hospice. It was an imposing complex of structures, most of which had remarkably high roofs to provide proper circulation of air. All the pilgrims knew where it was. I entered it alongside others, most of whom were ill. The attendant, thinking I was equally afflicted, asked me to describe my condition. I answered that I was not sick. I was looking for a member of the Order named Roland.

"Oh, you seek the 'One who is never silent'; that is what we call him. He will probably be among the ill, lecturing them on the grace of God. Some pilgrims have asked that we find another assignment for him."

The attendant directed me to a large room filled with straw pallets. Most were occupied by patients. I saw Roland at once. He was leaning over a man who was in obvious distress. I did not want to interrupt, but it seemed to me it might be to the patient's benefit if I did.

"Peace be with you, Roland," I shouted. "I have missed you!"

Roland turned from his victim, who gasped in relief for his rescue. By the look on Roland's face, I was not certain he recognized me. It took him a few moments. Finally, he did.

"My dearest friend Thomas, is it you? You have grown your beard. You look like you have been rolling in the mud. I almost did not recognize you. What has happened? You disappeared from the camp and no one knew where you were. Were you on another secret mission? Are you well?" He gave me no time to respond. As always, he continued to ramble on with his questions: "Have you heard the wonderful news?"

"I am well," I answered. "What is the news?"

"We have driven back the Turks! King Baldwin took five hundred knights and one thousand soldiers and joined with two thousand troops from Tripoli. Together they united with Tughtigin's warriors. Our new friends added at least five thousand to the army. Together, they came to the rescue of the Regent of Antioch, who was blocking the Turks from further incursion. They arrived just in time. When the Turks saw the forces allied against them in the field, they withdrew and, God willing, they will not be back. The

King is returning now. May God be praised! Come with me and I will tell you more about this great victory. Now that we have cooperated with the infidels against a common enemy, perhaps there will be peace in the land, and we can begin to convert our new friends to the true faith. Have you eaten anything?"

This was indeed good news. At least my journey to Damascus with Sukman had not been in vain. If Sukman had not given his life to defend me, King Baldwin might not have been victorious. I felt some relief at this realization. My own situation, however, remained tenuous. An assassin was hunting me and Jehan might have poisoned other Franj against me. The Deputy Master of the Order of Saint John might be of assistance. He knew I had faithfully performed my obligations. There was Queen Adelaide, but was reconciliation possible? My letter to Ruggiero would not have arrived yet, so she could not know the reasons for my departure from her service. The single friend I had in this place was Roland and I had no trust in his discretion. His love for discourse could be my undoing. There was little choice. I had to keep him close. Heaving a sigh, I answered him.

"This news is wonderful, Roland. Indeed, I am hungry. Let us find an inn and you can tell me everything."

"There is no inn nearby, my friend," he replied. "There is food in the market, but you will not like it. They call it the place of bad cooking! We can eat here instead. First, I must make certain that the pilgrims in my ward do not need me for now and then we can go to the scullery. We have much to discuss."

Roland took a great deal of time talking to each of the patients. As he did so, he often pointed in my direction and I was certain he was regaling them with tales. My hope to pass unnoticed was becoming just a dream. After an interminable period, he came to me and announced that he was free from his duties. In the scullery, we found an empty table. I steeled myself for the one-sided discourse to come. In as few words as possible, I told him of all that had happened on my journey to Damascus. Each sentence I spoke was met with a question and then a long treatise on whatever came to his mind. My head ached. I finally was able to ask a question myself. I had two.

"Roland, what has become of Brother Jehan? Where can I find the Queen?"

"Ah yes," he answered. "Brother Jehan is with the army. He should not have gone. Do you know about his leg? I will tell you. You know he always has limped. Now he has a large growth on his leg which causes him great discomfort. I think he is ill. Everyone told him to stay here but he insisted upon going with deputy grand master Raymond du Puy and King Baldwin. I do not know how he was able to do so. Perhaps he was given a horse. That would have helped. I am certain he wishes to speak to you, and he will most certainly return with the King. Why do you ask?

But wait, you also asked about the Queen. She will be at the Citadel. She looks old, you know. I do not think she leaves her chambers often. You were her friend, were you not? Do you wish to see her?"

"Thank you, my friend," I answered. "Now, all I want is rest. I have had a difficult journey. I do need to see her, but it will wait until tomorrow. Let me find a place to sleep tonight and we can talk again tomorrow."

"Of course," he said. "You are still on your mission, I'm sure. You can make use of the cells here. No one will object. Do you know how to find the Citadel? Forgive me. Of course, you know that place. Will you go in the early morning? I will be with the pilgrims when you return. Some of them are very ill and I know you can help them. We have few physicians here and I lack the skill to provide aid. All I can do is bring them comfort and companionship. I cannot tell you how much your presence brings joy to me. Bring your belongings and follow me."

I had no belongings. That fact escaped Roland, who continued to chatter on. He took me to an empty cell and, following even more comments, finally left me in peace. I fell asleep as soon as he departed.

The next morning, I walked to the citadel. On the way, using the last of the coin Sukman had shared with me, I purchased a new robe and cleaned myself at a public bath. My vestments were not appropriate for court, but it was the best I could do. By the time I arrived at the gates, I still did not know how to present my case to the Queen. I saw little choice. I would again entrust my fate to God.

A guard reluctantly granted me access to the citadel and directed me to an official from whom I could seek an audience. This man looked at me up and down, frowning as he did so.

"You seek an audience with the Queen?" he laughed. "What are you? A Rum pilgrim wanting alms? She has no time to deal with beggars."

"Just tell her that Thoma ibn Thomas, once her loyal physician, has a message. She will see me. If you do not, there may be consequences," I said, with as much arrogance and conviction as I could muster.

The official looked at me again, wiped his nose, sniffed and tersely ordered one of his servants to deliver the message. It was not long before a soldier arrived and commanded me to accompany him. I prayed I was not being led to a prison.

I meet with a Queen and discover a Cure for a King

Queen Adelaide looked me up and down and scowled. She sat on her high dais and stared at me with her piercing, cold eyes. "Well," she muttered, "our long-lost physician has returned. Tell me why I should listen to whatever you have to say; why I should not throw you in prison. That is where you belong." She steepled her fingers and waited for my response.

"Madam, forgive me," I began. "I have traveled far to see you so that I may confess all to you. I beg you to hear me out. My absence has not been by choice. My tale will take time. Will you grant this?"

The Queen said nothing. She simply motioned for me to continue. That was a small relief. Until this moment, I had not decided how to present my case. Only one path was open. I would tell the truth; all of it. And so, I did.

Other than calling for wine and fruit, Adelaide made no comment. She offered me nothing. She asked no questions. Sometimes she nodded in understanding. Otherwise she gave me no hint of her disposition. Despite the fierce demeanor I had come to know so well, I had faith in her wisdom and ultimate fairness.

When I had completed my tale, the Queen remained silent. She stared at me for what seemed an interminable time. Finally, she rose from the dais, ordered me to remain and left the room. Now I was nervous. It was not helpful that I had nothing to eat or drink. The rumbling of my stomach made my heart race even faster. I made effort to calm myself but to no avail. She was gone a long time. It was almost dark when a servant brought me a plate of fruit and a drink made from oranges. I had just begun to partake in this welcome feast when the door to the chamber opened with a loud bang and Adelaide stormed in.

"You miserable excuse for a physician! You ungrateful wretch! You creature of evil, I have missed you," she shouted. "My son missed you. We have all worried about your fate. I have listened to your excuses. Why did you not come to me in the first instance? I never believe the words of priests. You know that! You could have saved yourself from all of this. My son may forgive you, but I will remember. Now, let us truly talk." Adelaide smiled at me. I have never felt such relief.

We talked well into the night. She had her own problems. Three years ago, the Patriarch of Jerusalem convinced King Baldwin to cast aside his wife, Arda of Marash. Arda's father had promised a dowry of sixty thousand bezants. He only paid a mere seven thousand. To make matters worse, Arda was barren. With the shortfall in commitment from Arda's father, Baldwin needed coin desperately. He had made a grave error and sought the advice of his counselors. The Patriarch suggested that the King set Arda aside and send ambassadors to Sicilia to meet Adelaide and, on his behalf, ask for her hand. Everyone knew she was rich and that her duties as Regent were no longer needed. Her son, Ruggiero, was ruler in his own right. Adelaide saw the advantage in agreeing to Baldwin's proposal. She conditioned her consent for marriage to Baldwin on an agreement that their son, if they had one, would inherit the Kingdom of Jerusalem. As I knew well, Adelaide was clever. She was in her middle years and knew the chance of birthing a child was very small. Thus, she added a provision that if there was no issue from the marriage, the kingdom would pass to her own son, Ruggiero. This, she said, was the heart of her difficulty.

By this time, it was late at night. "I must tell you more, but not tonight. Do you have a place to stay?"

"I have been sleeping at the hospice. I have nowhere else to go."

"You told me you fear you are being hunted by an assassin," she said. "I will place you under my protection. You will stay here in the citadel. I would prefer not to lose you again and we have much to discuss."

I was delighted with this command. The citadel should provide some safety from unwelcome visitors and I needed sleep. As one of her servants began to lead me to my chamber, Adelaide had one more thing to say.

"Thoma, your clothing is deplorable. It smells like long-dead goat and belongs on a peasant. My servant will bring you something more appropriate to wear. Do not come to me in this condition again. Oh, and trim your beard. You look like an ape." With that remark, she swept out of the room.

The sun had barely risen when a palace official barged into my chamber and demanded that I attend the Queen at once. I took time to don my new vestments and trimmed my beard and hair as quickly as possible. Adelaide was pacing the room, waiting for me.

"You are late," she muttered. "Were you attacked by Saracens in the night? Never mind, you will have some excuse for your tardy arrival. I need to know if I can trust you again. Answer me!"

"Madam, you know you can," I answered. "I may have told lies to survive but I have never betrayed you. I never will, so help me God."

Adelaide stared at me. "Very well," she said. "You may sit on the cushion here. I told you last night that there was more to my tale and I have need of your counsel."

I sat as commanded and the Queen perched again on her dais. She ordered her retainers from the room and then began to speak softly.

"Thoma, it appears that my marriage is not valid. I do not know what to do. It seems the King never bothered to annul the union with Arda, his former wife. He simply banished her to the convent of Saint Anne, here in the city, and then permitted her to travel to Constantinopolis, where she still resides. I was not aware of this when I accepted his offer. I did that for the benefit of my son. Had I known of his sin – the Greeks call it 'bi-gamos' – I never would have made an agreement. The only one here who could help me resolve this situation, the Patriarch of Jerusalem, has been excommunicated for his role in the affair. I am at a loss for what steps to take."

"This is a grave problem, Madam," I said. "I do not know how to help you. Isn't this a matter for the Church and the law?"

"That is the difficulty, Thoma. You have not heard all I have to say. Remain silent and I will tell you. The King, you see, is ill. Some say his affliction is the result of an injury he suffered in battle. He believes, however, that his illness is punishment from God for his sin. If he is not cured, he will appeal to the Pope for absolution and you can guess what his penance will be. My marriage will be annulled. All I have strived for will come to naught. Cure the King. That is what I need you to do."

"Madam, I will do all in my power to do as you ask," I answered. "Can you tell me more about his illness? He should be here in the city any day now, is that correct?"

"Yes, I expect him soon. About his illness, I cannot tell you much. Our relationship is not close. He finds my demeanor too brusque and I am too old, he complains. Some wonder if he is interested at all in women other than for the wealth they can bring. He may have other preferences. But there is more. I brought one thousand soldiers from our army and a few of my best Muslim archers. They protect me here. He treats all of them badly and refuses to pay them.

Fortunately, he also has no faith in the physicians in Jerusalem. I think I can convince him of your skill."

My first question remained unanswered. I decided to ask again. "What have you noticed about his illness?" I asked.

"He coughs constantly. Often, we see blood on the rags with which he wipes his mouth. He has lost weight. Sometimes his body is hot. I know nothing else. Whatever it is, I expect you to cure it. I am certain you will not disappoint me again."

I tried to recall what I had learned at school. Galen had described some of these same symptoms and, if my memory served me properly, the King was a victim of a disease called phthisis. It was always fatal in the end. Aristotle, I recalled, named it 'The King's Evil'. I doubted that an old injury could result in the illness described. Without seeing him myself, I could not be certain. I said nothing of this to the Queen.

"Arrange an audience for me with the King and I will do all I can. In the meantime, I will need some medicines. I have none of my own."

"You have the large stock in Sicilia for which you never paid tax. Have you forgotten? Never mind, we will not discuss that now. Tell me what you require, and I will do my best to obtain it."

If my diagnosis was correct, Galen suggested milk, fresh air and a sea voyage. Salt air might be beneficial, but had I had no faith in the other suggestions. There was a plant, however, which might alleviate the most serious symptom.

"Madam, there may be someone in Jerusalem or a nearby coastal city that supplies medicinal plants and herbs. I need the leaves of a plant that grows on trees that some call lungwort. I also need another herb called marrubium. Both are covered in very fine hairs. Finally, I need spirea ulmaria. Shall I write these down for you?"

Adelaide agreed to send her servants to the market, or as far as Acre if necessary, to procure these ingredients which, I prayed, would help to relieve some of the King's complaints. If I could reduce his cough and excess heat for a reasonable time, there might be some hope. I needed more time to think.

"If it pleases you, I will accompany your servants. That way, I can judge if they purchase the correct herbs. I also must advise my friend Roland of my whereabouts so he does not worry."

She nodded her head in agreement and dismissed me from the room. I prayed my thinking was correct.

With Adelaide's servants, I walked to the hospice. I told them to wait for me outside and then looked for Roland. There were many large and heated rooms for the patients, a kitchen, baths, and rooms for bloodletting. There were even gardens where the sick wandered freely. As expected, he was in one of the large rooms providing 'companionship' to the patients. He apologized to his most recent victim and came to me in haste.

"My dear Thomas, I have good news! Brother Jehan survived his journey. He will return in a few days. Isn't that wonderful! I know he will want to see you. Why, I wonder, does he hate you so much? Of course, your other affairs may keep you away. Did you meet with the Queen? Her husband will arrive soon as well. Do you think he will reward you for all you have done?" Roland paused for a moment and then continued almost to himself. "How could he not? It is said he is ill. Where were you last night? I thought you were returning and found new straw for your cell. I have almost completed my duties here; let us find a place to talk. Have you eaten? I have not and I am hungry." He was going to continue with more observations and questions. I put up my hand to stop him.

"Roland, I am still engaged in my own duties and cannot spend time with you. I simply wanted to tell you that all is well and that I am staying at the citadel. Tell no one, not even Brother Jehan. I will see him but not now. I do, however, need your advice."

"Anything, my dear friend, anything at all. Just ask!" For once, Roland did not make further comment.

"Roland, my stock of herbs and medicines is gone. I must find a reputable merchant dealing with these goods. Do you know anyone?"

Roland put his head between his hands. Thinking was, for him, a great effort. Finally, he nodded to himself.

"Yes, there is a Jew who specializes in herbs. You can find him near the Dung Gate. Of course, he is no longer a Jew. He has converted to our true faith; or so they say. The brothers of Saint John deal with him and I have never heard complaint. Some say he practices magic. He has a few manuscripts written in the script of the Jews. I wonder why these haven't these been taken from him? They might contain words for the casting of spells. Do you think so? You never know about these people." Roland shook his head and raised his brows.

I chose not to answer. "Thank you, Roland. I will visit this man and share whatever opinion I reach." With that remark, I left him behind, collected my retainers and walked to the Dung Gate in the southeast corner of the city.

The city was littered with filth. The streets through which we walked were marked by hundreds of small booths selling gazz, dates, olives and merchandise of all kinds. There were shops selling spices, rancid cuts of meat and poor-quality amber. Many specialized in the sale of holy relics. Given the profusion of small bones and teeth displayed, I wondered just how many saints there were. The stench of rotting meat and offal pervaded the air. I was eager to return to the citadel.

It was not difficult to find the shop of the herb merchant. It was the only one that smelled sweet. Clay jars, each labeled as to their contents, were stored on the shelves. In one corner, rolls of parchment were stacked on a shelf. I assumed these were the manuscripts Roland had mentioned. The shopkeeper was a portly man with a jolly demeanor. Around his neck, he wore a large gold cross.

"Welcome to my establishment," he said in Aramaic. Seeing I had difficulty in understanding his greeting, he looked at me cautiously and then continued in Arabic.

"You are Rum, are you not? Let me guess. You are a physician from Constantinopolis. Have I guessed correctly? My name is Aubert. How can I be of assistance?"

"I am Rum," I lied. "But I am not from that city. My home is much further north. I have traveled far, and my own medicines are depleted. I need to replace them."

"You have come to the right place then," he said. "I have the only stocks in the city. Tell me what you require."

I asked for the herbs I had determined would be useful and, as good as his word, Aubert provided them. He paused when I asked for lungwort.

"That is an interesting request, sir. I have a small quantity here. I thought it would sell well but I was wrong. No one here knows anything about this plant, and they will not listen to me. I will give you what I have as a gift. I hope you will always come to me when you have need. My prices are fair, and it is always good for those of our faiths to aid each other."

I almost laughed aloud. The prices he asked were extravagant. It was then I remembered I had no coin. Entering negotiation without funds would be foolish. One of the servants, seeing my hesitation, withdrew a leather purse and, without speaking, gave it to me. It was filled with several gold and copper coins. Now I could haggle.

And that we did, from sext to nones. Every time I thought we had reached a bargain for one of the herbs, he would agree on the price providing I purchased others with the same property. For example, after we arrived at a reasonable price for the spirea, he suggested I also purchase white willow bark, which has the same effect. He also suggested that I should have stores of verdigris, that substance which arises from the weathering of brass and copper. Aubert claimed that verdigris was useful in treating a festering wound. Although I am certain the results of our bargains were not in my favor, I came to respect his knowledge. It occurred to me to ask a favor.

"Aubert, I have a message for a friend in al-Misr. Do you have a correspondent there?"

Until that point, Aubert had been jovial. He constantly smiled as we talked. My question provoked an unexpected reaction. He frowned with suspicion and, perhaps, a little fear.

"Why do you ask, sir? I was once a Jew but I am now a good Christian. See the cross I wear? I do no commerce with the infidel."

I thought for a moment and realized the nature of his concern. "Aubert, I am not trying to trick you. My friend is a Jew. His name is Jusuf Ben Abulafia. He is well known in al-Qahirah and Iskandariyyah. I only wish to have a message delivered to him. Any assistance you provide would be much appreciated. There is no danger to you."

He scrutinized me for a few moments as he attempted to judge my honesty. Eventually, he spoke.

"I may be able to forward your correspondence. Next time you come to my shop, bring it with you and I will do my best. You are a good customer and it is beneficial to my commerce to please you. Do come again, Hakim."

I turned to leave and had a second thought. It was a risk, but I needed friends here. I withdrew my parchment from Rabbi Ephraim and handed it to the herbalist. So that the Queen's servants did not know what I was doing, I said loudly, "Here is a list of what other herbs and potions I may also need. Please read it and, if you do not have enough quantity, perhaps you can find it elsewhere. I will purchase it from you."

Aubert read the directive with both shock and recognition on his face. The servants paid no attention. Again, he stared intently at me and then he whispered to me.

"I am at your service. You have only to ask. Perhaps we can talk more on your return." More loudly, he said, "God be with you, Hakim. May the peace of Lord Jesus be upon you. I will have these herbs prepared."

I bowed in thanks and returned with my herbs to the citadel. Queen Adelaide was busy with other affairs and curtly acknowledged me. She said the King was expected in a few days and granted me leave to conduct whatever business I had in the city. I was commanded to sleep in the citadel. She offered to send some of her soldiers to accompany me. I refused the offer; I needed to be alone.

During the days that followed, I wandered the city. Often, I accompanied pilgrims who were visiting the holy places. Without exception, these people were devout in their faith. They had all come from great distance on perilous roads to give thanks and seek salvation. I admired them. The soldiers remaining in the city were another matter. Most of them were far gone in drink. I also spent considerable time with Aubert, to whom I had delivered my message to Jusuf and Assad. That letter took time to compose. I wanted to relate all that had transpired since my last message, but what I wrote was brief. I could not risk having anything important fall into the wrong hands. I once again promised to find a way to come to them.

Now that Aubert had seen the directive from Rabbi Ephraim, he was open with me. I learned much of his story. When the Franj conquered Jerusalem, they systematically murdered almost all the Jews in the city. Aubert was fortunate. It was known that he possessed considerable wealth derived from his commerce. At the time, he was the sole remaining supplier of herbs and medicines in the city. That trade was of value. A leader of the crucesignati offered him a bargain he could not refuse. If he gave over his gold and converted to the Christian faith, he would live. If not, he would join the rest of the Jews in exile or death. Aubert felt great remorse for his decision.

"What else could I do, Hakim? Lord Jesus was a Jew, was he not? Could God abandon me if I merely gave words in return for my life? I changed my name to Aubert from the name Abrafim given me at my birth and converted to Christianity. That is what I did, may God forgive me. The King has many former Muslims in his court who have done the same. Do you understand?"

"Yes, my friend, I do," I said sincerely. "I too have had issues with faith. But let us talk about herbs. The past is the past."

And that we did. Aubert explained that the rule of the Franj had changed everything regarding trade. I knew that, of course, from the discussion I had so long ago with my uncles. Trade in spices had expanded enormously as the newcomers became acquainted with the products of the East. Many of the crucesignati were engaged in limited commerce, but merchants of Venice and Genoa dominated most of the trade. There was a special interest in al-sukkar. The quality of the sweet salt produced in al-Tawahin was inferior to the product originally supplied but no one cared.

"You know, Hakim, the spices delivered here come from far away by means of caravans from Persia. Because of demand, and the difficulty of the journey, prices have soared. I have the same difficulty with many herbs, especially Af-Yum."

"Is that why your prices are so outrageous?" I laughed.

Aubert did not find my remark amusing, but he ignored it.

"Thoma, if I may call you that, there is a solution. My people... well the people of my former faith have developed a new route by sea to al-Hind from where most spices are grown. It is safer and is far less costly. The rulers of al-Misr have cooperated in this endeavor. They too realize the importance of discovering an alternative that bypasses the control of the Franj. My people... I should say the Jews... have established outposts in Arabia and along the coast. Commerce is thriving. I am certain your friend in al-Misr is involved. Of course, we receive no supplies in this way. Someday this will change. Demand from the Franj in their own lands will drive it."

This was an interesting development. Long ago, my uncles had told me about the new trading route. From what I had seen in the Holy City, the most active commerce was in holy relics. Every monastery and church within Christendom desired such items to encourage pilgrimage and alms. Everyone believed these bits of bone, wood or iron had the power to bring direct blessings from God. For donations to the church and proper prayer, they might even cure illness. Their cost was recovered in months and then provided an opportunity for pure profit. Perhaps more importantly, relics were easily transported. They were almost as good as coin. There was a limit, of course. How many pieces of the True Cross could exist? Already, there were many forgeries.

Spices, however, were different. There was no limit except cost on their supply. There were no forgeries. The crucesignati and pilgrims, when they returned to their own lands, would bring news of the wonders of the East and their newly acquired taste for spices, especially al-sukkar. They would know something of the value of rare herbs in treating illness. All these things would become desired by the wealthy. As more was wanted, the more costly they would become. A merchant who bought cheaply and sold dear would make a fortune. My grandfather Terryn said that.

I shared these thoughts with Aubert, and he agreed with me. I even told him about my having sent sabun to Ruggiero.

"An excellent choice, Thoma," he said. "I had not thought of that. If the King is pleased and desires more, I can supply you. I still have friends who can assist me. I have no interest in pursuing commerce in spices. My herbs are enough. I belong here. Just advise me if I can be of use to you. You will never become wealthy as a physician."

That day, when I returned to the citadel, a guard was waiting for me. "Come now," he said. "The Queen demands your presence."

When I entered her chamber, she was pacing back and forth in the room.

"Ah, there you are. There is no time to lose. The King has returned. I have convinced him to see you. I told him you were my personal physician in Sicilia and that you perform miracles. I hope you do! Come with me!"

The King was most certainly ill. Despite this, he was in good spirits from his victory. He was much younger than the Queen and was a handsome man. His skin, however, was pale. There were dark circles under his eyes and, as I had been told, he coughed frequently. This distressed him greatly. He looked too thin for a man of his size. His skin was hot to the touch.

"My Queen says you can cure me of my affliction," he said. "She is wrong. Unless you are a priest yourself, I doubt there is anything you can do. My own physicians have explained to me why I am being punished by God. Nevertheless, I gave my word I would listen to you. Do what you must."

At this comment, the Queen raised her brow, silently asking if I understood the implications of what he said. I nodded, indicating that I did. The King then motioned for Adelaide to leave. "I need to be alone with this man," he said. We were not alone, however. Besides his attendants, two bearded priests remained in his chamber. Both were glaring at me with displeasure and suspicion.

Upon inspection, I saw that often his cough produced a small amount of blood. This he quickly wiped away as it appeared. More concerning was the fact he had a wound on his groin which, although old, had opened. The King complained that this wound was still painful, especially when he rode his horse. It was red around the margins. I began to wonder if my original belief was valid. A wound like this, if invested with rot, could make his heat rise. If untreated, the wound would kill him. That did not explain the cough or the loss of weight. If he did suffer from phthisis, that would kill him also. I decided to treat both ailments at the same time and pray for an acceptable outcome.

I took time to infuse the dried lungwort and marrubium in wine. To this I added spirea and, for good measure, some of the willow bark. I did not recall the correct quantities so decided that more was better. Thinking the taste might be disagreeable, I added some honey. I gave this mixture to the King to drink. One of the priests stopped me then.

"Drink it yourself first, Saracen. How do we know you are not trying to kill our King?"

I did so and angrily said, "I am not a Saracen, Father. Would you like to taste this yourself?" The priest turned to me, his face red with anger.

"I will not drink that potion. You are interfering with the will of God. We know the reason for his affliction and have already taken steps to resolve it. You are meddling in affairs of which you have no knowledge!"

King Baldwin turned to the priest and waved him to silence. He had promised the Queen to listen to me and cooperate with what I suggested. He would keep his oath. He grimaced as he drank my potion in one large gulp. He looked at me then and said, "This tastes better than potions I have been given before. Will I feel better soon?"

"Your Highness, I will make more. Drink it at least three times each day. In the meantime, you must eat. You will see the results in two days." I had no idea if that was true. The Persian physician Razes had written that patents, even if close to death, fared better if they were given assurance of cure. I turned next to his wound.

The wound itself was filthy. Someone had closed it long ago with cotton thread and, as expected, the wound was opening again. It was deep. The surrounding skin was inflamed. Yellow fluid leaked from it. This was serious. I asked permission to wash the area with vinegar and wine. I then applied a poultice of sheep's fat and blue-green verdigris.

"Your Highness, this wound requires care," I said. "If it pleases you, I will close it again properly with gazz when the skin is no longer red. Your servants should bind this with a clean cloth and clean it regularly as I have done."

"I have no time for that. al-Afdal is attempting to take Jaffa. I will ride again soon. We must control the trading routes between Aegyptus and the Levante if we are to maintain our Kingdom. I will take priests with me. They can pray. Leave me now."

Over the next two days, I visited the King several times to discover if my cures had been effective. Thanks be to God, his cough had calmed, and his skin became cool again. Although the wound was no longer red, I feared it would open again if he rode for any distance. He would not listen to my plea that he should rest. I had done what was possible. On my last visit, the Queen accompanied me. She immediately saw the improvement in the King's condition and quietly thanked me.

The King had not changed his mind. However, he did acknowledge the effect of my treatment.

"Physician, your potions have helped; but that will not last. God will not cease his punishment. He is only giving me more time to drive the Saracen from the

Holy Land. I have sought the intercession of the Pope himself. So has the Patriarch of Jerusalem, who wishes to be lifted from his excommunication. It is only his Holiness who can absolve me. I am waiting for his instruction."

Adelaide sadly shook her head and said nothing. I thought to make one more attempt.

"Your Highness, you know our Lord Jesus forgives our sins. Remember that your body is God's temple. The scriptures say so. Treat it in that spirit. If you care for your wound as I have proposed, and providing you eat the right foods, your condition will improve."

"My wound is of no import. I am concerned about my soul. Leave me now. I have much to do and little time. I am departing today and will not return until after Cristes Maesse. God willing, we will drive the Saracens away from our lands."

Afterwards, I spoke to the Queen and begged her to reinforce the directions I had given. I told her I would prepare more ointment of verdigris and would supply other herbs that might be beneficial. There was nothing more to do. No command from the Pope would cure him either. The King would not live long.

VI

A.D. 1116
A.H. 510
A.M. 4877

J ust as the King had declared, he was gone from the city through the days of Cristes Maesse. I spent those relatively peaceful days marking the birth of Lord Jesus by visiting the pilgrimage sites in the city. Once again, I was impressed with the devotion shown by the pilgrims and began to understand the power of faith. Jehan had again accompanied the King on his journey across the river Jordan, so I had the opportunity to reflect on my next steps. I needed to discover the fate of my father and vowed to do so after the beginning of the New Year.

Although I had no coin, I had a place to sleep and dine at the Citadel. Adelaide had no need for my services and, thus, I was free to conduct my inquiry. To begin, I decided to visit the deputy Grand Master of the Order of Saint John, Raymond du Puy. He would remember me and would, perhaps, know where I might begin my quest. It was not difficult to find him at the hospice. He was ensconced in his chamber, busily writing as he conferred with others of his order. He recognized me at once.

"Well met, Thoma. May blessings be upon you! I am delighted to see you and thank you once again for your assistance and, of course, the gold you so kindly delivered! What can I do for you? Is all well?"

"All is well," I said. "But I do need your help. Can we talk alone?"

Raymond dismissed his attendants from the room and asked how he could be of assistance.

"Lord Raymond, I am here in the city to learn of the fate of my father, Thomas Woodward. The Church sent him here to aid the Caliph of the Fatimid in driving the Turks from the city. I know he was present at the fall of Jerusalem. Some believe he died while performing his duties. There has been no word of him since. I would like to talk to the commanders who conquered the city. Perhaps they will have some knowledge."

Raymond considered what I had said. He had a strange look on his face, and I wondered what he was thinking. Finally, he spoke.

"I am not a Lord, so you need not address me with such formality. I have indeed heard the name. Brother Jehan mentioned it on our ride back to the city after we first met. What has transpired between the two of you that gives him so much anger?"

"We have had disagreements in the past," I said. "He believes I betrayed him by not following his orders."

Raymond shook his head. "I think there is more to this. For the entire journey back to Jerusalem, Jehan berated me for trusting you. He claimed you were a traitor just like your father. That is when he mentioned the name Thomas Woodward. He said that I could not know the depths of your betrayals. He claimed you were only pretending to be a Christian; that your loyalty was to the faith of the infidels. At the time, I told him I did not care who you were or what you had done as long as you delivered our message to the Atabeg. I was confident you would. When I refused to listen any further to Jehan, I remember that he mumbled that he would take matters into his own hands. When I was proven correct in my judgment, I dismissed all this from my mind."

I heard, but did not listen, to most of what Raymond said. The mention of my father was all that mattered. I rose and stood shaking before Raymond. "He told you my father was a traitor?" I said angrily. "That is not possible!"

"Be calm, I am only telling you what Jehan related," said Raymond quietly. "You know he has been ill for some time. It is his leg. I have often wondered if his illness is causing harm to his mind. He is fiercely religious; too much so, I think. His hatred for infidels and heretics knows no bounds. He acts like a man with great guilt on his conscience. I have some understanding of what prompts that guilt, but it has nothing to do with your father. At least I think it does not. This is a matter I must keep in confidence. I suggest you not judge until you know more. Unless he dies of his illness, he will return with the King. Talk to him then and perhaps he can tell you more."

Raymond was clearly withholding some information from me, but he was correct, I must meet with my enemy learn the truth.

As I turned to depart, Raymond spoke again.

"Thoma, we owe a debt to you. If I can help you, I will do so. In the meantime, we have need for physicians here at the hospice. It would please me if you found time to provide your services. Who knows, we may induce you to become one of us. Think about it."

I become a novice merchant

King Baldwin and his army returned to Jerusalem shortly after the New Year. I made plans to confront Jehan, but to no avail, as the King decided to set out again to drive the Fatimid back to Aegyptus. Jehan, against the advice of his own physicians, left with him. It was rumored that the King intended to capture al-Qahirah. I did not believe that. At the request of Adelaide, I had seen him before his departure to ascertain the state of his health. His cough was gone, and he appeared to be in good condition. His wound, however, had once again opened. I begged him to permit me to close it properly, but he would not listen.

"This is God's will," he declared. "If I suffer enough and correct my sin, I will be cured. My priests have all said so."

There was no arguing with him on this subject. Adelaide knew I had tried my best. I was certain that his wound, if untreated, would kill him. I expressed that conviction to no one.

Having no other obligations, I acceded to Raymond's request and paid a visit to the hospice every day. The pilgrims had the usual complains and ailments and I spent time doing what I could to treat their illnesses. I suspected many had come to the hospice for a free cot or a free meal and had nothing wrong with them other than poverty. Roland was there, of course, doing his best to alleviate his patient's distress through one-sided dialogue. I think many left the hospice before they were well simply to avoid Roland's continuing banter. Despite the frustration I felt every time I talked to him; it was comforting to know that I had a friend in this place.

I did ask Roland what he knew of Jehan and why he hated me so much. Roland was unhelpful in this regard.

"You ask me about Jehan; that is a difficult question. Indeed, he hates you beyond reason. He will not speak about this. He never has. You know the man; he keeps to himself and says little. I have my own suspicions, of course. He thinks you are an infidel. Why would that be? Once I heard him say you might be a heretic who pretends to be one of the true faith. That cannot be true, can it? Once he told me another infidel damaged his leg. He cannot walk properly, and it is causing him great distress. It is almost as if he blames you for his condition, but that is impossible." Without warning, Roland changed the direction of the conversation. "Did you hear we are constructing a fortress across the Jordan River? The king says we can control the roads from there to Arabia and collect taxes from the Saracens who travel in caravan to their own Holy City. What do you think about that?"

I started to answer, but Roland continued as if he had never asked his own question.

"The King is a good man, my dear friend. He is a terror to his enemies and a shield for all Christians. Everyone says that. I wanted to accompany him on his campaign against the Fatimid but my duties here are important. I do not know what my patients would do without me. I think I bring solace to their discomfort and I am sure my prayers for their health are heard by God. I am privileged indeed."

When I was unable to tolerate his continuing dialogue, I made an excuse and left him to continue his torture of the poor pilgrims. I did see him every day thereafter but avoided discussion. He seemed to understand I needed to address the needs of my patients and had no time to talk.

The hospice was not well supplied with the herbs and medicines necessary to treat the pilgrims and, when I pointed this out to Raymond, he provided me with coin to purchase all that was required. I thus had an opportunity to visit Aubert and strengthen our friendship. We spent long evenings together discussing various herbs and potions which were unknown in the land of the Franj. I discovered he had his own copy of Constantine's Antidotarium, which I had laboriously memorized at school. I re-read this manuscript and it became a subject of many discussions with Aubert. Together we studied the formulations suggested by Constantine and began to develop our own mixtures, based upon evidence of their effectiveness, derived from applying it to patients in the hospice. Although I could contribute no coin of my own, we began to develop commerce in those herbs and plants that were available in the east. Merchants from the city states of Genoa and Venezia became interested and, through my intercession, began to purchase rare medicines from our nascent enterprise. Because I could contribute nothing but my knowledge, Aubert gathered most of the profit. I earned enough to purchase the necessities of my own existence. I was not unhappy with this arrangement. I had existed so long without funds of my own, my own needs were little. When we made a large transaction, I contributed my share to the hospice. I could not take pride in this charity, however. It was impossible for me to forget the fact that I was wealthy already, if I could prove my father had died and thus secure my inheritance.

Our commerce was substantially enhanced after I received a letter from Ruggiero. His mother, Adelaide, had woken me one morning with a demand to seek audience with her. She had nothing to say herself. She just proffered me a letter sealed with wax and waited for me to read it. I was hesitant to open it then as I feared its contents, yet I was clearly meant to do so. The letter itself was brief:

"My dear Thoma,

It has given me great joy to hear that you are alive and well. Your explanations for your abrupt departure made interesting reading, but I cannot forgive you for abandoning us unless we can speak in person. My mother, the Queen of Jerusalem, has assured me that I will be King of that dominion upon the death of her husband. Thus, I will seek you out when the time comes, and we will talk. I command you to remain in the city until I arrive. While you wait, send more Sabun. This marvel has become popular at court and we need more. Everyone now sports a wonderful odor. I wish to keep it that way. I have granted a license to you to bring this substance to us without tax."

Ruggiero did not sign the letter with the customary flourishes. It simply ended. His mother looked at me as I read the letter and asked me to read it aloud to her. When I did so, I saw tears in her eyes. That this woman would react with such emotion was a surprise and I wondered why. When I asked, her answer was simple.

"He will not be King," she said. "I will fail in my duty to him. I do not know what to do." I asked her to explain but she shook her head and refused. "Whatever happens is God's will," she said. I was dismissed from her chamber without further discussion.

I put the Queen's concerns from my mind. That Ruggiero might forgive me was what occupied my thoughts. Perhaps, I thought, I could regain my reputation and once again gain favor. Ruggiero wanted sabun and that I would deliver. The question was how I could, without funds of my own, achieve this objective. The solution presented itself as I walked to the hospice. Raymond and the Order of Saint John would find such a trade of benefit to their coffers. I remembered how to make the substance and all the ingredients were available in the markets of Jerusalem. If properly supervised, some of the pilgrims cared for by the Order could be reasonably employed and thus pay for the services they received. The Order itself would benefit through profit from the enterprise and, in the process, strengthen an alliance with a powerful ruler. I sought audience with

Raymond and presented my idea. He recognized the opportunity immediately and gave his consent to contributing coin to commence this commerce. There was one more person I needed to recruit. Aubert would certainly be interested in participating and his understanding of the markets and transport would be invaluable.

I was deep in thought, walking to Aubert's establishment near the Dung Gate, when I heard the sound of a missile passing close to my head and then a 'thunk' as it struck a wooden door in front of me. I turned and, a short distance away, saw two beggars tussling with one another and arguing in Arabic. As I stood openmouthed, both beggars disappeared into an adjacent narrow lane. On the ground where they had stood was a short bow. I had forgotten the threat posed by the Hashashiyin retained by Jehan. I had avoided death by an exceedingly small distance and the intervention of a stranger. Had Abu Tahir dispatched someone to protect me? There was no answer to this question. When I was able to calm myself from this close encounter with death, I continued to Aubert's shop. He saw I was still distressed and offered a glass of wine. It took me a few more moments to relax and present the opportunity.

Aubert too knew much about sabun and how it was made. The ingredients, olive oil, wood ash, crushed seashells, and lavender, must be boiled in a copper pot for at least two days. It was then dried in the sun and cut into cakes. He had never done this himself but there were others who knew exactly what to do. The fact that the Order of Saint John would contribute to the costs and provide labor intrigued him and he saw the advantage of developing a commercial relationship. He did not hesitate in proposing to contribute half the costs to the venture. He asked about my own expectations for profit and I told him I had none. He thought I had lost my mind. I explained my reasoning and that seemed to mollify him. I said nothing about my encounter with the Hashashiyin. There was no reason to do so.

As I made ready to leave, Aubert stopped me. "Wait," he said. "I have something for you." He handed me a letter. It was from Jusuf.

"To my dear Thoma ibn Thoma, the Physician, may God grant you success and may you be in good spirits.

Your uncle Assad and I have received both of your letters and thank God you are well. We have shared your news with your grandfather Terryn and he too sends you his greetings. He is old now and prays he will see you before passing from this earth. He has, he says, written poems for you, as he believes that your education and experience have not given you sufficient guidance for life. We believe you should come to us when you have completed your quest in Jerusalem. There is much to discuss.

What I write to you is brief. It would not be wise to tell you all that is in our minds. We expect you to do what is right, to perform your duties faithfully and to guard your health. We pray for the day we see you in the flesh.

Your loving uncle in spirit, Jusuf

I thanked God my letters had been received and understood why Jusuf wished to keep his response brief. There was risk in disclosing too much, even though the letter was sealed with wax. I promised myself that one day I would join them in Aegyptus. My close encounter with death was forgotten in the happiness I felt having heard from my family. Aubert saw the joy on my face.

"Good news, Thoma?"

"Yes, very good news," I answered. "Thank you."

I left Aubert to make the necessary preparations for the production of sufficient quantities of sabun to fulfill the needs in Sicilia; then I walked back to the citadel. Although I lacked the skills of my father, I was careful on my return, stopping frequently to look behind me and paying close attention to my surroundings. I would not be able to stroll casually in the city again. It was wise that I took these limited precautions. I was being followed. To reach the Citadel from the neighborhood of the Dung Gate, I had decided to walk through a covered market known as the Suq-el-Attarin. The Street of Bad Cooking was located nearby. I thought that, within the warren of narrow lanes, I would be safe. I first noticed a young man, dressed as a Rum, as I entered one of these lanes. He looked directly at me and then lowered his eyes and walked in the opposite direction. A few moments later, I saw him again as I turned towards the citadel. I quickened my pace and so did he. I wanted to run but decided that would only convince him I knew he was following me. On my left, just as I left the Suq, I noticed a shabby inn. If I went in, perhaps I would be safe; at least until I decided what to do. As I was about to enter, I was startled to feel a tug on my arm. I turned to defend myself, only to discover I had been accosted by an old, white-haired woman, dressed in rags. A beggar, I thought, as I reached in my satchel for a coin to proffer.

The women startled me by speaking with authority. "You must take greater care," she hissed. "I bring news from the Moallim, may he remain in health. There is a place nearby where we can talk." With that remark, she took by be the arm and led me to a partially destroyed home nearby. I readily complied. If she was from Abu Tahir, then I should not be afraid.

She unlocked the heavy wooden door of the home and whisked me inside. "Hakim, you did not notice me as you walked through the souk, did you?" she asked.

"No, I was troubled about a beggar that was following me," I answered. "He stayed close behind and quickened his pace every time I walked faster. Was that a fida'i?"

"You have much to learn. If he was, do you think he would have been so obvious? Our men are better trained than that. He was merely what he appeared to be, a beggar hoping for alms from a well-dressed pilgrim. Unless you have studied our art, you will never know we are behind. You are being hunted. You know that. Today you were fortunate. We were watching over you in accordance with the Moallim's direction. The fida'i assigned to remove you nearly succeeded in his mission. Give thanks to Allah that you were saved!"

I hesitated to ask my question. "Sayyida, forgive me for my impertinence but I did not know women were..."

She interrupted me: "Hakim, do you think the women of Islam all sit in their homes, their faces covered, minding children and eating dates? I am not a fida'i, none of us are, but we do all we can to support our faith and our young men. In many things, we are much better than are they. I, myself, am a teacher. My art is the creation of disguise; a subject with which you men are woefully ignorant. Do you think this is my true appearance? Do not judge us by the convictions of the Franj."

It was then that I noticed the piercing clarity of her eyes, the eyes of a young woman. "Please accept my apologies, Sayyida. My ignorance is vast. Thank you for saving me. May I know your name?"

"You may call me Aunt; I am Umm Thoma for now. The Teacher sent word to halt action against you, but we have no way of knowing if his instructions have been received. I do not know who attempted to remove you and can do nothing to stop him myself. The brother who struck the bow from your assailants' hand, and I, will do our best to protect you; but be more careful. You are sleeping in the Citadel and we cannot help you there. Your assailant will, until he is relieved of his charge, find a way to gain access, so do not think you are safe there or, for that matter, at the hospice. Until his superior receives the Teacher's command, we think it best that you change your habits. If you cannot, leave the city."

"I cannot do that, Sayyida, or, as you ask, Umm Thoma. I have duties to perform here. Nevertheless, I will take greater care."

"What duties?" she asked. "What is so important that you are willing to risk your life?"

I gave the single answer that she might understand. I told her I had vowed before God to discover the fate of my father. There was, I said, a man here that I believed knew what had happened, but he was absent from the city. I expected him soon. Umm Thoma asked me to tell her more and so I did.

She patiently listened to my tale, deep in thought. Finally, she spoke.

"Hakim, you said your father was acting upon the instruction of a priest called Ogier, is that what you said?" I nodded my head in agreement. "Then you know something of the Frumentarii. Our people have often found it useful to cooperate with them. At times, we have the same interests, but many Franj do not trust them. At the beginning, the Frumentarii believed al-Quds should remain in the hands of the Fatimid; that it should be spared from the disaster the Franj have vested upon it. The leaders of what they call the armed pilgrimage disagreed. The Christian Pope listened to all of them but did nothing. If you desire to fulfill your oath quickly, I think you should introduce yourself to a priest called William. You will find him at what the Rum call 'Saint Jacob's Church' near the Zion Gate. It is now being constructed. Do not disclose that we have met. It is best that you know nothing about us." She hesitated for just a moment and then said, "You say your father was a Christian. Is it known you are a Muslim?"

How to answer this question, I wondered? Fortunately, she had given me an opportunity to be truthful. "No one in the city knows anything of my faith. Do not worry; I will be careful."

She accepted my response, asked me to wait until she left the house before I walked out into the street, and wished peace upon me. I never saw her again, but it was comforting to know she was somewhere behind me.

I meet a former Holy spy

The Frumentarii, the secret intelligencers of the Church, were here! I knew my father had performed many services for them but, I thought, it was likely Bartolomeo, who caused my downfall in Sicilia, was a member as well. I had been told to trust no one but what choice did I have? Until Umm Thoma talked to me, I had given up hope of discovering anything about the fate of my father from these people. I abandoned my decision to return to the Citadel and determined to seek out Brother William at once. I took a winding route to Saint Jacob's Church, as cautious as possible. Often, I stepped into shops and pretended to be interested in the merchandise on display. Where I could leave through a door other than one I entered, I did so. I knew that such caution would be insufficient but, at least, I was making the best effort possible.

When I reached the church, I interrupted a stonemason in his work and asked where I might find Father William. The man I addressed wore a large silver cross over his shabby robe. He was in his late middle years, but his arms were well muscled, as were all practitioners of his trade. He was, of course, covered in stone dust.

"Who is asking?" he asked gruffly. "Why do you seek him? Can't you see I am busy?"

I was taken aback by his surly response but, indeed, I had disrupted his labor. "My name is Thomas," I answered. "Father William can provide guidance to me on an important matter. I do not wish to delay you further; all I ask is that you tell me where to find him."

The mason looked at me carefully, as if inspecting the surface of a stone to be hewn. He put down his tools and beckoned me to a completed corner of the building being erected. I saw no other workmen near. He looked at me and smiled.

"I am who you seek," he said. He wiped his hands on his robe. Seeing the look of disbelief on my face, he said simply, "Now that I have time, I love to work with stone and am happy that I can help build this new Church. And you are the son of Thomas. I have known of your presence in the city but did not wish to contact you. We have common enemies. I considered it best that you seek me out yourself. The alternative was too dangerous. I will not ask how you found me. I can guess the answer. I do not wish to enter into discussion here. Listen carefully. There is a house opposite an inn in the second lane to the left of the Zion gate. A small cross is scratched on the top of the door. When the bells calling for vespers ring, go into the inn and look for a heavily bearded priest of the Eastern Church. He will raise his glass to ask for more wine if all is well. When he does, go immediately to the house I have described and knock three times. I will await you there. If he does not raise his glass, leave at once. You have been followed. Do not arrive early. Until then, Godspeed."

William raised his brows to ensure I had understood his directions. I nodded my head in acknowledgment. Then he shook his fist at me, shouting that I should find someone else to bother with questions. He turned on his heel and walked briskly away, leaving me speechless. I assumed all would be explained when, and if, I saw him again.

I returned to the Citadel, where I changed into my old robe. It had a cowl which I never used, but this time, I would. My face was thus partially shielded, and I took care to be sure no one noticed my departure from the Citadel. I knew how long it would take to arrive at the inn and measured my pace accordingly. I passed a decrepit soldier who had obviously been crippled in one of the many conflicts. He asked for alms. I reached into my purse to comply, but he simply turned away. Before he did, I saw him wink. I sighed with relief that at least someone was watching over me and made my way to the inn just as the vesper bells began to chime. As I had been told, a priest sat at a table near the door. He briefly made contact with his eyes and raised his glass, demanding more wine. I turned and swiftly walked across to the house opposite and saw the cross I had been told about.   I knocked three times. Brother William opened the door and dragged me in without saying a word.

When I was inside and the door was bolted, William motioned for me to kneel on the carpeted floor. Without preamble, he began to recite a prayer of Saint Ephrem of Edessa that I had never heard.

O Lord, Heavenly King, Comforter, Spirit of Truth, have compassion and mercy on Thy sinful servant and pardon my unworthiness, and forgive me all the sins that I humanly committed, and not only humanly but even worse than a beast - my voluntary sins, known and unknown, from my youth and from evil suggestions, and from my brazenness, and from boredom. If I have sworn by Thy Name or blasphemed it in thought, blamed or reproached anyone, or in my anger have detracted or slandered anyone, or grieved anyone, or if I have got angry about anything, or have told a lie, or if I have condemned anyone, or have boasted, or have been proud, or lost my temper with anyone, or if when standing in prayer my mind has been distracted by the glamour of this world, or if I have had depraved thoughts or have thought evil, or said indecent things, or made fun of my brother's sin when my own faults are countless, or been neglectful of prayer, or have done some other wrong that I cannot remember - for I have done all this and much more - have mercy, my

Lord and Creator, on me Thy wretched and unworthy servant, and absolve and forgive and deliver me in Thy goodness and love for men, so that, lustful, sinful and wretched as I am, I may lie down and sleep and rest in peace. And I shall worship, praise and glorify Thy most honorable Name, with the Father and His only begotten Son, now and ever, and for all ages.

I joined him in saying 'Amen'.

William looked at me carefully and said, "Consider these words in silence, Thomas, or as you sometimes call yourself, Thoma, and then we can talk."

There was much to ponder in these words. The sins I had committed were beyond count. I decided to meditate upon them when it was possible to do so. The room contained little furniture; only cushions on the floor and a small table between them. William brought a flask of watered wine and two cups and positioned himself comfortably on a cushion. I did likewise. He poured the wine and offered me a cup.

"So, Hakim Thoma, what can I do for you?"

I decided to be immediately forthright. "I vowed to discover the fate of my father. He bequeathed me a large fortune which is held by the Church pending proof of his death. That is the reason I came to this city. He wrote a letter long ago claiming he had performed certain duties for the Frumentarii. If you can help me, I will forever be in your debt."

William took a long sip of his wine. "There is little I can do but your quest is noble, and I will advise you as best I can. You must be wondering about the secretiveness of our meeting. Perhaps it would be best if I explained matters more clearly. Then you will understand the limits of what is possible."

I most certainly had wondered about the great care William had taken to arrange our meeting. "I did want to ask you why we have taken these elaborate precautions. You said we have common enemies. How could that be?"

"You have knowledge of the Frumentarii, did you not?" I nodded my head in agreement. "And you know something about the Knights of St. John?"

"Their order is charged with providing aid to pilgrims, is that not so? They have managed a hospice here for many years. All their brothers are of the laity, but they take vows of chastity, obedience, and poverty. Some of them are armed and they tell me their duties are to protect the pilgrims from the Saracen. I have met their deputy master and several others, but that is the extent of what I know."

"Then permit me to tell you what has happened since the days when your father aided us. About three years ago, Pope Paschal issued a bull in which he recognized the Order of St John and authorized them to elect their Grand Masters without interference from Church authorities. He granted them both independence and sovereignty over their own affairs.

That is when the problems began. Many in the Church, and even among the Frumentarii, believed the apocalypse was nigh. They claimed that the evils of the world were God's punishment for permitting the depredation of the Holy City by non-believers. Some were convinced that unless the world was rid of the idolaters, and even the Jews, the Anti-Christ would assume power. Those who believed this most strongly were from the province of Narbonne in the south of the Kingdom of France. They were amongst the first who took the cross. I and a few others did not think these beliefs were true. Are you following me?"

"Yes," I answered. "But what has this to do with my question?"

"Everything," he said. "You see, once the sovereignty of the Order of Saint John was recognized, they gained control of the Frumentarii. The Pope agreed to this. We had his ear for many years but, following the conquest of Jerusalem, our services became less valuable. The Pope had other sources of information upon which he came to rely. Although the Frumentarii were well funded, the yearly cost was significant. You must know that the Pope had his own difficulties. He needed all the coin he could amass to achieve his purposes. He could not continue to support us. A solution presented itself. Once control of Jerusalem and the Holy Land was regained, many nobles donated significant property to the Order of Saint John: manor houses, estates, and even churches with Holy Relics. The Order possessed the coin necessary to support the Frumentarii."

"I understand what you are saying, Father. Why does this matter?" I asked.

William sighed with exasperation. "Do you not have a mind of your own? I have already answered your question. The Order of Saint John is independent of the Church. They assumed control of the Frumentarii, or at least they thought they did. I do not think they realized what evil would result. Many of my former associates ascribed to the false beliefs I have explained. Brother Jehan is one of them. He wields significant influence."

I still did not understand but, this time, maintained silence and waited for William to continue.

"You see, at the beginning of the armed pilgrimage, we thought it best to honor the agreement reached with the Fatimid regarding Jerusalem. Christian pilgrims could then freely visit the Holy City. We were certain an attempt to capture the city for ourselves would result in the destruction of the city and the loss of many lives. As you know, we were proven right. Father Ogier and others believed it best to find reconciliation with the followers of the Muslim and Jewish faiths, so they could one day understand the truth of Christianity without coercion and violence. These thoughts were branded traitorous. Ogier died of illness after the fall of

Jerusalem and, without him, we had no leader. That vacuum was soon filled by the likes of Jehan who, some say, reports to a priest in Rome. In any event, I could no longer justify my position. I abandoned the Frumentarii, an act which many condemn. I became, once again, a simple priest and, as you have seen, a competent stonemason. Do you understand now? I cannot be seen with you. If I am, you may be branded a traitor as well. I fear that may already be the case."

I nodded my head in understanding. My own faith was already suspect. I had become the target of an assassin; an association with Father William would make matters worse. I decided to speak forthrightly. "Thank you, Father, for explaining all to me and, yes, I do understand. I have already told you of my own need to discover the fate of my father. He would, I believe, have been one with you. Can you advise me on how I can learn more about what happened to him?"

William furrowed his brows and looked at me. "Speak with Brother Jehan. He knew Ogier (May he rest in peace) and he hated him. Jehan participated in the siege and capture of Jerusalem. It is rumored that he personally dispatched some of the Jews. He has access to the records of the Frumentarii. I regret I cannot offer you advice as to how to persuade him to divulge anything."

"What can you tell me about Jehan?" I asked. "He has a deep hatred of me, and I do not know the reasons why."

"That," said William, "is a longer story. I will disclose what I know. Let us have more wine."

It was growing dark and my stomach ached with hunger, but if William could bring me clarity, I needed to stay longer.

"You ask about Jehan? That is a long story, but I will try to be brief," he said. "I do not know what he has told you. His story is complex. It might be best if I start at the beginning. He was the third son of a minor noble in Toulouse. When his father died, he left a few small parcels of land to Jehan but nothing else. Like other young men at the time, Jehan was trained in arts of war. When Pope Urban called for the armed pilgrimage to aid the Greeks and reclaim the Holy Land, Jehan had few options. He borrowed funds against his meager lands to purchase arms and joined the Count of Toulouse on the first incursion into the lands of the Saracens." William paused to ensure that I was following his tale.

I signaled my understanding and asked him to continue.

"Count Raymond of Toulouse was one of the first to follow Pope Urban's call for an armed pilgrimage. I have never seen a copy of that speech but some amongst the Count's following claimed he preached the Antichrist was emerging from hell and would soon move against Christians. The Antichrist would not make war against either Jews or pagans. Rather, he would seek to dominate those of our faith from his throne in Jerusalem, as though he was God himself. The only way to prevent this from occurring would be to establish Christianity in all places where pagans rule. I do not know if the Pope said anything of the sort but, as I told you, many believed he did. Jehan was certainly convinced."

"Is that why he had such hatred for the Jews and Saracens?" I asked.

"I think those beliefs had great influence, but they were not the reason," said William. "Jehan desired to emulate the deep faith of the Count of Toulouse. He fought bravely during the long pilgrimage and rose in stature. Some say he executed Jews along the pilgrimage route, but I do not know if that is true. His experience at the battle of Dorylaeum was a turning point. There began his hatred of the Turks. It was not until later that his world fell apart. He was among the armed pilgrims who insisted upon extending their march all the way to Jerusalem, despite agreements made with the Fatimid and the Greeks. Jehan honestly believed the Antichrist could not be defeated otherwise. He willingly participated in the massacres of nonbelievers and this too colored his vision. He was wounded at that time and, reluctantly I think, returned to Toulouse. There he was confronted by his creditors, who demanded repayment of their loans. He could not pay and his lands, small as they were, became forfeit. I think he felt this to be a grave injustice. He had sacrificed everything for God, only to be ruined by Jews."

"He told me something of this, Father," I said. "But why did he have such hatred for me? I suspect he has hired assassins to end my life."

"That is a question for which I have no answer, Thomas. When Jehan lost everything, he joined the Frumentarii. I think he believed that by so doing, he could seek revenge for his misfortune. Given his wound, he was unable to immediately return to the Holy Land. Instead, he was given duties in Rome, where he served under a priest at St. John Lateran. Rumor has it this priest now directs the Frumentarii. Beyond this, I have no knowledge. I regret I can help you no further."

"God will show me the way," I replied. If I only knew in my heart that He would, I thought. There was no reason to question William further. How could I convince Jehan to help me? He clearly hated me and, I suspected, wished for my death. If he did have knowledge, why had he said nothing for all these years? I thanked William for taking such pains to talk to me. I was about to leave through the front door when William stopped me with his hand.

"Do not leave through that door. There is another in the rear of this room. I see your father was unable to teach you how to protect yourself." I turned in the direction he pointed and saw a small door, which I assumed led to an alley behind the house. "Go in Peace, Thomas. Remember the words of Saint Ephrem and, if you need to speak with me again, you know where to find me. I am worried about your soul. It is the duty of a priest to help you in matters of faith. I will do so if you ask."

Once again, I thanked William for his aid and then walked back to the Citadel. There was much to consider, and I was so deep in thought I forgot to exercise proper awareness of all around me. I had walked about two hundred paces when a milky-eyed blind man obstructed my path. He was trying to avoid holes in the lane by using his walking stick. The lane was narrow, so I moved aside to permit him to pass. As I did so, he seemed to stumble and, faster than I could think, he grabbed my arm, spun me towards him and placed a thin dagger against my throat. At that moment, I prayed to God with all my soul.

"Keep still, keep silent," my assailant whispered. "This time, your guardians lost you. This time, I have not failed in my duty. You must thank Allah for your life. The order for your removal was rescinded; but I will have no one say I was unable to discharge my task. If I receive such an order again, you will discover paradise. Go in peace. Allahu Akbar."

As fast as he had attacked, he sheathed his dagger in the walking cane, turned away and staggered down the lane. It took many moments for my heart to stop its rapid beat. Then my entire body began to shake from the aftermath of terror. I had to lean against a wall to regain my breath and calm my shaken nerves. This was as close to death as I had ever been. I gave thanks to God for my deliverance.

I reached the citadel and proceeded directly to my room. I needed time to collect my thoughts. I won't claim my experience was at all like that of Saint Paul on the road to Damascus, but the result was the same. Our Lord Jesus has died in this city for the salvation of all. He promised his followers everlasting life. I too desired the promise of heaven. I wanted to know that, after death, there was hope for resurrection. I had lost my honor; I had told many lies and even denied my faith. My fortune was lost and what pride I had once possessed was long gone. Remembering the words of the prayer Father William had taught, I prayed silently for forgiveness. Although my goal to discover my father's fate and recover my fortune was unchanged, I swore to be a different man.

As I waited for King Baldwin and Jehan to return from their expedition across the River Jordan, I devoted more time to my uncompensated commerce in sabun with Aubert. Demand for this product had overwhelmed his ability to supply it and, as a result, he increased prices. This did not reduce demand. I also assisted the brothers of Saint John at the hospice. Roland had begged me to engage in this latter pursuit as the hospice was not well served by properly trained physicians. Brother Raymond had already requested my assistance so I readily agreed. There were more pilgrims needing aid than the hospice could manage, and my services were desperately needed. Most of them were Rum, but many more were now arriving from the lands of the Franj. With few exceptions, these pilgrims were sincere in their faith. They wanted nothing more than to follow in the steps of Lord Jesus and the Saints. They believed that by doing so, their sins would be forgiven and entrance to heaven assured. No matter how ill they were, they accepted their pain with dignity. Their long journey to the Holy City had been one of hardship, depredation and danger. When I inquired about this, the common response was, "Did not the Savior suffer as well?" Their hardship, they said, was nothing compared to what He had suffered to save their souls. Some were convinced that the greater their distress, the greater was the chance their souls would be saved. I too had endured hardship. Was this travail sufficient to save my own soul in the eyes of God?

Each evening, I returned to the Citadel and often met with the Queen. We talked well into the night. I confessed my difficulties with matters of faith and, although her own faith was clear, she listened patiently. During one of these discussions, Adelaide confided in me that at times she had doubted her own convictions, especially with respect to her worries concerning the King and the future of her son. She said there was only one priest in the city she trusted. He had provided comfort to her during these troubling times.

"I believe he can help you as well, Thoma. His visits to me are kept in strict secrecy. The excommunicated patriarch of Jerusalem would be greatly displeased if he knew of this. He would tell my husband. I will ask if this priest would be willing to speak to you."

The following evening, one of her personal guards summoned me to her chambers. I expected that she wished to engage in our customary conversations so was taken aback to see a second person in her room. I saw only his back, but I thought by his dress he was a Rum. When he turned to face me, I was even more surprised. It took me a few moments to recognize him when he was not covered in dust.

"Father William," I exclaimed. "What are you doing here?"

"I see that you did not expect me," he laughed. "Do you think I spend all my time building churches? I am, after all, a priest. During the day, I work stone. In the evening, I work souls. How fortunate I am!"

Adelaide smiled. "Thoma, Father William has, as he says, been crafting my soul for the past year. He is the only priest in this place I can trust. He knows my sins. He knows my worries and the Patriarch of Jerusalem hates him. We have much in common."

I nodded in understanding but wondered what all this had to do with me. I had no opportunity to ask as the Queen continued.

"Forgive me, Thoma, but I have shared some of your story with Father William. You have done little to hide your doubts about faith and your own conflicts. I am sincerely concerned about your soul. If you are to continue to be my physician, this concern must be alleviated. This priest can help you. I am commanding you to speak honestly with him. You may meet here any time you wish. Father William knows how to enter the citadel and my chamber without the knowledge of any but my most loyal servants." With that, Adelaide left us alone.

Before I could say anything, Father William asked me to pray with him. When we finished, he looked at me for a few moments. Finally, he spoke.

"Thomas, I know much about you. Not only what you have told me but what the Queen disclosed. I share the Queen's concern for your soul. Do you attend mass?"

"I did when I was not in the lands of Islam, Father. I have not done so here," I confessed. "You should know that I have many times joined in the prayers of the Muslims."

William absorbed this admission and held his head in his hands while he considered it. "At the school for physicians, you learned about the humors, is that not correct? You were instructed that for health and well-being, they must be in balance. You learned how to address imbalance. That is what a physician does. Did they also teach you about the 'ordines', the Orders? They too must be in balance."

"Father, I understand the role of humors but learned nothing about what you call 'ordines'. Is this important?"

He gave a long sigh and stood. I started to rise as well but he held me back. "Stay seated. I am going to give you instruction and it is easier to do so standing. First, I must think."

"Where to begin," he mumbled to himself. "Listen carefully. There are three orders of humanity, Ordo Ecclesiasticus, Ordo politicus and Ordo economicus: the ecclesiastics, the warriors or temporal rulers, and the workers and peasants. The first of these involves a concern for matters of faith, the second, matters of war and the third matters of food and trade. These orders must be in balance if we are to achieve peace and avoid alienation between ourselves and the world in which we live. That is what God expects of us. Are you following me?"

Taking my silence for acknowledgment, William continued.

"You need to understand more. If we are to gain salvation and do God's will to achieve peace and prepare for the end of time, spiritual order must exist. There is only one true faith and all of mankind must be brought into its fold. That is what our Savior has taught us. Until that occurs, there will be neither peace nor harmony. There is no room here for ambivalence. Our world is clearly divided between those who believe and those who do not. You are either a Jew or a Muslim or a Christian. Some say Greeks and the Rum cannot be true Christians. I have my own doubts about that. What is clear is that you cannot be something in between. I am talking about you, Thomas, do you see that?"

"Yes Father," I said. "I have dealt with disease. I have witnessed death and have seen it coming to me. That there can be hope for something after life has occupied my thoughts. I have told many lies. I have failed to adhere to the laws of both Islam and Christianity. My preoccupation with the events of each day, and my own interests, left me no time to reflect properly on these matters. I will do my best to avail myself of your teaching."

William folded his hands in prayer. "May God grant me wisdom to teach and may He open your eyes and ears to what I say." William stood quietly, deep in thought.

"I have explained what is meant by Ordo. God requires balance in all things. Our Lord Jesus has instructed us how to achieve eternal life and forgiveness of sin. I need you to understand there is no salvation until the Jews and Muslims are brought to the true faith. I told you some believe this can only be done through war and violence. They forget that Saint

Paul and the apostles devoted themselves to the peaceful conversion of the Gentiles. They did not convince idolaters of truth with the edge of a sword. They sought to convince nonbelievers of truth through words and example. I want you to begin reading Holy Scripture for yourself. You are privileged that you can read Greek. Begin with the gospel of St. Mark. When we meet, I will explain what I can. It is dangerous for me to come here too often. I will find a way to arrange meetings with you. Do you accept?"

"I do, Father," I answered sincerely. "It has been too long that I have lived in two worlds; too long that I have failed to consider matters of faith. I am concerned for my soul. I have told you the reason for my being in this city, but I can do nothing until Brother Jehan and the King return. Call for me and I will come."

William nodded his head in agreement. "That is good," he said. "The King will return before the New Year. I am informed he became ill during his campaign; so ill, in fact, that he was convinced he would die. He gave orders to begin distributing his wealth. It seems his old wound reopened. Even now he is being carried back to the city, where he wishes to be buried. Brother Jehan is with him, I am certain."

William left that evening, leaving me a scroll containing Saint Mark's gospel. It was well worn but written in a fine hand. William asked that I treat it with care as it was his only copy. Over the next few evenings, I read it by candlelight.

The King returned just before the following Cristes Maesse. He and his army had traveled all the way to a sea the Greeks call Erythra Thalassa on the border of the Fatimid lands. Along the way, he had constructed castles to protect the Holy Land from further incursions. He had indeed been ill but was recovering in the citadel. I asked Roland if Jehan had returned as well. Roland claimed he was resting in the ancient town of Ayla on the seacoast and would return shortly after the New Year. Roland confirmed that he was terribly ill. I prayed he would not die before I confronted him.

VII

A.D. 1117
A.H. 510–511
A.M. 4877

The Queen is deposed and, once again, I am bound in captivity

I had not seen Adelaide since my meeting with William, so I was not surprised when she called me to her chambers. I assumed she wanted to know the outcome of that meeting. This was not the case. The first thing I noticed were the tears in her eyes, which were red with weeping. I had the good sense to say nothing. I stood in her presence for some time before she spoke.

"All is lost, Thoma," she said. "My husband has returned. Our marriage has been annulled. Pope Paschal offered to rescind the excommunication of that scum of a Patriarch if he voids my union with the King. Now he has done so. As for the King, the fool, he believes his recovery from illness is God's reward for casting away his sin of bi-gamos. I am to be sent home as soon as proper provisions are made. My former husband is a coward. He has not even bothered to tell me of this himself. All I have worked for; all I have planned has come to naught." Adelaide began to cry again but her tears were not those of sorrow but of rage. "I never should have trusted these people; I never should have bound myself to such an idiot. Everyone calls him the shield, strength and support of his people. Nonsense! What has he done; I ask you? Oh yes, he is skilled at war and clever with peace, but his ambition and arrogance know no bounds. He cared about my wealth; not me. Much of what he has done threatens to rip apart the Holy Land. It does not take a wise man to see that. Everyone says he has honor, but how is what he has done to me and my son honorable? If he does not die of his wound, I would be happy to kill him myself. God forgive me but that is how I feel."

I understood her anger and I told her so. She had certainly been betrayed. It occurred to me, however, that she had brought this upon herself. She had coveted power, not for herself, but for her son. She had sacrificed her own well-being to achieve that end. How easily we can seek such a false god and how easily our seeking can be in vain. I thought about the prayer of Saint Ephrem. I repeated it to her. She listened and wiped away her tears.

"Thank you, Thoma, but those are the words of a Saint and I am not that. I cannot hide my anger. Perhaps, one day, I will forgive Baldwin. Not now. He is in the hands of God. I have written to my son and he will dispatch a vessel to collect me from this place.

Ruggiero will be angry at what has happened and, I am certain, will demand reparations. I fear you and anyone close to me here are in danger. The King is convinced that the treatment you gave him was a fraud. God saved him, not you, he says. You cannot remain here. You will leave this city with me."

Her last words were not a question but a command. It only took me a moment to realize she was correct. Without her support I had no place here and was in danger. Yes, I had duties at the Hospice and was confident my services were needed, but others could do the same. Roland, for all his words of friendship, was too absorbed in his own duties to miss me for long and, in any event, could be of no help. I could continue my commerce with Aubert from Sicilia. I truly had no place in the city. Most importantly, in Palermo I could freely see my family, Assad and Jusuf, again. That was not possible here and I did not belong in Aegyptus. I decided then to obey her command. I would begin my life on the island once again, hopefully as a new person. But I had to fulfill my oath. I needed to discover the fate of my father.

"I will do so," I said. "But first, I must complete my tasks here; with your consent, of course."

"The vessel to carry us home will not arrive for many days, so you have time to complete your affairs. Until we depart, you may continue to sleep here, where I think you will be safe. However, do be on your guard. I do not know what action the King might take."

Once again, I lose my freedom

It soon became clear what action the King would take. As I left the citadel to walk to the hospice, three soldiers clad in mail accosted me.

"You will come with us peacefully," commanded a soldier as he gripped my arm. I started to protest but he silenced me with a blow of his mailed fist. My knees gave way and my head spun. "I said peacefully," he growled. "I did not give you permission to speak. The King charges you with treason and fraud." I wiped the blood from my face where he had struck me and said nothing. What, I thought, could I do now? My former protectors were gone, and the Queen deposed. I tried to think of a solution, but my head was still spinning, and I had to focus upon my steps to avoid falling. The soldiers dragged me back into the citadel, down some stone stairs. The next thing I remember was being thrown into a dark cell below ground. The cell had one small window; filthy straw covered the dirt floor, and it was otherwise empty. At least I thought it was empty. As my eyes adjusted to the gloom, I saw I was not alone. There were two other figures huddled in the corner of the cell.

"Well met, Thomas. I did not expect our next meeting to be in this place," said one of the figures. I looked closely in the dim light. The man who addressed me was covered in grime and smelled of stale urine. I could not believe my eyes.

"Father William, what are you doing here? You are a priest! How can you be taken by the King?"

"It seems the Patriarch of Jerusalem has determined that I suffer the fate of laicization. This means I am no longer a priest and am subject to the King's law. Unless the Pope intercedes, you and I are the same. I told you many in the Church disagree with me. I thought my meetings with the Queen were secret, but, sadly, I was mistaken. I am accused of treason. That must be why you are here as well. The Patriarch has convinced the King that he must rid himself of Adelaide and all of her advisers if he is to escape the punishment of God for his sins."

That explained what had befallen us. At least I was in a cell with a friend. It was difficult to speak given the pain I had suffered from the soldier's blow. I was till bleeding and two of my teeth were loose in my jaw. "It seems our fates are intertwined," I said. "I too have been accused of treason. Will we be granted an opportunity to defend ourselves?"

"That, Thomas, is in the hands of God. We will pray for deliverance. It is all we can do."

The other occupant of the cell had remained silent while William and I conversed but now he spoke.

"Hakim Thoma, I had hoped you would be spared. I am truly sorry to see you in this place. I have been here for several days. Father William joined me only yesterday."

Through the gloom, I looked at the man who had spoken. "Aubert," I cried. "What are you doing here? I did not recognize you in this dark."

"No one has told me, but I think for the same reason. I was unable to get word to you. Before my arrest, two monks accompanied by armed soldiers visited my shop and remarked upon the sabun we were making for Sicilia. It was, they claimed, poisoned. They ransacked my stores to see what I possessed and, to my regret, discovered a nine-branch candle. It had been in my family for generations. I kept it in memory of my ancestors. They claim I was using it to celebrate the Jewish celebration of Hanukah. I am accused of apostasy. My conversion was a lie, they say. I do not know what the future holds for us but at least we three are together."

Days went by and then weeks. Each day was the same. When clouds obscured the little light from the opening above us, it was often not possible to tell the difference between night and day. Each morning, we were brought a pot of thin porridge, a piece of stale bread and a bucket of water. That was the extent of our sustenance. To relive ourselves, we used a single space in the far corner of the cell. It was not long before the stench became overwhelming. We slept on the filthy straw floor. All of us suffered the bites of what seemed thousands of insects. William kept reminding us that what we suffered was nothing compared to what Lord Jesus had suffered for our salvation. That was small consolation as our bodies began to develop sores from bites and our teeth loosened from our poor diet. We were thankful there were no rats.

The reason we did not all become mad during those days of horror was due to the teaching of Father William. He had an incredible memory and, each day, would recite a passage from the gospels and then explain its meaning. Aubert listened, but rarely asked questions. He did remark on how closely the gospels themselves followed prophecies contained in the Torah. My own contribution consisted of drawing parallels between the gospels and the words of the Holy book of Islam. William's teachings were our sole consolation. I remember that his discourse on the concept of hope as reflected in the resurrection was particularly comforting. It was here, in the Holy City of Jerusalem, that our Lord Jesus Christ rose from the dead and promised salvation to all of us. Father William encouraged me to confront my doubts and conflicts and, over time, I became more committed to my own path to seek the forgiveness of God if I were ever to be freed from this hellish cell.

I confront my enemy

I do not know how long we were confined in squalor. We did notice that the guards, whose voices we often heard outside our cell, were now absent. We began to wonder if we had been forgotten, especially when we no longer received our daily food and water rations. Without water, we would soon die. Just as I began to lose hope, a guard opened the door and commanded me to come with him. He bound my arms in chains and dragged me up the stone stairs. I was certain I was being led to my own execution and, perversely, I found this comforting. At least my trials would be over, and I could look forward to joining God in heaven and finding peace. Perhaps I would even join my father and mother in paradise. At least, I hoped that was the case. My hope was soon dashed.

"Brother Jehan has need of you," said the guard. "Clean yourself first," he ordered as he led me to a bucket of tepid water. I wanted to drink some of it, but the guard insisted that I wash my face and hands. After the long confinement, I was covered with filth and smelled of urine and excrement. What, I wondered, did Jehan want from me? I summoned the courage to make my own demands.

"Call for Brother Raymond," I said as forcefully as possible. "I will not see Brother Jehan without his presence." I stopped in the hall, fell to my knees and lifted my head. "You can kill me now, but I will go no further unless this is done." The guard was uncertain as to what he should do. He had been ordered to deliver me to Jehan but had not been told to kill me if I refused. It took him several moments to decide it might be best if he acceded to this request. He called for another soldier and told him to convey my demand to Raymond. That was, he said, all he could do. Thanks be to God, Raymond agreed and, when I entered the small room where I was taken, he was there standing over the cot upon which Jehan lay. He looked at me with suspicion but said nothing.

Jehan was in obvious pain. His eyes were closed and he was moaning. A linen sheet covered his body. My guard whispered something to him and Jehan turned his head towards me.

"Thomas or Thoma, whatever you call yourself, I am dying. The infidels are killing me slowly. You must help me. It is because of me you were trained as a physician. You owe me everything. No one here knows what to do. Cure me of this affliction and I will see that you are released from bondage."

Infidels are killing him? How could that be? Jehan's illness was affecting his mind. I decided to ignore this and permitted my own training to take command. "Unchain me and I will do my best," I said. Raymond nodded his head, signaling to the guard to do as I asked.

I uncovered Jehan and saw that his damaged leg was marred by a large lump the size of a small melon. No wonder he was in pain, I thought. It was obvious what afflicted him. Hippocrates of Kos, the ancient Greek physician had first described this condition. He named it 'karkinos'. Galen had called all swellings of this kind 'oncos' and claimed only certain ones were 'karkinos'. These, he wrote, were the result of an excess of black bile. Most writers claimed rebalancing the humors through bloodletting and diet was the proper treatment. I recalled the physician Abulcasis who wrote that prospects of a cure are improved if the karkinos is found early. If the growth were small enough, it could be removed with a knife. The famous Persian Ibn Sina (the Franj knew him as Avicenna) wrote:

'When this condition begins, it may be possible to maintain it as it is so it will not increase and keep without ulcers. It may happen sometimes that the early form may be cured, but when it is advanced, verily will not.'

That was the case with Jehan. His growth was indeed advanced; it was too large. Had it been removed long ago, there would have been hope. When I examined it with my hand, I was certain it had grown into his bone. I knew of no cure. He would die.

I was at a loss as to what to say or do. Jehan's claim that infidels are killing him was disturbing. If his mind was gone, then that presented a significant complication. I needed time to think.

"Brother Jehan, if you can hear me, what do you mean by saying infidels are killing you?" I asked softly.

Jehan groaned and his face became red with anger. He grimaced in pain and spoke through gritted teeth.

"How can you ask me that question? How do you think I became crippled so long ago? They placed a curse upon me. I am certain of that. You must lift it." Jehan grimaced and whined. "I carried out my duties towards you. My superior forced me to collect you from Eynsham and become your guardian until you completed your studies at school. I did that. What else did anyone expect me to do? Then you betrayed me. You are no Christian!"

Following this diatribe, he sank back into his cot, moaning with pain. Raymond, who heard these words raised his brows and shrugged his shoulders. "What is he saying, Thomas? This makes no sense."

"Brother Raymond, I beg you to be a witness to what is said next. Will you do so?" Raymond nodded his head in agreement.

I turned to Jehan, doing my best to hide my own confusion. "I will give you something to alleviate your pain, but now you must rest. This will not take long." I asked for someone to fetch Af-Yum from the hospice stores and a glass of raw wine. A few moments later, these ingredients were brought. I mixed them in the correct proportions. For a moment, I was tempted to make a lethal dose and, as my friend Sukman said, remove this man who had retained others to kill me. Thanks be to God, the words of Saint Ephrem came to mind and I could not. I gave the liquid to Jehan and told him to drink it slowly. He did so. I saw that his muscles had relaxed so spoke softly to him again.

"Brother Jehan, your pain will become less. Please explain to me how you became lame. What happened?"

By this time, Jehan was becoming groggy and I feared he would fall asleep before he responded. Thankfully, he could still speak, though in little more than a whisper. I motioned for Raymond to come closer so he too could hear.

Jehan's eyes were glazing over. "Look what the Moor did to my leg. I heard the crack; my bone shattered. It has never been the same. See the growth? It is in the same place. It is killing me. The Moor is killing me. All of them must be destroyed; why do some blame me? God directed everything."

This was not the response I wanted. Now I panicked. I had made a long and difficult journey to discover the fate of my father and Jehan was my last resort. I needed an answer. I should never have administered Af-Yum before I questioned him.

"Brother Jehan, stay awake! What do you know of my father? Did he die here? What has happened to my trust?"

Jehan's eyes began to close and he stopped speaking. I was so angry that I could barely speak. I was convinced he knew the answers to my questions. Did he know what happened to my father? I was certain he did. If so, he had lied to the Abbot of

Eynsham. He claimed my father was a traitor, but he had been acting on the instructions of the Church. It was then that I noticed Raymond looking at me. He was shaking his head side to side and his eyebrows were raised in confusion.

"Thomas, I have heard him, but he said nothing of import. I do not understand. I have never trusted Jehan. He is like a mad dog. He belongs to a separate group under command of our Order. They are obliged to report to us, but they do not. They act as they wish. Help me to understand. Who was your father? Why do you think Jehan knows anything about him?"

"My father was known as Thomas Wood-Ward," I answered. "The church sent him to assist al-Afdal in recovering Jerusalem from the Turks. Brother Jehan has always claimed he knew nothing about my father. I think he lied. If I cannot prove my father's death, I will be dispossessed of all I inherited." I was about to go on, but Raymond interrupted.

"I am beginning to understand. That name is known to me. There was a priest named Ogier who came to the city a month after we conquered it. He was an old man and looked frail. Ogier was searching for a man named Thomas who had acted on his behalf. I do not remember what happened or if he found answers to his questions, but Ogier died of illness shortly after his arrival." Raymond paused and then continued: "So, you have learned nothing from Jehan?"

"No, Brother Raymond, I have learned nothing." I hesitated with my next request but there was no choice but to state it.

"I have demonstrated my good faith to you and your Order. You know that. Now I need your help. I know something of the Frumentarii, the group you say is under your authority. Jehan was one of them. My father acted at their direction. There must be someone here who has the answers to my questions. My father was no traitor to the Church. I must discover his fate."

Raymond raised his brows in shock. "You know of the Frumentarii? Few do. It was a grave error to bring them into our fold. Yes, they provide us with information. We provide them funds. Otherwise, we have no control over what they do. Their leader is in Rome. I will make inquiry. That is the least I can do for you."

I had reached an impasse. I knew nothing more than when I had first commenced my journey. I had come this far only to fail. I needed to think. If Jehan survived, perhaps I could ask my questions again, but I held little hope for answers. "There is one more thing," I said. "Can you free me and my friends from confinement? I believe we have been unjustly imprisoned."

Raymond hung his head in shame. "That I cannot do. You have been confined on the command of the King. It is only he who can free you. But no one has told me that you are to be kept in chains or denied sustenance. I will also demand that you be given fresh straw. With this I can assist. I will tell your guards that the Order has determined you must remain in good health. I regret this is the best I can offer."

That response was not what I had hoped, but I knew he was doing his best.

"Thank you, Brother Raymond. Pray for us," I answered.

I had not forgotten Jehan, who was now fast asleep. Reluctantly, I suggested that he be given the tincture I had made with Af-Yum if he experienced more pain, which I was certain he would. I hoped that whoever prepared this medicine would make an error and deliver too much or give far too little. Such a hope was in itself a sin, but I felt no remorse. Raymond asked if there was anything else. I answered that there was a plant in this part of the world called hindiba. A physician named Ibn Baytar suggested that if the leaves of this plant are squeezed to make a juice and then heated to a foam and drunk by the patient, it might have a positive effect on growths of this kind. But, I said, there was no final cure for his affliction. It was too late. He had just days to live. Perhaps, I said, there was a priest to pray for him. Before I left, I could not resist explaining to Raymond that there was no curse. In all my studies, I had never read that an old injury could result in karkinos. I wondered, however, if this was true. Of course, the fact that I had read nothing about this possibility meant little. Most likely,

I thought, this was punishment from God. There was no question that Jehan had committed mortal sins.

I was marched back to the cell in the citadel; this time unbound by chains. These few moments of walking in the fresh air gave me time to think and calm my nerves. Although I had suspicions, my quest had been in vain unless, somehow, I could speak to Jehan again. My oath to discover the fate of my father had cost me everything; my position at the court of Sicilia, my fortune, and one of the only true friends I had ever had. My worry was the fate of my companions in prison. How angry must be God with my sins?

We receive a visitor to our cell and hope is restored

William and Aubert joyously welcomed my return to the cell. They asked what had transpired in my absence and I told them. That I had secured a promise for better food and drink and even clean straw was, to both, the best news of all. Because I had cleansed myself, I now found the odor of my companions and our abode loathsome. It took me all night to become accustomed to it. Our spirits were lifted the next morning when, for the first time, we received hot porridge, warm bread and even a piece of meat. The latter was rancid but, to us, it was a gift from heaven. For the next few days, we received food of this kind and, for once, had sufficient water for our needs. The new straw, however, did not arrive and our cell became even more odiferous, if that was even possible. There was no place to dispose of our eliminations. The pile in the corner became higher and more fly-blown each day. The insects plaguing us multiplied each day and our bodies became masses of open sores. No one came to us other than the guard who delivered our sustenance. We heard no sounds of anyone outside the cell. We were left alone.

William never complained. He reminded us that our sufferings were nothing compared to those of Lord Jesus. Aubert suffered in silence as William's attempt to lift our spirits seemed not to have meaning for him. He responded that those of his former faith suffered through all the ages and, perhaps, that was God's will.

One night, following another interminable day, our cell door was quietly opened. None of us slept soundly so we all awoke at the noise, wondering what was happening.

"Shhh," said a voice. In the dim light, we could not see who addressed us. "Remain quiet. It is me, Roland, I have come to save you," said the voice. I could not believe my ears.

"Roland, is that you? What are you doing here?" I whispered.

Roland was holding his nose to avoid the stench. "I am to clean your cell and deliver the straw Raymond promised," he said in a loud voice. Then he whispered, "Stay quiet, I beg you."

For the first time in my memory, Roland was silent. Still holding his nose, he threw us a bag containing old but serviceable robes for common laborers. He motioned for us to dress and follow him. He quietly locked the empty cell door behind him. Outside the cell, a bale of fresh straw lay on the stone floor. In silence, we walked through the empty hall and then ascended a stone stairway at the far end. This led to another hall. Roland peered around the corner and, seeing no one, beckoned for us to continue in his footsteps. We finally reached another door which opened to a narrow alley behind the citadel. We were free! It was a dark night and Roland silently gestured for us to stay close as we walked. Eventually, we reached a place in the city wall piled high with rubble. Roland climbed the pile and led us through an opening in wall itself. Once outside, we saw a mule-drawn cart filled with dirty straw and other rubbish. Roland indicated with his hands that we should bury ourselves beneath the straw. If the cart smelled of filth, we did not notice it. We had become used to evil odors. Roland, still holding his nose, then led the mule down the road towards Jaffa.

It took the rest of the night and a good part of the next day to reach Jaffa. Roland had brought water but nothing to eat, so, by the time we reached to port we were starving. No one stopped us on the road. The smell of the cart was sufficient to quell the curiosity of any passerby. Normally at any port, guards inspect all who enter the area and the goods they bring with them. Our cart was no exception. A guard shouted to Roland, who was, of course, wearing the robes of the Order of Saint John.

"State your business in the port and what, pray tell, are you carrying in that cart. It smells of evil!"

"I am carrying out the commands of the Order of Saint John," he said with resignation. What you smell is a body. I covered it with straw to prevent further rot in the sun on our long journey. It is the deceased kinsman of the captain of the vessel at the dock." Roland pointed vaguely at a ship nearby. "Perhaps it is his brother. I do not know, nor do I care. The body is going home for burial." Roland was true to form. He had more to say. "Can you imagine why anyone would go to these lengths to bury the dead? What are they going to do to preserve the body on a sea voyage? Perhaps they will use salt. They will not use wine or vinegar. That is expensive. I have heard that the oil of olives might work. But who knows? Who cares? Don't you think it will smell even worse? My Order owes a debt to the captain, so we had to accede to his request but, believe me, I do not understand. Do you wish to see? Come closer to the cart and I will show you my cargo. It has not fully putrefied. At least I do not think it has."

The guard immediately shook his head and backed further away from the cart. "Go on then and do what you must. I do not wish to come any closer than I already have. Move quickly! How can you stand it?"

"It is my duty," Roland replied gravely. As we continued, I heard Roland snickering to himself. He was not as foolish as I thought. No one would want to inspect a rotting body if that could be avoided. I was unable to see William or Aubert, but I was certain they thought the same.

It was not long before the cart halted, and Roland told us to rise and follow him again. This time, we proceeded up the ramp of a waiting ship. There were crewmen aboard, but they ignored us as they went about their duties, preparing the ship for sail. Motioning us to move faster, Roland led us down into the hold. In the dim light, Roland sighed with relief and congratulated himself on a task well done.

"If I don't say so myself, I think I have accomplished my mission with perfection. Don't you think so too? Did you hear that guard? I thought he would die of the odor. I think my ruse was clever! Who would want to come closer and inspect the dead? And did you notice I had you dressed as workmen? No one notices workman as they board a ship. Will anyone wonder why you did not return to shore? Of course not." Roland was going to go on, but I stopped him.

"Roland, stop for a moment. We are forever in your debt for delivering us from confinement, but where are we?"

"Yes, we are free. You will soon discover where we are going, but for now I have been given further instructions." With that response, Roland pointed to several buckets of fresh water and, God be praised, two cakes of sabun. "We are to wash ourselves and stay here until our vessel leaves the port and enters safe waters."

I looked at the sabun with amazement and gave silent thanks that we were able to clean ourselves properly. I suggested that William do this first as he was the filthiest among us. I would clean myself last as something bothered me and I had a question.

"Roland, you said 'we'; are you not staying here?"

"Of course not," he said. "Members of the Order who followed Jehan consider me to be a risk, given my friendship with you. They forbade me from working with my patients. They gave me nothing but menial chores to do. I had to clean the floors of the hospice and change straw in the beds of the ill. Many demanded my removal from the Order. I had no future. Brother Raymond assigned me to deliver your new straw to your cell. I wonder if he knew what I would do once I had a key to the locks. Perhaps he did. No, I am certain he did. When the King's men discover you are gone, who do you think they will blame? I could never return, nor do I wish to do so." Roland paused for an instant. "Brother Jehan is dead," he said flatly.

"Dead?" I exclaimed. "I did not think it would happen so quickly." Before I could ask another question, Roland answered a question I had not yet asked.

"He refused to take the potions you suggested. He said they were the work of Satan and only God could help him. He died in terrible pain. It is unthinkable you would ever suggest something that was not to his benefit. He was a fool."

So it has ended, I thought. I almost committed a sin by smiling, but I did not. That man had lied to me and brought about my ruin. I suspected he had stolen my inheritance. He attempted to have me killed. He committed atrocities during the fall of Jerusalem, and I wondered what other evil he had done. But it was up to God to judge him, not me. I did not make any comment to Roland. I simply acknowledged what he said.

What continued to trouble me most was my failure to fulfill my oath regarding my father. All the perils and hardship of my journey to Jerusalem had been for naught. Now, I would never find answers to my questions nor recover the fortune left to me. My future was as uncertain as it had ever been.

I sail home at last

We were unable to leave the hold for the following two days. A member of the crew delivered food and water to us each day and even flagons of wine. The wine was most welcome at first, but all of us indulged in too great a quantity. That was an error as the ship was constantly rocking in the seas and we became ill in our stomachs. The sabun helped to clean up the sorry mess we made of ourselves. At least we were cleaner than we had been in many, many days. Over time, we noticed that we all smelled of lavender and that was even more welcome. In that dark hold we were regaining our place among civilized men.

During those days, Roland had been strangely quiet. I resisted asking him about this for as long as I could. His silence was so unusual I began to wonder if he was ill.

"Roland, for the first time in my memory you have nothing to say. What is wrong?"

Roland looked at me, tears emerging from his eyes. "My dearest friend, I have been thinking, and I must beg for a favor from you. I know I will never be able to achieve my dream of becoming a knight. The Order will never accept me back. I have no future unless you can assist me. I do not wish to burden you, but I must ask."

"Roland, you liberated us from prison," I said. "You have been a dear friend. If it is in my power, I will help you. What do you wish me to do?"

"I want to become your assistant," he said. "I can help you with your duties as a physician. I have learned to provide aid to patients at the hospice. You are my only hope. Please say you will not abandon me."

This request was not easily granted. Roland could drive even an angel mad with his ramblings. I had no idea what my own future would be. As I pondered his request, I thought perhaps he could be of assistance; and I did owe a great debt to him. One thing I had learned is that if a patient has hope of being cured and resuming normal life, their recovery from illness was enhanced. In the case of Roland, perhaps his incessant chatter would drive a patient to wellness, if only to escape his care. This thought had merit. I also knew Roland was intelligent. He could learn to aid me. He might even be able to prepare medicines. In any event, I had already told him I would help him.

"Roland," I answered. "If God wills, I resume my trade, I will make you my assistant. Perhaps that is your true calling."

Roland commenced to weep and thanked me in so many words that I lost count. He was finally acting normally. I might regret this decision, but I had given my word and that I would keep, regardless of my annoyance with him. I worried about my own future, but I said nothing of this.

On the morning of the third day, we were liberated from our confinement in the hold. On deck we reveled in the fresh salt air and the beauty of the deep blue-green Middle Sea. We had sailed clear of the waters controlled by the crucesignati. We had not been on deck long before I noticed Adelaide, standing near the rail at the stern of the ship. She motioned for me to join her. When I got closer, I saw that she looked many years older than when we had last met. Although we were in the light of the sun, her skin was pale, and I thought she might be having difficulty breathing. Her eyes were red, but she did smile at me. She looked at me directly and said: "Well, Thoma, I told you that you would come with me. Did you not believe that?"

"Madam, I heard your words as a command; did I have a choice but to obey? Had we not been rescued, I do not wish to consider what fate we would have suffered. We are in your debt. I can speak for Father William and Aubert. We will serve you as best we can. May I ask *where* we are going?"

"Thoma, we are going home."

VIII

A.D. 1118
A.H. 511
A.M. 4878

Adelaide died in the year of our Lord 1118. I was with her at the end, as were her son Ruggiero, and Father William. Her health had rapidly declined since our return to Palermo. There was nothing I could do. There was no cure for her grief for lost dreams and the ravages of age. I thanked God for her peaceful demise and for the privilege of my having known and, yes, loved her. As might be expected, her son was inconsolable. His rage at King Baldwin and the people of his kingdom knew no bounds. In the summer of that year, we received word that Baldwin had died. I assumed his wound had reopened and that he failed to follow guidance on keeping it clean. Clearly, God had not absolved him of his sins. Baldwin's death mollified Ruggiero's hatred and he began to devote his time to creating and defending a new Sicilia, under the wise tutelage of my old friend Christodulus. Ruggiero became a great ruler. Most of Sicilia's population followed the faith of Islam and Ruggiero not only tolerated this but encouraged scholars and philosophers of all faiths to reside in his domain. To my surprise, he was in the final stages of completion of the book of knowledge he promised to produce so long ago. He also did not forget his dream of conquering Ifriqiya.

Over time, the Emir Christodulus regained his trust in me. My herbs had long since been sold and taxes paid from the proceeds. The balance had been transferred to the Treasury for the benefit of the island. To my great relief, he soon reinstated my former position as court physician. Roland, of course, was appointed my assistant and followed me everywhere. I learned to ignore his long diatribes and kept him occupied with regaling our patients in the palace with his tales of adventure, woe, and the lives of the saints. I had guessed correctly that Roland could drive a patient on his deathbed to rise from it to avoid him. Eventually, he learned to formulate medicines and became proficient in both the process of preparation and their correct use. When it was no longer possible to tolerate his banter, I ordered him to study the great works on this subject alone, and that he did with sincere interest and enthusiasm. To my great surprise, I found him to be most useful. I never regretted my decision to employ him.

I spent many days with Christodulus, and we came to know one another well. So well, in fact, that he introduced me to his family, one of whom, his youngest daughter, Tamura, was incredibly beautiful, with tresses of raven black hair and eyes the color of amber. My experience with women, other than Adelaide, had been limited but when I first saw her, I was mesmerized. When she spoke, I was transfixed. Her father, unlike many others, had insisted that she learn to read and write and, even at her young age, she had become an invaluable assistant to him in the conduct of state affairs. I visited his villa many times and when I overcame my initial trepidation, I enjoyed brief, supervised discussions with her. I was fascinated not only by her beauty but her quick mind. Indeed, her knowledge of many subjects far exceeded my own. She was skilled in drawing and even wrote beautiful poetry. I could not get her out of my mind.

Father William was also a godsend. King Ruggiero had him reinstated as a priest. The right for a temporal king to take this action was a matter of serious dispute. But Ruggiero, like so many sovereigns at the time, claimed he had the authority to appoint whomever he chose. Like his mother Adelaide, Ruggiero took action he believed to be correct regardless of the consequences. Father William devoted considerable time with me, and we spent many hours together discussing matters of faith. He aided me greatly in resolving my questions. He insisted I continue to read the Gospels in their original Greek and I grew in understanding.

About sixty days after my return to al-Madinah, I received letters from my uncles in Aegyptus. They praised God that I had escaped from Jerusalem and was now ensconced in Sicilia. They wrote of the latest success of their new enterprise and, again, begged me to come to al-Qahirah. What, they asked, had become of my trust? Did I discover what happened to my father? Did I wish to resume the trade in herbs? There were many other questions and I did my best to answer them all when I wrote to them. I had no desire to travel again. I had done enough.

Despite all this, I remained unhappy. I had heard nothing from Brother Raymond and thus knew nothing more about either the fate of my father or the status of my inheritance. I had betrayed my oath in this regard. Further, I was dependent for my position upon the good will of the Emir and King Ruggiero and possessed no funds of my own. My failure had cost me everything.

During one of my discussions with Father William, I told him all and confessed my concerns.

"Has God punished me?" I asked. "I failed to fulfill my oath. Will I be damned for this?"

William sat back on his cushion and placed his head in his hands. He was silent in contemplation for some time. He looked at me carefully and said: "Thoma, God is not punishing you. You are punishing yourself. Let me ask you a question. Did you do everything in your power to discover the answers to your questions regarding your father? Was your failure the result of error or laziness on your part?"

"I tried my best, Father," I said without hesitation. "Perhaps I am blinded by my own ignorance, but I cannot think of anything more I can do."

"Think again," William declared. "You say the Deputy Master of the Order of Saint John wrote to the Pope about this?"

"Yes Father, but I have heard nothing more."

"Well, there is one more thing you must do. Do you know what has transpired in Rome?"

I admitted that I did not. Once again, I had been preoccupied with my life on the island and knew nothing about events outside.

"Did you hear that Pope Paschal has died and we have a new Pope?" he asked.

"I know nothing of this," I answered.

"Once again, the answer is simple. Brother Raymond's letter never reached him. That is why you have heard nothing. Believe me when I tell you the Pope would have paid close attention to any request from the Order, had he received it. Of course, our new Pope will eventually see it, but he has difficulties of his own. Perhaps you should give this more time."

"Who is the new Pope?" I asked.

"He is named Gelasius II. Formally, he was called Giovanni da Gaeta, the Chancellor of the Church. Why do you ask?"

I was taken aback by this revelation. "I have met His Holiness, Father! He came to me long ago and told me my inheritance could not be located. He asked for my help to find it. I told him that Jehan would know and that seemed to disturb him. He said he would investigate this matter. But I never heard from him again."

William thought about this for a few moments and shook his head. "I can understand his dilemma, Thomas. I agree there is little you can do. I am sorry. Rest assured, however, that God will forgive you for not honoring your oath. You have done your best and that is sufficient."

"But I have not, Father," I said. "If the Pope received Raymond's letter, I am certain he would see me. I cannot rest without at least making an attempt."

William shook his head again in denial. "You will find that difficult if not impossible, Thomas. The Church is in serious difficulty. Only last month, the Emperor, Henry V, pronounced the election of Pope Gelasius null and void. He has driven him to exile in Gaeta, on the mainland, and appointed another in his place. Even if he would see you, what could you accomplish?"

"I do not know," I answered. "But I will try. I cannot claim to have done all in my power to fulfill my oath unless I do that."

Once again, I would travel. If it came to nothing, so be it.

I meet the Pope

Gaeta is a small city on the mainland coast, three days from Rome by horseback and two days by ship from Palermo. I requested the Emir's consent to travel there and he agreed, providing Father William accompanied me. I think Christodulus wanted to ensure my return and thus assigned an escort. At first William was reluctant.

"Thomas, I am not certain my presence before the Pope will be well received," he said. What if he knows that the Patriarch of Jerusalem defrocked me? What if there are members of the Frumentarii in his company? The Emir has asked this of me so I will go. I pray, however, my joining you does not interfere with your mission."

I assured William that would not be the case, although I had my own doubts. We left the following day. The winds were not favorable, so our voyage took longer than expected. When we arrived in Gaeta, all was in turmoil. Tension in the air was palpable and there were many soldiers in the streets. Long ago, the city elected its own ruler. Now it was governed by a succession of Norman princes, none of whom were beholden to the Emperor. The town itself is dominated by a grand castle and, from the port that is where we decided to go. Christodulus had given me a letter of introduction and my companion was a priest. I hoped that would be sufficient to gain audience with Pope

Gelasius. If he remembered me, perhaps I would finally discover the answers I sought.

After gaining entrance to the castle, a guard took us to a great hall which served as the Pope's audience chamber. I recognized Gelasius at once. He was engaged in animated discussion with other members of the church and Norman nobles. Whatever they were debating was causing him to frown. I heard him shout.

"Enough, my mind is set. I will excommunicate the Emperor himself, along with his minion. What Henry has done is against the will of God!" Turning to the Normans, he said, "I expect your support. The usurper, Burdinus who calls himself Gregory VIII, is a fraud. He is not even from Rome. Yes, he took the cross and made pilgrimage to the Holy Land, but so have others. He has spent his life in Toledo and the land of Portugal. What does he know of our Empire? He is your enemy as he is mine! If you value your souls, I demand your support!"

The nobles nodded their heads and bowed in submission. The Pope signaled that the meeting was over and glanced in our direction.

"You have business here?" he asked.

"Your Holiness, I do," I said. "Several years ago, you came to me in Salerno, where I was a student. You asked if I knew the whereabouts of my trust. I told you a lay brother named Jehan would have the information you sought. At the time, you told me to trust no one. Do you recall this?"

Pope Gelasius did not respond. Instead, he motioned for us to follow him to his private chambers. As I did so, I remarked on the fact that he appeared much older than when we had first met. He walked with the gait of an old man and I was certain he had not yet reached sixty years of age. His skin was pale, and I wondered about his health.

The Pope remained silent until we reached his chambers, where he sat not on a cushion but on a simple wooden chair. He directed us to sit on a low bench opposite.

"I do remember my visit with you. It was many years ago. It seems you listened to my warning. You are here to ask about your trust. Is that correct?"

"Yes, Holy Father, you told me then you would explore this matter. I wrote to you myself, but I never heard from you. But that is not so important. I traveled to Jerusalem hoping to discover what happened to my father, Thomas Wood-Ward, when he helped open the Holy City to the Fatimid. The deputy grand master of the Order of Saint John wrote to you about this when you were Chancellor of the Church. Did you receive his letter?"

"I did receive a letter from him," he said. "I regret my lack of response. But you say you also wrote to me many years ago? I received nothing. As you must know, other affairs of the Church have occupied my attention. These are troubling times. Who is this with you?" he asked, pointing to Father William.

William kissed the Pope's ring and said that he served as a priest to King Ruggiero and had agreed to accompany me. He said nothing further and this simple explanation seemed to satisfy the Pope, who then turned back to me.

"You recall my telling you of the Frumentarii when we first met. Have you learned anything further?" he asked.

That candor was required was without doubt. I was meeting with God's representative on earth. There was no higher authority. Thus, I told him everything I knew. William did not speak. When I had finished, Gelasius sighed and spoke again to me.

"When you disclosed that lay-brother Jehan administered the funds in your trust, my suspicions were aroused. That Eynsham Abbey had been told to remit the funds elsewhere only added to my concern. You recall you authorized me to use funds from your trust for the benefit of the Church, given our need for coin. To access the funds, I needed to know where they were kept. That was a problem. The Frumentarii always kept their affairs close, but I assumed there must be some record. If the funds were in their possession, I would need help from the Pope to recover them. They would not willingly cooperate with me. At the time, notaries in Rome prepared and held most documents for us. Without knowing which notary was involved, finding anything was impossible. Thus, without the aid of the Frumentarii, my search would be futile. Of course, as Chancellor, I changed all that. A full staff of clerks now works directly for us to prevent this sort of difficulty from occurring again."

"Then you found nothing Holiness," I said.

"I did not say that," he answered. "In fact, I confirmed the Frumentarii had taken control of the trust. I learned that they had commanded their friend, the Bishop of Lincoln, to transfer the funds to a canon of Saint John the Lateran. The amount was large. By that time, an additional one hundred thousand gold dinars had been sent from Eynsham. This, combined with the fifty thousand I knew to exist, was a substantial sum. When I was elected Pope, I needed those funds. My dispute with the Emperor came about so quickly I could not take additional steps until a short while ago. I think it is time I called for someone else who can better explain what transpired." With that pronouncement, the Pope signaled to his attendants, who seemed to know what to do.

A few moments later, a man wearing a filthy brown robe entered the chamber accompanied on either side by guards. This man kept his head down, staring at the floor.

"Have you met this man?" asked the Pope. "I think you may recall him from earlier times."

The prisoner, for that is what he was, looked up. He said nothing but I recognized him at once. The first time I saw him, he was smiling. The last time, he was not. Now, he was hanging his head in shame.

"Yes, Holiness, I know this man as Father Bartolomeo. He caused me great difficulty in the past. I thought he was acting on your behalf."

"He is no longer a priest," declared the Pope. "Do not call him Father. He was certainly not acting on my behalf. When I left Rome, it seemed best to bring him with me so he could do no more harm. It has taken some persuasion, but Bartolomeo has helped me to understand what has become of your funds. Perhaps he can tell you himself."

Bartolomeo looked at the floor and mumbled, "We took the funds, Holiness. What choice did we have? They were needed to serve God's purposes."

"Serve God?" shouted the Pope. "Who determines the purposes of God? The Frumentarii? These funds were held in trust for Thomas. Were you going to repay him?"

"Holiness, I have already admitted my sin," said Bartolomeo. "The coin is gone. I have told you everything. There is nothing more I can say."

"You did not answer my question," said the Pope, his face turning red with anger. "Were you going to repay Thomas?"

Bartolomeo did not respond. William, who had remained silent, could not contain himself. He looked directly at the Pope and said, "Holy Father, I can shed light on this matter. I too was a member of the Frumentarii. Thomas has told me stories regarding his experiences in Jerusalem. Now I can guess the answer. May I speak?"

The Pope motioned for William to continue.

"Holiness, Thomas has told me of his suspicion that Brother Jehan paid an assassin to kill him. I have wondered why and now understand. The funds belonged to Thomas if his father had died. If Thomas were no longer living, everything would be the property of the Church; is that not so?"

"That is true," admitted the Pope. "I saw this danger long ago."

William turned to Bartolomeo and addressed him directly.

"Jehan acted on your instructions, did he not?"

Bartolomeo shook his head. "I told Jehan to resolve the problem. I did not instruct him how that was to be done. We had already used the coin for our purposes. There was nothing left. Repaying funds owed to an infidel would have been wrong in the eyes of God. I wanted this matter resolved. I never told him to have anyone killed. That would have been a sin."

"So Jehan's solution was simple," said the Pope. He paused and grew even angrier. "You knew Jehan. You knew what he would do! You have already admitted grave sins. This act was truly evil. You will be damned for this. I can only thank God that Jehan failed. Take him away," he ordered.

The guards seized Bartolomeo and dragged him roughly from the chamber. The Pope raised his hands and prayed aloud, "Great God, deliver us from evil!" Then he turned to me.

"Thomas, you have an answer, but there is nothing I can do. I must restore my position in Rome. Even then, there is no way to repay you."

I thought about this for a few moments and said, "Holy Father, what is done, is done. I have lived without coin for years and have no needs that can be purchased. But that is not the only reason I sought audience with you. I made an oath to discover the fate of my father and have failed to do so. You told me you knew Father Ogier well. It was he that gave directions to my father. I know he attempted to find him after the fall of the Holy City. Is there anything more you can tell me?"

"My son, I knew Ogier well. I told you that long ago. When I was Chancellor, he explained the betrayal of the agreement with the Greek Emperor and the Fatimid. He directed your father to assist the Fatimid in taking Jerusalem from the Turks. It was at that time he told me about you. He did not know what happened to your father but had suspicions. I asked what these were, and he would not tell me. He assigned a new lay-brother member of the Frumentarii to take you to Salerno and become your guardian. This, brother, he said, had committed sins in Jerusalem and would undertake this task as an act of penance."

The Pope hesitated for a few moments deep in thought. "I remember now," he said. "Ogier was concerned that many within the Frumentarii believed the decision to leave Jerusalem in the hands of infidels was a grave error; that those who aided the Fatimid were traitors to the Church. I raised this matter with Pope Urban, who assured me he knew of this and would deal with it when he could. I never heard anything further. I am sorry; that is all I can tell you."

Clearly, there was nothing more I could learn. William and I gave our thanks and prepared to take our leave. Pope Gelasius, however, had something more to say. He must have seen my disappointment reflected on my face.

"Thomas, I see you remain concerned. It has been so long that we have heard anything of your father, he must be in heaven. You should not question this. If you told me when we first met you needed to prove his death in order to claim your inheritance, I could have easily resolved that for you with a simple document. There was no need for you to provide proof. If I regain my position, I will prepare such a document for you so there is no doubt. The coin, however, may never be recovered. For that I am sorry."

I tried my best to keep my emotions in check and simply thanked Gelasius for his time. He gave us his blessing and William and I walked back to the port in silence. We found a vessel returning to Palermo and paid for passage. For the first day, I stood alone at the railing, deep in thought. William seemed to understand my need for solitude. He devoted himself to converse with the crew and other passengers. All I could think about was the futility of my quest. I had lost everything, including the best friend I ever had, for nothing.

On the morning of the second day at sea, William approached me and placed his hand on my shoulder.

"Do you want to share your thinking with me, Thomas? If I can provide you comfort, I will do so."

I was so deep in thought I barely mumbled the answer. "I have failed, Father. The cost has been great."

William nodded his head in understanding. His grip on my shoulder grew stronger. "Thomas, I learned long ago that often God shows us what we so desperately seek is only a mirage. You have traveled in the desert and thirsted for water. You have seen the shimmering reflection that lies just ahead and have pushed yourself onward to reach it only to find nothing there. Am I right? That is a blessing and leads to wisdom. Once I sacrificed everything to preserve the Church, only to discover my true calling was to be a simple priest. I found happiness in carving souls and stone. I understand your grief but, in the days ahead, think not of what you have lost but what you have gained."

IX

A.D. 1120
A.H. 513
A.M. 4880

During the year following Adelaide's death, I devoted most of my time to treating the various afflictions of members of the royal household. Roland accompanied me everywhere and happily took charge of preparing the various herbs and potions needed for our art. King Ruggiero was in good health and rarely needed my attention. We did, however, spend time together discussing his various plans for Sicilia and, of course, his book of knowledge on which he earnestly labored. He is a remarkable man.

Whenever my duties were few, I seized the opportunity to visit Christodulus at his home. I confess my visits had little to do with the Emir himself. I wanted to see his daughter. Eventually, Tamura and I were permitted to speak alone and, on these occasions, I basked in the beauty of both her physical presence and her spoken words. It was far easier to listen than to speak for myself. Once, and only once, I took Roland with me. That was both a blessing and a curse. Roland was fascinated with Tamura and took the opportunity to regale her with stories of our adventures together. In his telling, I was described as a true hero; brave, noble, and a man of honor. I did my best to dissuade Tamura from believing these myths, but my denials only fortified her conviction that Roland was telling the truth. I prayed that she would eventually discover and accept the person I am.

I will never forget the day Christodulus offered me her hand. He had seen a common attraction between us and, I think, realized an alliance between me and his family would have value. The dowry he proposed was large, but I neither needed nor wanted anything. I suggested instead that the Emir fund the construction of a hospice for the benefit of the island. There I would be chief physician in addition to my duties at the palace. I suggested that such an institution would bring wealthy visitors to the island and produce added revenue. I would draw my own compensation from fees charged to those who could pay. Christodulus considered this solution for only a few moments. The benefits were clear and he readily agreed. I was overjoyed at the prospect. Not only would Tamura and I be joined forever, but our future would be secure.

Preparations for my marriage and the establishment of the new hospice were time-consuming and I had less time to spend with Roland. He continued diligently to study my manuscripts and even treated patients with minor ailments on his own. His dedication gave me pause. Perhaps, I thought, he had finally discovered his true calling. If only he could listen more than talk. Thus, last year, I recommended Roland to my friend Matthaeus, who was now head of the school in Salerno. He responded to my letter by appearing himself in Palermo. We spent many long hours together, relating our respective tales over numerous cups of wine. The day after his arrival, Matthaeus wanted to meet Roland to discuss his potential acceptance at the school. "Let me meet this man who you so favor. If he meets our standards, I would be happy to approve his admission," he said. "Call him to me now. Our discussion should not take long."

I had not expected Matthaeus to seek a personal meeting with Roland before agreeing to admit him to school. This constituted a risk for which I was unprepared. I regretted having indulged in so much wine the day before. There had been no opportunity to tell Roland of my plans and he might well ruin his prospects by talking too much. I swallowed hard, prayed that Roland would speak only when spoken to, and sent a servant to fetch him. Much to my surprise, he came quickly and then stood silently, waiting for me to introduce him to my visitor.

"Roland, I have recommended your admission to the Schola Medica Salernitana so you too may become a physician. This gentleman here is my old friend Master Physician Matthaeus Platearius, who is head of the school. He has questions for you. Please answer him truthfully." I wanted to add that a warning that he should provide only brief answers but, of course, I could not.

Roland gave an elegant bow but had the good sense to remain quiet. From his face, which had turned white, I knew that he was shocked by the news I had just given. I had never before discussed the possibility of his becoming a physician or attending a school.

Matthaeus did not waste time. He acknowledged Roland's silent greeting and extracted a manuscript from his traveling bag.

"This is a copy of a treatise written by my father and I called Liber de Simpliei Medicina. Please read the first pages to me." I assumed that Matthaeus wanted to judge Roland's ability to read fluently.

Roland took the manuscript but did not open it. Instead, he began to recite the Latin words from memory. I gasped in awe. I had a copy of the manuscript in my possession but did not realize that Roland had not only read it but memorized the text. Matthaeus waved his hands to stop. "Do you know all this by memory?" He asked.

"Yes, Master Physician, I do," said Roland. I expected him to continue with further explanation, but he did not. Instead, he remained silent. Matthaeus raised his brows in surprise and innocently asked if Roland was familiar with the work of Dioscorides on medicinal plants. This question finally prompted the lengthy response I feared. Roland appeared to relax and gain confidence. That could be dangerous. I held my breath as he answered.

"Of course!" he said. "Your work relies on his teaching. His volumes of De Materia Medica list almost six hundred plants and their benefits to health and the cure of illness. Unfortunately, I have not memorized them all. I promise to do so if I can continue my studies. Many of the plants have names which I do not recognize. His work is written in Greek and that language is difficult for me. Do you read Greek? Never mind, of course you do. Have you identified all of them? I have wondered about the proper use of the dried seeds of cuminum and the anethum plant, which he says were useful to early physicians. Anethum helps the body avoid rot, does it not? This is a subject I would like to explore further. Have you done so? Then there is blackberry. It is sweet to eat but can be used to treat bleeding gums. Have you studied that cure? Forgive me, I am being foolish. I do not doubt you have opinions on this."

I could see that Roland was going to continue. I prepared to interrupt, but there was no need. Roland stopped himself. "Master Physician, I apologize for speaking so much. Your time is valuable. Have you other questions?"

Matthaeus, his eyes open wide in astonishment, shook his head. "I have no further questions. The new term begins soon. Collect your belongings and travel back to Salerno with me. We will train you to become a physician."

Roland's smile was so broad I thought his face might break apart. He turned to me, asked permission to leave and almost ran out of the room. Matthaeus looked at me with wonder.

"You have hidden a sparkling gem from us, Thoma. I will not only approve his admission but we will charge nothing for his fees."

I chose not to disclose anything further about Roland's unfortunate habit in speech and breathed a sigh of relief. I had no conception of the degree to which he had followed my counsel to study my manuscripts. Roland left for Salerno the next day. He hugged me in his arms and thanked me for granting him this extraordinary opportunity. He swore to be my faithful friend forever and promised to tell me all that happened at the school. This oath was disconcerting but, I thought, Roland would indeed become a competent physician.

Recently, Matthaeus provided me some assurance of Roland's future. After his first year of study, he was assigned to provide instruction on medicinal plants to younger students. With his long-winded but lively lectures, he had become popular. Matthaeus wrote that upon completion of his studies, Roland might be offered a teaching position. Matthaeus claimed that his students became so eager to rid themselves of his long diatribes they studied all the harder to pass his course and remove themselves from his lectures.

Shortly after Roland's departure, the day of my marriage arrived. There were two issues that presented difficulties. The first related to Christodulus' conversion from the faith of Islam to that of the Greek Christians. Tamura, of course, was raised in that persuasion. I spoke at length to Father William and it was determined that, as a condition of marriage, she would convert to the faith of Western Christians. That presented little difficulty as the two branches of Christianity were close. It was, I thought, a matter of a few unimportant doctrinal disputes and, of course, fealty to the Pope in Rome. The other issue was more troublesome. I remembered I had been baptized by Captain Rowan as a child. Presumably, there were witnesses to this fact, but it would be impossible to prove it. I was gravely concerned about this, but Father William did not find it important. To question the validity of a baptism, he declared, would be to question the legitimacy of the rite itself.

"So long as you swear before God that you were, indeed, baptized, that will be sufficient," he said with a smile. "However, I will want one more oath from you when I bless your union. I will ask you to affirm your convictions. You will repeat the response spoken by your guardian at your baptism. Do you know the words? If not, I will provide them to you."

I agreed. This act would confirm my beliefs not only to myself but to everyone else. No more would I navigate between two faiths. Those days were forever past. The day I made my oath and became husband to Tamura was the happiest of my life. For once, I felt complete. For once, I felt at home.

But what, you may ask, happened to my fortune? That is a longer story. Of course, I could not travel to Aegyptus to meet with my uncles in person to resolve matters. Such a journey would have been dangerous. Although Sicilia was safe for both Muslims and Jews, Assad and Jusuf were too old to travel to me. Instead, they dispatched their eldest sons, who were a few years younger than me. The Collegantia had passed to their hands as, by this time, their fathers no longer wished to be engaged in day-to-day commerce.

Abdullah, Assad's son, was named for our grandfather who, may he rest in peace, died in the same year I returned to Sicilia. I will always regret that I never met him. There was no question that Abdullah was the son of Assad. They shared the same girth and an affinity for fine clothing. Both had voracious appetites. Most importantly, my cousin inherited our grandfather's skill in commerce. The mill for al-sukkar in Aegyptus was under his control and he had developed new markets to better compete with the Franj. I was delighted he was my close relative and we have become fast friends.

Elazar, Jusuf's son, was more serious. I immediately saw the likeness to his father. He was equally quick with numbers and had studied the arts of defense known to Jusuf. Although he was born in Marrakech, Elazar studied the Talmud and law in Qurtuba for several years. He had also traveled the new trade routes to al-Hind and developed relationships in that far-off place. Now, he said, he planned travel to Lisboa to establish a trading venture there. Lisboa, he argued, was tolerant of both Jews and Muslims and provided an opportunity to expand commerce to Christian cities.

Both Abdullah and Elazar wished to settle accounts with me. Although the Pope had promised to recognize the legitimacy of my inheritance, I was reluctant to accept anything from the church. In any event, the one hundred fifty thousand dinars in my account was unlikely to be recovered. What remained was the value of the mill in Aegyptus and the makhzans. The solution was simple. I introduced them to Aubert who, now that it was safe to do so, called himself Abrafim. He was then fully engaged in making sabun for Ruggiero's court. There was an instant liking between them. When my cousins recovered from shock that this substance was only now becoming popular in Sicilia, Abdullah suggested that the introduction of other fragrant additives would increase demand. These could be supplied from Aegyptus.

"You will find that buyers will demand more if you provide them choices," he said. "In Aegyptus, we add an extract from roses and rare woods. Did you know the ancient queen Cleopatra enjoyed the perfume found in the blue lotus? No one will have thought of that.

Hakim Thoma can confirm that oil made from the seeds of a tree the Greeks call 'balanos myrepsike' could also be added. We can establish a shop in the Suq al-Attarin where spice merchants ply their trade. We must keep the secret of making sabun close. There are many possibilities if we think carefully!"

I agreed with Abdullah's judgement. Dioscorides had written that the oil mentioned by Abdullah was useful in treating many ailments and I remembered the words of the Lady Trota regarding the benefits of cleanliness and good odor to health. The hospice would want a significant quantity of the improved product. This prompted further discourse regarding opportunities for trade, particularly in al-sukkar and medicinal herbs, between our island and the Muslim world. The cane of al-sukkar was now being grown in Sicilia, but its quality was less and its cost more than in Aegyptus. The talk between these new commercial partners lasted for several days. Other than listening, I contributed little. When it became clear that a lasting relationship would develop, I suggested that my remaining interests in the Collegantia be invested in a new Commanda enterprise.

"If profits from trading accrue to me, I ask that you supply medicinal herbs and spices having an equal value to the new hospice, at no cost. That is all I desire." This arrangement would, I thought, resolve any remaining issues with the Church and benefit the hospice. Elazar was shocked at my proposal.

"Have you lost your senses? How can you abandon this opportunity to increase your wealth?" he asked. "If we expand this trade properly, there is no limit to what we can achieve!" Abdullah shook his head in agreement.

"Elazar, I do not need more than what I possess at this time. If the hospice can benefit, that is sufficient for me," I said.

Unless one has lost everything, one cannot understand how little value can be ascribed to the accumulation of coin. It was enough, I thought, that I could sometimes cure the ill. I was not a merchant nor would I ever be. By the grace of God, I was a physician. That was my calling. But, God was not done with me. He gave even more.

My son was born this year. It is through the miracle of birth and the joy of holding an infant in one's arms that the true meaning of life is understood. He was baptized into the Christian faith, with Ruggiero acting as a witness. With Tamura's consent and blessing, I named him William.

Now, my life is complete. I no longer wish to travel anywhere. Here in Palermo, I have everything I could ever desire. I no longer covet fame or wealth or security. These false gods are, I have discovered, fickle and easily lost. That I have a loving wife, a healthy child, and the knowledge to help others is more than enough. My grandfather's favorite poet, the Persian Khayyam, wrote that the greatest waste of a day is one without love. That is what is important. Nothing else. My life would have been easier had I understood this truth long ago.

God is great!

الله أكبر

Allahu Akbar!

GLOSSARY

Aegyptus – (Latin) Egypt

Af-Yum – (Arabic) opium

Al-Andalus – (Arabic) Muslim Spain

Al-Hasba – (Arabic) measles

Al-Hind – (Arabic) India

Al-Iskandariyyah – (Arabic) Alexandria, Egypt

Al-Luban – (Arabic) frankincense

Al-Maghribiyah – (Arabic) modern-day Morocco, literally "the West"

Al-Misr – (Arabic) Egypt

Almoravids – the ruling dynasty of al-Andalus and al-Maghribiyah

Al-Qahirah – (Arabic) Cairo, Egypt

Al-Quds – (Arabic) Jerusalem

Al-Shaam – (Arabic) Syria

Al-Sukkar – (Arabic) sugar

Anethum – (Latin) dill weed

Atrabulus – (Arabic) Tripoli, Libya

Atabeg – (Turkic) governor

Ayla – (Arabic) modern-day Aqaba, Jordan

Bangha – (Persian) henbane

Balanos Myrepsike – (Greek) ben tree (horseradish) seeds

Bezant (Old French) = ¼ oz. of gold or 3.22 oz. of silver or approximately 46 English Pennies

Caliph – (Arabic) chief Muslim civil and religious leader

Cardamomum – (Latin) cardamom

Cipros – (Greek) Cyprus

Colchicum – (Latin) crocus

Collegantia – (Latin) early form of joint stock company

Commanda – (Latin) early form of contractual trading enterprise

Constantinopolis – (Greek) modern-day Istanbul, Turkey

Cowl – the hood of a monk's robe

Crucesignatus – (Latin) an armed Christian pilgrim, "crusader"

Cuminum – (Latin) cumin

Dimashq – (Arabic) Damascus

Dinar (Arabic) = 1.5 Bezant or 1 Al-Qahirah Bezant

Ellaen – (Old English) elderberry plant

Emir – (Arabic) a Muslim military or political commander

Erythra Thalassa – (Greek) the Red Sea

Fatimids – the ruling dynasty of Aegyptus

Franj – (Arabic) Western Christians, literally "Franks"

Frater Conversus – (Latin) lay brother, a member of a Catholic religious order who is not an ordained priest

Funduq – (Arabic) an enclosed compound used and owned by foreign merchants

Gazz – (Arabic) silk

Hakim – (Arabic) physician

Hammam – (Arabic) bath house

Hashishi – (Arabic) an assassin, a member of the Hashishiyyin

Hindiba – (Arabic) flowering plant found in the Near East known to have cancer fighting properties (chicory)

Ifriqiya – (Arabic) modern-day Tunisia

Jaffa – modern-day Tel Aviv, Israel

Kalaripayattu – (Malayalam) the oldest Indian martial art

Kabbaba – black pepper

Kanab – (Persian) cannabis

Lazaward – (Persian) lapis lazuli

Levante – (Italian) the lands of the Near East along the Mediterranean coast

Leymun – (Arabic) lemon

Londres – (Old French) London, England

Madrassa – (Arabic) an Islamic school

Makhzan – (Arabic) warehouse

Marrubium – (Latin) horehound

Meṛṛakec – (Berber) modern-day Marrakech, Morocco

Moallim – (Arabic) teacher

Nazarene – a medieval Muslim appellation for Christians

Peirates – (Greek) pirate

Phthisis – (Greek) tuberculosis (consumption)

Quadrivium – (Latin) basic medieval education in arithmetic, geometry, music and astronomy

Quarib – (Arabic) seagoing barge used to transport heavy cargo

Qutun – (Arabic) Cotton

Qadi – (Arabic) judge of Islamic law

Rum – (Arabic) designation for Eastern Christians living under Muslim rule

Sabun – (Arabic) bath soap

Sayyid – (Arabic) sir; milord

Sayyida – (Arabic) madam; lady

Sharab Alshuwkran – (Arabic) hemlock

Sharq al-Urdun – modern-day Jordan, literally "East of the Jordan"

Sicilia – (Latin) Sicily

Silphium – (Latin) laserwort, used as both a perfume and aphrodisiac

Solidus – (Latin) gold coin (bezant)

Spirea Ulmaria – (Latin) meadwort

Suq – (Arabic) market

Tari – (Arabic) Sicilian coin worth about ¼ Dinar

Tulaytula – (Arabic) modern-day Toledo, Spain

Yeriho – (Hebrew) Jericho

Zarniqa – (Arabic) arsenic

Zingiber – (Latin) ginger

Zirids – the ruling dynasty of Ifriqiya

From the Same Author

The Sugar Merchant

When Thomas's family is annihilated in a raid, his life changes forever. Wandering for days, starving and hopeless, he is rescued by a monk and is taken to live at the abbey of Eynsham. There he receives a curious education, training to be a scholar, a merchant and a spy. His mission: to develop commerce in Muslim lands and dispatch vital information to the Holy See.

His perilous adventures during the 11th century's commercial revolution will take him far from his cloistered life to the great trading cities of Almeria, Amalfi, Alexandria and Cairo.

Published by New Generation Publishing in 2018
Paperback ISBN: 978-1-78955-320-8
Hardback ISBN: 978-1-78955-321-5

Praise for The Sugar Merchant

Publishers Weekly: "This complex and fascinating portrait of medieval life will appeal to history devotees."

Finalist - Chaucer Award for emerging new talent and outstanding works in pre-1750s historical fiction

Bronze Medal for The Coffee Pot Book Club Historical Fiction, The Early Medieval Period, Book of the Year Award